THE NUN AND THE DOCTOR

A conversion love story at midlife

A NOVEL

RICHARD P. JOHNSON

AGES PRESS
St. Louis, Missouri

ISBN 0-9743623-2-8

10 9 8 7 6 5 4 3 2 1

Cover Design by Craig Johnson

Printed in the United States of America

Dedication

This book is dedicated to the spirit of Dr. Stanley Zawalnicki, DDS. His life, taken in its prime, gave bright hope to all those who knew him. His zest for life, his infectious enthusiasm, his perseverance in the face of terrible loss shall inspire us all. His ever-vibrant, vital, and "fun" personality stands in effervescent counterpoint to the personality portrayed by Dr. Stanley Renowski in this novel. Stan, the world is a better place because of you ... we shall always miss you and always love you. Thank you for being you.

Other books by Richard P. Johnson ...

- *Adult Development in the Five Life Arenas*
- *The Fifteen Factors of Retirement Success*
- *Caring for Your Aging Parents*
- *A Christian's Guide to Mental Wellness*
- *Body, Mind, Spirit: Tapping the Healing Power Within You*
- *The 12 Keys to Spiritual Vitality*
- *Creating a Successful Retirement: Finding Peace and Purpose*
- *Honoring Your Aging Parents*
- *All My Days: Writing Your Spiritual Autobiography*
- *Loving for a Lifetime: The Six Essentials for a Happy, Healthy, & Holy Marriage*
- *The New Retirement*

Acknowledgements

I want to thank all the consecrated religious sisters and nuns whose benevolent accomplishments and unwavering commitment to the noblest parts of humankind has made our American culture what it is today. So much of the American social infrastructure: schools, hospitals, orphanages, social service agencies, eldercare organizations, and so much more stand today as a direct consequence of the dynamic and selfless work of these gifted women. I thank you all; you have inspired so many hearts and minds, and led so many souls to God. I know that I stand on your shoulders.

I would also like to thank my editor, Hope Rowold Johnson (no relation) whose sharp eye, sensitive heart, and intelligent editing guided me in ways that have measurably improved this book. Her husband Craig Johnson gave life to the theme of this book by designing the cover. I want to thank Rita Zawalnicki for her accurate and compassionate editing that caught many mistakes that my eyes missed. But, most of all, I want to thank my wife Sandra for everything she contributed to this book directly by her excellent computer, editing, and grammar skills, not to mention her wakefulness as I read and re-read this book aloud to her many times in the middle of the night, and indirectly by her unquestioned commitment to me and my work. There is no way I can thank her ... I give to her my undying love.

THE NUN AND THE DOCTOR

Chapter One *Dr. Stanley Renowski*

"Will you wake-up! What do you think you're doing? Either follow my lead or get out! When I request an instrument I expect it immediately. If you were any good at all, you'd anticipate my moves ahead of me!"

Dr. Renowski's comments exploded in the surgical suite like hand grenades lobbed onto the floor. The nurse had assisted Dr. Renowski many times before, and had come to view him with a fearful adulation. He seemed to sense her glorification of him and took full advantage of it by using her, some might say abusing her, to buttress his undisputed power and total command of the OR.

"Move your hand away! I can't see the surgical field with your fat hand in the way! Don't bother to assist on my next case," Dr. Renowski said with contempt to the now cowering assisting nurse.

Dr. Stanley Renowski had been wooed to the Medical Center seven years ago after he received the *National Cardiac Surgical Honors Award* for perfecting what's now called the Renowski technique. The simplicity of the technique was its genius. By-pass surgery patients not only spent one-half the time on the table, but they could be discharged up to two days earlier from in-patient care. Since his arrival he's improved on his technique several times.

Last year, Dr. Renowski received the *National Cardiac Surgical Honors Award* for a second time, an honor never before given any individual. This year he snared the *International Surgical Honors Award.* To accent the honor the Society of Surgical Arts International has come here to Detroit to award it to him tonight. This too has never happened; every other award was given in formal ceremony at the society's headquarters in Switzerland. The ceremony will be held this evening at the Renaissance Center Hotel next to the convention center ... the best Detroit has to offer.

A tear formed in the eye of the nurse Renowski attacked, the only evidence of which was a slight fogging of her surgical goggles. Everyone in the room took silent note of it. Renowski seemed to gloat. Everyone also knew that the nurse would have a dozen roses waiting for her in the surgical suite reception area on Monday morning. Renowski never missed an opportunity to abuse, nor to assuage.

With surgery completed, Renowski punched his stopwatch signaling yet another triumph, not over heart disease, but over the other surgeons in the Medical Center, in the city, the state, the country ... everywhere! Renowski lived to conquer, for both the pleasure of the hunt, and the spoils of being on top ... unquestionably on top.

Chapter Two

Renowski bolted out the OR door and almost ran over Dr. Tom Dubac, assistant director of cardiac surgery.

"What are you doing here, I thought you left hours ago?" demanded Renowski.

Ignoring Renowski's question, Dr. Dubac asked, "Well, have you decided? Are you going tonight, you know, to accept your award?"

Renowski had played with the surgery staff by intimating that he didn't intend on accepting his award in person. He floated the notion that he was too busy, and that "it didn't mean anything anyway." He kept up the ruse even to today. Tom Dubac knew however that nothing could keep Renowski from the glory of the ceremony. Renowski lived for adulation; his ego had trampled over everyone just so it could gloat in the spotlight as he received the crown laurel of surgery. He saw himself as the emperor.

Renowski's favorite quip to surgical residents on rounds was, "You have to be a cut above!" This comment wasn't meant as motivation for the residents, but as a slightly disguised but still clear self-accolade. Indeed, all of Renowski's interactions were of this genre. He really didn't interact, his life was a monologue; others' thoughts and words were inconsequential, of no use except to provide the backdrop for Renowski's one-man show, as the floor upon which he trod, the rungs of a ladder that led to his throne.

"Yeah, I guess I will," Renowski almost sneered to Tom Dubac. "I don't want them calling my house looking for me." Renowski's words jolted Tom. Normally unflappable, Tom emotionally winced at Renowski's remark. He tried to keep his reaction to himself, but even so, a bit washed over the top and contorted his face into the hint of a stare of condemnation.

Renowski shot back at Dubac, "You only wish it was you, don't you?" Renowski's eyes narrowed, his eyebrows curled as he patronized his colleague, "Tom, you're the best back-up I could ever have." Here was Renowski at his best, the master of paradox; his compliments were always put-downs. Tom Dubac was again relegated simply to support staff. Emperors always needed lots of support staff.

Renowski quickly debrided himself of his surgical garb and raced down the surgical wing hall toward the underground doctor's parking garage. His black Mercedes SL 500 filled his private parking space. Renowski brought it to life and streaked off the Medical Center campus with stealth.

Cold rain scoured the pavement and turned the street gutters into torrents as Renowski spun his tires out into the press of the Friday drive time traffic just beginning to thin. Onto the connector Renowski directed his Mercedes toward Westerleigh. He drove with abandon, wielding his car as a scalpel cutting through the traffic like a wave-bladed stiletto. He punched on his favorite CD, the final two minutes of Ravel's *Bolero* that played over and over as his tires erupted the water awash over the road. The wipers on high kept time to his heartbeats; he imagined himself ascending onto the stage tonight. He calculated the length of time he would pause between receiving the award and beginning his speech, a time when he would survey the audience without expression; a gesture designed to cement his new status as their undisputed commander-in-chief.

Off the connector onto Wellington Street, past Portland Place, Renowski turned onto Westmoreland. He accelerated past the gaslight, missing the curb on the turn by a half an inch as he did every night. Garage door opener pushed, he didn't break the stride of the Benz until he approached his driveway. He saw the jaws of the garage opening revealing the sheen on the garage floor. He blasted out of the car and into the house. As he bounded up the center hall staircase, he bellowed, "Anne, are you ready?"

Chapter Three

The twice oversized Williamsburg chandelier that illuminated the entrance hall quivered as Renowski once again filled the manse with his question: "Anne, are you ready?"

Anne didn't answer, she had long ago learned to withhold response, communicating both affirmation of herself, and power over him.

They met 14 years ago when Anne was Renowski's defense attorney in a malpractice suit. Renowski was then still experimenting with his new technique. The widow of a 54-year-old mayor of a small town in Indiana, who didn't make it off of Renowski's operating table alive, sued him and everyone else her lawyers could conjure-up.

The case was dismal; Renowski's new procedure was not yet approved as a standard-of-care. Renowski had phenomenal results in many cases but they hadn't yet been verified. The mayor probably wouldn't have survived any surgery; Renowski's procedure was his best shot. Renowski was well aware of the risk before the surgery, but whatever prudent caution Renowski possessed was eclipsed by his bravado.

The surgery "went south" almost from the start. The mayor struggled to hold-on, but his heart damage was simply too advanced. He died. Renowski wouldn't call the death, he never did if he lost a patient; his pride precluded him from even sewing the mayor back up. The fact that the chief surgical resident, and not Renowski, called the death made for great courtroom dramatics by the prosecution. But, in the end, Anne captured the jury by describing her client as the next Dr. DeBakey, a surgical giant who went farther in attempting to keep the stream of life alive in the mayor than any other surgeon could have.

Anne successfully transformed Renowski's arrogance into compassionate determination and a haloed steadfast stamina. When she had finished her summation, Renowski had been beatified as the patron saint of surgery, smart, stalwart, savvy, and oh so contrite. She apologized to the jury, not for any failure on Renowski's part, but because medicine had simply not yet progressed far enough to save the mayor ... something Renowski had dedicated his life to rectify. Anne even convinced herself.

The attorney-client relationship morphed into a kind of mutual veneration dynamic. In Anne, Renowski saw an intellectual heavyweight and a person who revered power. She could never equal his prowess in either of these two traits, reasoned Renowski, but she was just the right combination of a high horsepower professional and an adoring partner to give his life style, passion, social status, and most of all continuous adulation. The wedding reception was held in a half-acre size tent pitched like a castle on the grounds of Anne's grandmother's mansion. The couple entered Detroit's social elite with panache.

Chapter Four

Renowski attacked his closet where his tuxedo hung neatly with tie, cummerbund, and shoes placed strategically giving the impression of a stick man in formal attire. He swaggered as he approached the mirrored wall in his palatial dressing room. He ran his fingers through his graying temples, and said to himself, 'Damn, I look good.'

"Are you ready yet?" he screamed from his dressing closet. Still no answer from Anne.

"Answer me!" he commanded as he burst into her bath where she was seated in front of the mirror, eyes fixated on herself, cigarette burning in the ashtray, and a half glass of gin next to it.

"How many of those have you had?" he barked.

"Will you calm down?" She replied as she twisted around toward him revealing her shape that appeared both pointed and rounded as her slip clung to her body.

"How many?" he retorted.

"This is my first ... just for you," she demurred.

"I'll bet it's your first!" he said with a scalpel-sharp sarcasm. "Anyway, hurry up, we need to leave in five minutes. I told you to be ready and waiting for me when I got home."

"I know you did," she answered, in a tone that seemed to reprimand him for his presumption.

"I'll be in the car waiting!" he said as he marched out of the bathroom.

He sank into the leather driver's seat of his Mercedes. He flicked on the radio switching from NPR to a smooth jazz station. He noticed that his taste in music was changing. In his younger years he'd listen to hard rock only. He then went through a long period where classical ruled his airways. Now he was leaning toward smooth jazz. He wondered what that meant, if anything.

He looked around inside his car, still in the garage. He congratulated himself on his distinguished taste. Each gauge in the dash, each piece of finely turned walnut trim, each stitch on the leather steering wheel, each squeak and creak of the deep leather seats seemed to cry out the same song for Renowski: "You are good! You are better than good. You are the best!" Renowski smiled a smirky smile of congratulations to his success in life. He was, after all, the renowned Dr. Stanley Renowski.

He imagined what was to come tonight. He would sit in the honor seat at the head table. He would nod in agreement as each guest congratulated him throughout the evening. He would slowly and regally rise from his chair when he was introduced. He wondered how many introductions there would be; surely at least three: one general one giving glimpses of his personal history, a second giving an overview of his accomplishments, and a third designed to inspire the audience about the primacy of cardiac surgery and anointing Renowski as the profession's new crown prince.

Renowski punched out of his reverie and checked the time. "Damn, it's been more than five minutes that I've been waiting."

He arched out of the car and raced upstairs. Anne was still in the bathroom.

"Will you hurry up!" he fired. "I want to get there just late enough to be fully noticed, but not so late that they are already settled in at the tables."

He had planned this for months, his attire, his demeanor, his slight tardiness, all of this designed to let the spotlight of adulation shine on him just a little brighter and just a little longer.

"Anne, I'm going to the car; be there, now!" he barked.

As he marched down the hall and again, Anne made no attempt to move any faster. Instead, her movements became all the more slow and deliberate. In his car, Renowski was alone with his thoughts. Even the sound of the electric motor that reclined his seat said quality. Renowski liked that, he related to that motor. He thought there was some small part of him that aligned with that seat motor. After all, reflected Renowski, it's the best automobile seat motor there is.

After another five minutes, Renowski resisted the surging impulse to go inside a second time. 'She always does this! This is deliberate on her part; simply an extension of her courtroom power posturing,' he reasoned, 'only an attempt to gain the advantaged position.'

In the beginning, their marriage seemed a continuous reiteration of the question, 'who has the right to decide what?' Renowski demanded Anne's unquestioned loyalty, but more than that, he demanded her 'agreement' that his career, his needs and wants, his whims, his whole being took precedence over hers. In exchange, she had free reign over all domestic decisions and social schedule. Naturally, there were clashes. One time, Renowski forced Anne to have a newly paved patio completely torn-up and replaced. Renowski didn't want the new interlocking paving stones that Anne had picked out; he had to have the more traditional red brick patio ... just like the one at the country club.

Money wasn't discussed; Anne was supposed to know what was a prudent expenditure and what wasn't. Renowski chose her car, she the color; he chose vacation times, she picked out the place; he chose his favorite food; she made sure it was there. In the 12 years they'd been married the division of labor and decision was now operating with deft, yet unspoken efficiency. Renowski didn't like talking about things ... he liked disposing of them. For his purposes the relationship worked well; it was only times like these, when he sensed that Anne sought some ill-defined power advantage that unnerved him. Renowski never could go deep enough inside himself to ask what Anne might be trying to communicate with her apparent indifferent behavior.

After another five minutes the laundry room door to the garage opened framing Anne as a backlit silhouette. The picture provoked a level of awe in Renowski. Ann glared at her husband through the windshield, took the last sip of her gin and set the glass down without breaking her stare, giving Renowski just enough time to gloat over his crown achievement. If he was wearing a heart monitor it surely would have registered a quickened pace as the stimulus of Anne's physical form cascaded over him. He prized Anne as he would a statue; he appreciated her fullness, her aristocratic nose and chin, her arched brows, her delicate but strong fingers, her confident poise, and her commanding yet sensitive gaze. He drank her in as a part of himself, not unlike how he ingested the idea and the quality of his Mercedes. Both the woman and the car stood as props on his stage; each echoed his achievements, his exclusiveness among men, and his quest for "the best."

Both the car and the woman required exquisite attention. The Mercedes was maintained immaculately, double maintenance was accomplished; the car was detailed every six months, washed and polished weekly by a service that actually made service calls at the medical center doctor's parking garage.

Anne too was expected to do double maintenance. In addition to her "normal" personal grooming, Anne saw her hair stylist weekly; she visited the day spa twice a month. She is on a first-name basis with her cosmetic surgeon who has had the pleasure of putting Anne under no less than six times. Personal maintenance was all but Anne's full time occupation; virtually everything she did, read, discussed, thought about, and worried over revolved in some way around her need to remain absolutely the same. That's what Renowski wanted, and that's what Anne delivered.

Chapter Five

Anne eased herself into the Mercedes raising her leg and exposing her lower thigh. This snapshot imprinted on Renowski's mind and ratcheted his heart rate higher. She settled in and without a word from either of them, Renowski turned the ignition key. In expressionless silence they slid out of the garage and into the night.

The rain had now turned nasty, bleating down on the windshield with a roar. With wipers going double-time, Renowski coaxed the Benz out into the street, but gunned it once they passed the stop sign. Even in the rain the speeding Benz raised the leaves into a billowing wake behind the car. The weather turned ominous; Renowski, however, was intent on making up lost time.

He always drove with intensity, but tonight in a state both intoxicated with himself and numbed with irritation at Anne, his usual intensity evolved into abandon. He began rolling through stop signs and ignoring speed limits; he stopped at a red light, but went through it after he visually cleared the intersection. Onto South Lake Shore Drive the water swirled around the speeding Mercedes making it appear more a submarine than a car. Weaving between, around, and through Renowski now exceeded Anne's limits.

"Stanley, would you please slow down before you kill us both?" she said.

As if to show her who was in charge, Renowski accelerated. Anne slumped in her seat, crossed her arms, and scrunched her lips to one side.

As the car negotiated the transition from South Lake Shore Drive onto Jefferson, Renowski's driving morphed to reckless. Going 70 mph on Jefferson into the city in a piercing rain was Renowski's response to Anne's insinuation that he was not in absolute command. Finally they reached the downtown area and headed toward the Renaissance Center.

'Six more blocks and we'll be there,' thought Anne.

Yet Renowski didn't let up. As though to prove his mastery of everything he disregarded the lights. He'd slow down a bit approaching the inner city intersections, but would punch right through the lights regardless of color. As he approached the Mt. Elliot street intersection with Jefferson, Anne could make out the lights of the Renaissance Center ahead. This observation was the last cognitive impulse that coursed through her.

A city trash truck delayed by the weather was making its way back to the yard, perhaps going a bit faster than normal; the driver wanted to get to his high school son's wrestling match on time. The trash truck driver didn't see the black Mercedes at all; his light was full green. He knew well how to time the lights on this city thoroughfare; he'd driven it thousands of times.

The trash truck struck the Mercedes squarely on the passenger door. The impact of the crash embossed the car onto the front of the truck that then drove it across the intersection until both vehicles, now joined into one, veered through a street light and through the front wall of the Immigration Building. The Mercedes came to rest inside the building with the trash truck nosing into the building as if nursing from its mother.

Anne's body lay on top of Renowski. He opened his eyes to her death stare back at him; her look seemed to say, 'How could you do this, you imbecile?' Blood dripped from the crown of her head onto Renowski's face. He tried to gather his consciousness. Several times he forced his eyes to focus only to have them blur again. He took an inventory of himself. He felt no pain except for his left ear that was stinging. He was wedged between the door, the steering wheel and the dash, his seat and Anne's body. Strangely the only sound he could discern was the sound of the seat motor, which squeaked in fits and starts. Finally, a voice rose from the darkness.

"Are you alive?"

"Yes ... yes!" Renowski blurted. "Get me out! Get me out!"

"Are you alone?" came the voice.

"No ...no!" he exclaimed. Inside however, Renowski knew that he was alone.

Renowski could now see the reflection of the flashing lights on the thousands of glass shards all around him. He heard the undulating wail of sirens coming closer.

Another voice came at him: "Sir, be calm, we're working on getting you out! Is that your wife? Is she unconscious?" The voice was slow and deliberate, well modulated with authority. The voice cracked some internally protected space of silence in Renowski, a strange silence deep within him.

All Renowski could say was, "Yes."

"Can you give me a hand, sir?" came the voice. "Can you give me a hand?"

Renowski tried but his hand wouldn't move. "I'm trying to, it must be stuck somehow."

"OK, sir, sit tight," came the voice "I'm going to get the jaws."

Now Renowski was alone; he felt alone in every way. He tried to move but couldn't. He could move his head, but couldn't get response elsewhere in his body. He tried his fingers ... no response; he tried his toes ... no response. He tried his legs ... nothing! Thoughts raced through him, but nothing else. All he could feel was Anne's blood still dripping on him and his left ear stinging more acutely now; but that was it. Renowski had no other sensations! 'This must be some temporary reaction,' he thought, 'some trauma reaction ... kind of a physical amnesia ... my body has temporarily forgotten how to move,' he reasoned.

The voice returned. "OK sir, you're gonna have to help us! Do you feel any pain?"

"Only my left ear," said Renowski.

"Yeah, I can see that," responded the voice. "Any place else?" it demanded.

"No ... I can't feel a thing."

"Nothing, you can't feel anything?" quizzed the voice.

"No!" Renowski responded, with exasperation ... and fear!

Chapter Six *Sr. Theresa*

I felt the other sisters enter the chapel even before I heard their black habits rustle through the still air illuminated only by the night light and single candle burning on the altar. Matins at 3 AM was not my favorite of the seven formal prayer times of the day; some nights I even resented the mid-night awakening for which I always did penance, but right now I tried to focus my heart and mind on God.

"*Help me Lord! Gather–up my thoughts. I'm so scattered in my thinking. Help me focus only on you.*"

My thoughts scrambled to all the tasks and worries of running the monastery. As each sister filed past me finding and settling into her place, instead of seeing her as a beautiful child of God, tonight I thought only of her personality quirks, her demands both spoken and unspoken, her interaction patterns with the other nuns, or what her needs might be next year. Lately, each of my sisters seemed more a burden than a gift.

"Lord grant me simple harmony, help me avoid distractions invading my focus on you."

They were all in their places, settled, and ready to begin. I remembered all the passengers finally getting settled in their seats ... the memorized greeting I'd recite welcoming them, closing the door on the 727, demonstrating the seat belts, safety features, and smoking rules. For 10 years this was my life, flying. We used to be called stewardesses, now I understand they're called flight attendants. I liked my job; I got away from home, away from my mother, away from her direction, her domination over us kids and over my dad. I had to get away. The airlines kept me moving, ever moving, always busy – the same busyness over and over, the same runs, the same pilots, planes, and airports; sometimes even the same passengers. Everything became the same, yet everything was so different too.

Matins begins. *"Dear God let me stay focused!"*

Was it possible to say perfect matins? Was it possible to remain fully awake and aware of every word without my mind wandering? Each word of our prayers goes deep; could I ever hope to penetrate the full meaning of matins? I hadn't seen these words for a full year and yet it seemed it was only last month when they were in front of me. Can time be so elastic? Does this time compression mean that I'm aging faster, or was the same thing happening here in the monastery that happened with the airlines? At some point it all seemed the same.

Sister Ignatius was restless tonight. She had not been feeling well; her cancer was back. She had refused chemo and radiation; she claimed her refusal was out of obedience, but I've assured her that if she wanted it she could have it. However, she does take her cancer meds ... faithfully! But it was back and the whole community, all 12 of us, were already mourning her pain. What will her course bring? Will she linger like Sister Ramunda, who hung on to life for four years, or will she cut off her suffering by going quickly?

Chapter Seven

I love the psalms; they capture my mood so well. Take for example, Psalm 10

Why, O Lord, do you stand far off?
Why do you hide yourself in times of trouble?

How often had this been my own lament? Wasn't it paradoxical that I've been a cloistered nun for over 25 years and I still haven't mastered the art of praying? When I was a novice I believed that the day would come when my prayer would be like a masterpiece of perfection, a hand sewn quality tapestry. But instead, I still groped for words, I stumbled over my own distraction, I condemned myself for my insufficiency even as I mouthed the most beautiful phrases ever put together. What a conundrum I weaved. But, I was a reflection of all women and men; I suffered the same confusion they all share, I struggled the same struggle. I expected perfection, but I needed to remember that if I didn't struggle I'd never stretch beyond myself. Without struggle, I'd stagnate.

Matins was over; I walked to my cell past the statue of the Blessed Virgin in the hall, around the crucifix, and up the stairs, each one I punctuated with a prayer as I was taught so many years ago. Sr. Matthias opened her cell door (she must have heard my footfalls on the hall floor) and greeted me with our usual greeting.

"God's charity is in your heart." She strained to speak, knowing that she was breaking the great silence, only to say, "Don't forget Mother, tomorrow we're cleaning the chapel ceiling fans."

"I haven't forgotten." I responded and made my way to my bed.

Chapter Eight

At 6 a.m. I found myself in the chapel again, as I did each day, for Morning Prayer. The sun appeared luminous through the colored windows of the chapel. Our stained glass windows were lost before they arrived; a casualty to a brutish budget tightening caused by construction cost overruns. I liked the colored windows; stained glass always seemed too hierarchical to me anyway, a connection to the old church. I wanted the new church!

Sister Madeline hobbled to her seat in chapel; the pain of her osteoarthritis weighted her down. She is totally without complaint. She saw her suffering as a sacred connection with the passion of Jesus. In my younger years I would have seen this as absurd, today I stood in awe before it. I revered her; she's a spiritual giant among us mere apprentices. Can I ever reach her spiritual heights? She seemed possessed by the positive energy of the universe, a benevolence of charm, grace, and patience well beyond our human boundaries. She filled me

... gave me hope ... settled my soul that can be so easily agitated ... too sensitive to the world and so obtuse to what was real ... what was true.

We processed out of chapel. Most of us headed directly to the refectory for breakfast, some detoured to their cells or sidelined themselves to the community bathroom. Another paradox of the cloister was that we seek contemplation; a sense of being with God, yet the cloistered life was not one of privacy. We live in constant community; aloneness is somehow suspect. Only our sleeping cell was solitary, most everything else is communal, bathrooms included.

Breakfast, as all our meals, was served buffet style ... eggs, toast, cereal, and juice. Simplicity demanded we eat all we took, so we took only what we were sure we would eat. Much of our food was donated, adding in our minds to the sacredness of it, someone served God by giving us this food. The food then was a double gift, first a gift from God in itself, and second, a gift bestowed through God's grace by God's children. The act of giving was sacred. We continued God's love by our gracious acceptance and the honor we gave to the givers, God and our benefactors.

The act of eating was also sacred. We prepared and ate our food with as much honor as we could find inside us. Each day, indeed each meal was different for me. Some days I could honor with a genuine holiness that satisfied me deeply. On other days I struggled to reach any depth at all, as though the escalator down to that noble place in my soul was broken. I've tried to figure out what factors or forces pushed me one way or the other, but even now I was flummoxed ... I had no sense at all whether my days of felt reverence arose as a triumph of prayer, sacrifice, toil, tolerance of ambiguity, patience, or virtue. Perhaps those halcyon days were some mere happenstance of chemical change in my brain caused by whatever allowed it to fire with greater spark. I only accepted the days of deeper awareness of God's presence as gift, and those days of struggle as my own overactive residue of the human condition. In any case I was called to accept them all without comparison and without complaint. I only wished that I could.

Sister Michael Marie raised her spoon with a deliberateness that spoke more of compulsiveness than her holiness. She proceeded, with her cereal spoon in hand, in slow motion, eyes fixated on some illusionary object as though mesmerized. Her struggle with food and with the function of eating was real. Scrupulosity tortured her. Each morsel she ingested presented a potential for punishment. Was the size of the morsel correct? Did she separate the morsel from the whole with the precision it deserved? Was the angle of ascent to her mouth precise enough? Was the prayer in her mind appropriate? Was the sequence she chose for her food giving freedom to virtue or vanity? Her internal questioning never relented. Sister's struggle was real, and her actions of grace belied the torment in her mind. Attempts to calm her cognitive tempest only intensified it.

After laborious and ineffective remedies for Sister's problem, we arrived at a psycho-spiritual accommodation. Sister Michael Marie and all of us, have come to accept her travail as part of her spiritual journey, and therefore as an occasion for goodness. This new frame on her problem gave her the opportunity for advanced spiritual growth and deepened understanding of herself, a perspective far more healing for her than seeing her problem as an egregious pathology that needed to be swept out of her life. The first perspective expanded Sister's life; the second one only drained her of life's energy and richness.

Sister did not seek to quash her torment any more than she would swat a troublesome fly or step on a roving spider in her room. All was honored as God's presence in her life. If something was troublesome ... so be it; we were not called to control our universe, only to find God and live in it. Sister had somehow found God even in her scrupulosity. In some paradoxical way sister found solace in her tempest, peace in her turmoil, and simplicity in her complexity.

Chapter Nine

Sister Matthias knocked on my office door. She was finished with her breakfast clean up in the refectory. It took longer today after cooking the eggs a minute or two over caused the pan to scorch, and necessitated that she scratch the egg pan clean. Scratching the pan was not a phrase that my mom used in our home, somehow the word scratch connoted damage, but here in the monastery the word carries an entirely different connotation. Scratch meant to remove any and all scorching or baked on residue.

We had two chapels in the monastery; one was for the sisters and the other for public worship. A brass grill above the altar divided the two chapels. The grill was rolled open when public mass was offered each morning.

There was no air conditioning in the monastery; it was thought a violation of poverty for us when the monastery was constructed in the late 1950s. In today's world this action seemed an unnecessary omission, nonetheless we offered up the discomfort from the heat of the summer for the poor souls in purgatory.

"Your charity is appreciated. Are you ready to attack those ceiling fans, Mother?" Sister Matthias greeted me as she knocked on the door sash of my office and visually scanned my desk for anything new.

She brought this habit into the monastery with several others. Over the years I've pointed out the impropriety of this indiscretion. Another sister's space, as it were, was private until permission was offered, but sister's habit seemed intractable. Today I only took note of it and decided to let it pass. I flashed a mental prayer of thanksgiving for the slight patience, if patience can ever be so, that God has granted me this morning.

"Your charity is returned." I responded, as I rose from my chair and followed Sister Matthias downstairs to the maintenance closet on the other end of the monastery from the kitchen, which was also on the basement level. The closet was perfectly arranged in exact order by Sister Maria; she currently held the office of maintenance prefect for the monastery. This was the perfect job for Sister Maria; she suffered from, or perhaps reveled in, a slight obsessive-compulsive disorder. Sister craved order, cleanliness, harmony, and peace. Anything that disrupted these gave rise to an anxiety in Sister that she showed in crying. Sister was easily provoked to tears. Periodically, but regularly, she succumbed to a "jag" of crying. Most of the other sisters reacted to her crying in much the same way as die-hard baseball fans reacted to an obvious bad call by an umpire in the second to the last game of the World Series. The best spiritual and psychological care had made not a dent in sister's crying behavior. Most of us have simply come to accept it as a regression to childhood

Chapter Ten

Sister Maria had the required cleaning materials ready for us, a bucket with water and cleaning solution, two towels, and, in case we should required it, a sponge. She explained that she knew that the sponge is not required for the job, but perhaps, only perhaps, we might find it useful to give the fan blades a final swipe after the initial cleaning and before the final drying.

The three of us proceeded up the stairwell past the first floor receiving parlor and down the hall to the nuns' chapel. Sisters Maria and Matthias managed the 12-foot stepladder out of the nuns' chapel, through the sacristy, and into the public chapel. I followed behind with the cleaning supplies. We set up the stepladder straddling over a pew, but there wasn't enough room to open the ladder fully, it was too big to open over one pew, and too small to fit over two pews. This configuration left the ladder somewhat less than stable, but with two of us holding it, and the third climbing it, we agreed that it was safe.

Even though I was the eldest of the three of us, I was still the most limber, and so I volunteered to climb while Sisters Maria and Matthias steadied the ladder. I climbed up as both my sisters offered suggestions of caution. As I ascended, each step became somewhat less stable than the previous one due to the awkward angle of the two sides of the ladder over the pew. Once at the top, I sat on the apex and reached my hand down to retrieve the cleaning cloth from Sister Matthias. We both extended as far as we could but still couldn't reach. As Sister Matthias stepped on the first step of the ladder extending her reach, the ladder heaved to one side and threw me off. I stretched to grasp for the fan blade that served only to twist me farther away from the ladder, and flipped me. As I fell, all I saw was the chapel ceiling twirling in space.

When I next opened my eyes, both Sisters stared down at me, as I lay on the chapel floor between two pews.

"I'm all right." I stabbed at them, as though they were over-involved in a trivial matter inflating it beyond reality.

Once again I protested that I was fine. "Just move away and let me get up out of here. I'm fine; I'm all right I tell you."

Now it struck, I felt the pain in the center of my back. It gripped me, squeezing out the life below it. I strained to get up. I tried again. Nothing happened! My brain sent the message but nothing moved below the pain in my back.

I reach for my sisters' hands. We prayed. "*Dear Lord, give us the strength to move beyond this impasse. Thank you that I still have my breath, my mind, my life. Help me to gather up myself and proceed in your divine will.*"

"Sister Matthias!" I commanded, "Go to my office and call 911 right now. Tell them we need an ambulance here immediately."

She stared at me as though my words had no meaning. "Go ... now!" I direct.

Sister Matthias jumped to her feet. I heard her running down the hall.

"Sister Maria," I said, "Don't let me pass out, keep me awake. It's very important."

"I will," she responded.

Once again we began to pray. *"Lord Jesus, help me in this time of need, wash away my fear. Cleanse me of my doubt."*

I broke into the prayer from the 23rd Psalm. *"Shepherd me Oh God, beyond my wants, beyond my fears, from death into life."*

Sister Maria now joined me. Over and over we said the prayer. I heard footsteps running toward me. One by one all the sisters appeared over me. They were kneeling on the pew seat in front of me as they peered over the pew back. They looked to me as unattached heads craning over a fence.

"What happened?" they exclaimed almost in unison.

I put my finger to my lips and continued to pray the 23rd Psalm. Gradually they all joined in.

When the EMTs burst through the public chapel door, they witnessed a huddle of black veils shrouding an unseen victim of mystery, all praying together,
"Shepherd me Oh God, beyond my wants, beyond my fears, from death into life."

I heard clanking and squishing sounds coming toward me. "How many are there." I wondered.

A mere boy, encased in what looked like a football helmet with a visor, and the most bulky rain suit I had ever seen peered down at me as the sisters untie the knot they had knitted around me. He slid one knee onto the pew seat and planted his other foot against the upturned kneeler.

He asked, "Does anything hurt?"

"Yes." I said. "My back ... and sir ..." I don't know why I addressed him as *sir* except for the bearing he wielded and the hope in my bones that this boy-man could help me. I grasped his hand and pulled him close to whisper without the sisters hearing ...“I can’t move my legs!”

Chapter Eleven *St. John's Rehab Hospital*

"Hi Jan," said Randy, the medical tech on the floor.

"Hey Randy, how are you doing this morning? What's on tap for today?" said Jan, the head nurse.

"Big day, two new patients, both pretty fresh from their trauma site," said Randy.

"Oh yeah, what do we have?"

"You won't believe the first one, a nun! Not just a regular nun, but one of those nuns who doesn't ever go out. You know, what do they call it, closeted?"

"You mean cloistered," Jan replied. "How could a cloistered nun break her back, did she fall off her kneeler or something?"

"Well, something like that. It says here she fell off a stepladder in a chapel."

"How bad?"

"T9 complete; no movement from the lower back down," said Randy

"How about number two?"

"Number two is unusual as well. He's a surgeon, but not just a general surgeon; evidently this guy is a very, very famous heart surgeon. His trauma was vehicular. He was on his way to receive some big award and - *wham* - a garbage truck puts his wife's light out and sends him here!"

"Oh no! Doctors can be such difficult patients, and I'll bet they just get even more difficult when they're famous," said Jan. "How bad is he?"

"He's a lot worse than the nun. He's a C5-6; no movement from the neck on down, but perhaps the hope of some slight right shoulder sensation."

"When are they due in?"

"Admitting says they're both arriving at the airport around the same time," said Randy. "St. John's is sending an ambulance for each of them; that means they'll probably get here around 1 p.m. or so. We better get back-up coverage for their arrival."

Chapter Twelve

Jan Seifert gazed down the hall. It was quiet now; patient census was only moderate, but these two new admissions, the nun and the doctor, would almost fill the floor. Something, or someone caught Jan's eye at the door of room

11. "That's strange," she thought. "Room 11 is where the nun will go. Who could be in there?' she wondered.

As she walked down the hall to check on room 11, she passed all the patients and mentally said a little prayer for each. This was the spinal cord injury rehabilitation floor; each patient had serious trauma; only the site of their injury on their spine was different.

Room 1: Bob Shands, a 43-year-old executive from Portland. A boating accident left him paralyzed from his mid-back down. Room 2: Dan Felter, single, 27, farmer from Iowa. Dan's tractor overturned on him. Room 3: Emily Hartbeck. A fall down the basement steps in her home fractured her spine. Room 4: Michael Renati, 34, ironworker. A fall from construction site scaffolding brought him here. Room 5: Tommy Hernandez a high school senior athlete was run over by the school athletic bus after a big night game win. Room 6: Wyman Ernst, accountant, 52, ran off the road in his new Corvette, charged with DWI. Room 7: Harry Pond, 63, spinal cyst surgery left him immobile. Room 8: Brian Odilini, 37, telephone lineman jolted off a pole by electrical surge. He's burned and paralyzed. Room 9: Sarah Barthols, 42, ER nurse from Charlotte, NC injured in a med helicopter hard landing. The other six passengers, including the patient on-board were not injured. Sarah broke L4; she'll never walk again. Finally, room 10: Jack Cimino, 28, high school history teacher and tennis coach. He ran into the tennis court fence going back for a long hit by one of his students.

As Jan walked into room 11, she felt something strange. It wasn't exactly a physical feeling; rather it was a sensation she felt on another level. The room looked brighter than it should on this overcast day; a very soft golden glow gave the room an otherworldly look. Jan even felt the hint of euphoria, a pleasant uplift as she walked past the bed toward the window. 'What is that?' she thought. Just then her beeper buzzed. It was Randy; the nun was on her way up from admitting.

Chapter Thirteen

Jan liked to meet new arrivals at the elevator, somehow that just seemed right to her. Patients were coming to their new home for the next 3 to 4 months, welcoming them at the front door of the floor was Jan's way of letting them know they were valued. She arrived at the elevator just as the doors opened. The face that protruded from the body coverings in the wheelchair seemed to glow just like room 11; it emanated a sweetness that Jan could almost smell. The nun smiled as Jan squeezed her hand.

"Welcome to your new home, Sister Theresa. I'm Jan, the head nurse this afternoon. Let's get you down to your room."

Sr. Theresa smiled and said, "Thank you Jan, you're very kind."

Jan had heard that voice before; it wasn't so much the voice itself, but the tone of her voice that seemed so familiar to Jan. 'Where had she heard a voice like this before?' pondered Jan. Jan submerged into her memory for what seemed a long while, but was actually only several seconds. When she surfaced, it came to her. 'Of course, this was the tone, the same inflection, the same sense of peace she had experienced many years ago. It was the voice of her 5th grade teacher, Sr. Mary Agnes McGinnis.'

With an aide on either end, navigating the wheelchair down the hall, Jan began her pre-orientation speech.

"Sr. Theresa, this is the spinal cord injury floor, all the patients here have back injuries. We're here to help them start living new lives."

Chapter Fourteen *Sr. Theresa*

I caught the strange wording Jan used. The words that I expected, and the words that would seem normal would be; "...and we're here to help you *get back on your feet.*" Words are powerful, they can motivate when well placed; they can also destroy when used thoughtlessly. Jan used her words carefully.

I tried to catch a glimpse of each of the patients as I was wheeled past each room. How calm, how peaceful: I like peace, I like things harmonious. I wasn't always like this, finding peace wasn't a skill that ever came easily for me. I worked very hard seeking the peace that I believed under girded the whole world and everything in it, even those things that seem chaotic, as my life once was.

I listened intently to Jan as she guided the wheelchair into room 11.

"Sister, do you see anything strange in here? The light seems different in this room – more glowing somehow."

"No Jan, I don't notice anything; of course, I've never been here before."

"This is very mysterious; it's like there's a sensation of a slight emotional updraft in here, some ... I don't know ... something! Do you feel it Sister?"

"No Jan, I can't say that I do."

"There is something here – it's almost like some welcoming sentinel protecting you."

I let the idea pass without further comment. I was as surprised by Jan's sensations as I was by the prospect of some presence in the room.

Jan squeezed my hand again and said, "Sister, we're now going to transfer you from your wheelchair onto your bed. When we pick you up try to grab the trapeze bar over your bed, this will make it easier to bring your body around and place it squarely in the center of the bed. "Are you ready, Sister?"

I wasn't at all sure; I had never heard anyone refer to my body so objectively as though my body was somehow detached from me. Then I realized that in a very real sense even though my legs were still firmly attached to the rest of my body, they were sensationally detached from it. This realization cascaded over me and triggered an internal reaction that culminated in a small tear forming in the corner of my eye.

Jan saw the newly generated emotion and moved closer to me. With words as tender as rose petals, Jan asked, "Are you doing all right, Sister?

I felt Jan's compassion. My smile of appreciation squeezed the tear out of my eye; it rolled down my cheek. I reached up my right hand and caught the tear just below my ear lobe. "Yes, I'm all right, Jan. Thank you."

"Sister, I have to leave you now, but I'll be back soon; we have another admission today. He'll be in room 12, right across the hall from you."

"Does this mean I'm in room 13?" I asked.

"No Sister, you're in room 11. We have no room 13; there are only 12 rooms on this floor.

"That's a good number." I say. "It was good enough for Jesus, so I guess it's just fine for me, too."

I watched Jan smile in agreement. As she left the room she said, "Sister there are some days when you just know that God is around, you can feel it coming up from your toes.

"I know Jan, when you feel like that you know you're on holy ground."

"It seems like some spark of divinity is nodding at you. For me it's very comforting, like a little voice inside saying, 'I told you that this job would bring you riches far beyond gold.'"

"Jan, you must be a pretty special person if you can hear God talking to you that plainly."

"Well, I don't know about that, but at times like these, when I feel light on my feet with appreciation, I just say a little prayer of thanksgiving for all the gifts God has showered upon me -- including you, Sr. Theresa."

"Jan, I know I'm in the right place."

Chapter Fifteen

Jan left and I was alone. I surveyed my room where I would spend the next few months. Just then I heard a commotion down the hall. I heard the elevator door open, quickly followed by a tirade of what sounded like orders being barked by some deranged person.

"You kept me waiting for five minutes in the ambulance. Is this the quality I can expect in this place? Take me someplace else; get me out of here."

There was silence for a bit.

I then heard Jan say, "Good afternoon, Mr. Renowski, welcome to your new home!"

"Who are you?" Renowski snapped.

"I'm Jan Seifert, the head nurse on this floor. I'd like to give you a short orientation as we get you settled in your room."

"I want a room with a view. If I have to be here I want to see something of interest out my window," said Renowski.

"Don't worry, Mr. Renowski," said Jan, "All our rooms have a view. You'll have a wonderful perspective from here."

"Nurse, it's not *Mr.* Renowski, it's *Dr.* Renowski. Don't you know who I am?"

"Oh, I'm very sorry, of course it's *Dr.* Renowski."

"Just get me settled, this trip has been horrendous!"

Chapter Sixteen

Jan escorted the gurney down the hall and into Room 12. Perhaps because Room 12 was at the end of the hall, it was larger than the other rooms. Room 11 was also at the end of the hall, but for some reason it was the same size as all the other rooms. Renowski's room was bigger, probably a third again bigger than the others. He got this big room by pure chance, but once Renowski realized its size, he naturally thought it was given to him in deference to his prodigious medical accomplishments. Renowski always sought, expected, and generally received special, even exclusive consideration; it just seemed to work out that way.

Renowski's transfer had to be done without his assistance; he couldn't steady himself on the trapeze bar above his bed because he couldn't use his arms. The transfer procedure required two attendants. On this very first transfer at St. John's one of the attendants inadvertently lost grip of the lifting strap. Renowski's body jolted onto the bed. Renowski screamed, not in any pain; he couldn't feel anything in his body. His reaction was simply his opportunity to spit a little more emotional venom, and spit venom he did very well!

Jan apologized but thought to herself that the attendant's mistake was probably due to all the tension caused by Renowski's own strident demands and caustic attitude. The attendants were not used to such irate patients especially on admission, but Renowski's display was well beyond what any of them had witnessed before.

Renowski dispensed an angry face to everyone, turned his head, closed his eyes, and disappeared into himself in defiance of everything and everyone. His thoughts were indiscernible, even to himself. At his point his cognitions were blotted-out by the rush of emotion invading and controlling his being. Paradoxically, Renowski prided himself as a deftly programmed computer, a rational thought machine capable of anything. Yet, right now, and perhaps always, Renowski's logic was driven by raw emotion, emotion that was unclarified, unheeded, and unwanted. Blindedness and denial had served Renowski well.

Chapter Seventeen

I said a silent prayer for Dr. Renowski. My reaction, rather my response, was one of pity instead of condemnation for his uncaring attitude. I understood ego-centrism; I had experienced it for 10 years in my former life, but long ago I had dedicated myself in contrast to it, having come to the conclusion that no good could come of pride. In previous years, I reacted against it. Now I simply recognized it, pitied its possessor, and prayed for him to somehow open himself to God's illuminating and healing grace. There was no other real choice for me. Egotism was the bane of the world, an insult to the noble parts of the human spirit; it was a lapse in memory of our true and primary holy nature. I prayed for Dr. Renowski; I prayed he could find peace, could emerge from his emotional hell and discover the real power of the universe.

"Dear God, help this man find himself by finding you. Let him accept your grace, your power, and your healing. Open his mind, dear Lord, and let your Spirit stir him up. Let his injury be his vehicle to peace; let his paralysis give him a new freedom of movement of mind and heart. Loosen him up, dear Lord, and give him humility."

I also prayed for myself.

"Dear God, you have brought me here to this place; you have allowed my body to lose its former mobility. I do trust that your Spirit will bring more good than evil from this event. Oh, that I may participate fully in your will for my life right now. Help me in my time of need, help me to see you in

everything, to love you ever more deeply, and to find your love/patience in every corner of this place, and every corner of my heart."

I fell asleep, and I lapsed into a dream where an ice cream man, the same one who came around to my girlhood neighborhood, stopped outside the rehab hospital. His yells bounded up the stairway and echoed up the elevator shaft, and finally stumbled into my room. He shouted for me to come down; he had my favorite ice cream on the truck today, orange sherbet and vanilla swirl. This was my heavenly combination. He kept yelling for me, again and again. "Sister Theresa come down, come down. I have your special treat today. I saved it just for you. I want you to have it; it's the very last one. Please come down!" I answered him over and over again, "Hank, I can't come down. I can't get out of bed. Hank, can you come up? I'd love the orange-vanilla swirl, but I can't come down Hank!" Hank responded, "Sister I can't leave the truck, you know that I can't, I'd be fired if I left the truck. Sister, you have to come down!" "I can't, I can't." I repeat over and over again. "I can't, I can't."

Chapter Eighteen *Ahead and Behind*

Renowski was restless! He flung his head from side to side, wet his lips, and alternately stared at the ceiling. He memorized the dot pattern of the holes in the ceiling tiles, thinking they appeared random and yet standardized one to another. The dimmed light from the lamp in the corner of the room cast a shadow in each little ceiling tile hole that made each look different than it did in full florescent light. Like so many things, when we see them in a different light we can notice patterns that were formerly hidden from us.

Renowski's mind wandered to the epidemiological studies on heart disease. The scatter grams that showed the incidence of heart attack age by gender in any population always looked random at first, but at a closer investigation the randomness was transformed; patterns emerged where only chaos existed before. Renowski changed the heart disease patterns with his miraculous surgery. Was spinal cord injury random, or did the same patterns emerge as with heart disease he wondered? Patterns seen in retrospect give us clues as to what to expect in the future.

Chapter Nineteen

I'm in the middle of another dream, a dream that isn't new for me; I've had it many times in the monastery. The dream had first dawned into my psyche more than 10 years ago, a time when I was walking a valley of doubt about myself, my vocation, my sexuality, my worthiness, even my faith.

I'm jogging on a sidewalk, passing a park. The park is thick with large trees, and it appears dark and foreboding. But it's very early in the morning and I have jogged this stretch of street many, many times without incident. Perhaps 75 yards ahead of me a big black dog bounds onto the sidewalk from out of the park and begins walking directly toward me. My long-standing fear of dogs growls from within me; my heart beats faster and faster, my thoughts blur, and a primal feeling of something about to end shivers through me. All this is happening, yet I feel little, if any fear. Should I turn-around, cross the street, stop in my tracks, or simply keep running forward? I choose the later, and as I do, the dog begins to run toward me, baring its teeth, lowering its ears, raising the hair in line down its back. The quiet, stealthy approach of the animal unnerves me, yet I seem compelled to keep running straight at the approaching menace. It comes closer, closer, closer and yet closer. The dream now slows to a pace well below slow motion. I focus on the dog's face, its teeth, flying saliva, its wild eyes, and the flesh of its jowls bouncing as the dog bounds up at me. Just as its paws, claws extended, are about to find home on my chest, and its jaws ready to clamp shut over my face – I awaken.

The feeling that I was left with was not fear; rather it was simple relief, a gratitude for being saved from a savage attack. Instead of being threatened, the dream somehow affirmed me; it gave me a sense of safety as though I was protected from some unseen, but not unknown force.

I was jolted out of my reverie by Dr. Renowski's bellicose demand, "Nurse, get down here!" Again he ranted, "Nurse, get down here!"

I was reminded of the shouts for help that day when the workman was repairing the natural gas line coming into the monastery. Thankfully I heard his muffled shouts laboring out from the bottom of the trench he was digging as it was collapsing around him. I could still hear his shouts in my mind, 'Help, help, help!' Dr. Renowski's demanding shouts sounded similar. I realized that Dr. Renowski couldn't press his call button; he couldn't move his arms, so I pressed the nurse's call button on a wire connected to my bed rail.

Nurse Jan shot her head into my room and said, "Sorry, I can't get to you right now sister, Dr. Renowski is having a problem."

"Nurse, that's fine, I rang my button for him anyway." I didn't need to strain to hear Dr. Renowski across the hall.

Chapter Twenty

Renowski bellowed out, "Nurse, I'm uncomfortable ... do something! I can't stand this; this is horrible. What kind of place is this, some kind of torture chamber? Are you SS or something?"

"Dr. Renowski, what can I do for you? How can I help?" Nurse Jan replied.

"I don't know what you can do; you're the coordinator here, you suggest something," snapped Renowski.

"Well, let's see," said Jan. Jan knew that there was little she could do. She can only adjust his body position slightly; she knew that for the rest of his life Dr. Renowski would be confined.

"Let me wipe your face with this cool cloth," she said.

"I don't want my face soothed with water; that's nothing. I want something substantial. I want something to make me feel better. Do something!" Renowski blasted.

"Would you like something to eat or drink? Perhaps you'd like a bit of ice cream, Jell-O, or some chips and soda?" queried Jan.

"What I want is a Manhattan ... a perfect Manhattan."

"Oh, you're partial to Manhattans. Once we get an order from your doctor that alcohol is indicated for you, I'd be glad to make you a Manhattan. Tonight, I'm sorry Dr. Renowski, I can't honor your request, but I can get you a cool drink of some kind ... how about that?"

"I want a Manhattan! I am a doctor; I can give my own order. Alcohol is indicated. I've given more orders than all your doctors here combined. I know what I want and need. I have a Manhattan every night and I want one now. Get me a Manhattan."

"Dr. Renowski, I know how you must feel, but please understand that I simply cannot give you alcohol without a prescription. You know that alcohol is a drug and I don't have the authority to write a scrip for you, or for anyone."

"Nurse, you don't get it, do you? I give the orders, I always have and I intend to continue. Neither you nor anyone else can or will change that."

"Dr. Renowski, all I can tell you is that I'll check with your doctor," said Jan, as she backed out of Renowski's room.

Chapter Twenty-One

Jan appeared in my room and closed the door behind her. With exasperation written all over her face, she said, "Sister, I think I've already lost."

"What do you mean, Jan?"

"I need to change my tactics with Dr. Renowski if I'm to help him, and keep my sanity at the same time. It's common to see patients, especially males, exhibit an adolescent attitude the first few days, but I'm afraid the Dr. Renowski might be worse."

"He doesn't seem to be easily soothed."

"For him at this point, our conversation is simply a power play; he's the MD, and I'm only the lowly RN. It's that simple for him. In his dependent state all he can do is demand."

"But he is in a dependent state, much more dependent than he's ever been before."

"Oh, I certainly know that, but I have a feeling that he's always been in a dependent state, dependent on his rank, title, power, and medical prowess. What is he left with now that all that formerly propped him up is now taken away?"

"I'm sure you're right Jan, you have lots more experience in this area than I do."

"Sister, I think I need to take a risk. I hesitate to ask you, it's not really regulation here, but something tells me you could help a fast unraveling situation with Dr. Renowski before it cascades out of control."

"He certainly seems flummoxed by it all. How can I help?" I asked.

"I don't know Sister, it's against our usual procedures, but you seem so at peace, in control, somehow knowing. Dr. Renowski needs some of that, his agitation feeds on itself."

"Thanks for the compliment. Is there anything in particular that you think he needs?" I asked.

"I guess I'm hoping that you can distract him a bit. Right now I just stir him up; he sees me as the resident authority and he resents it. You're neutral, on that account anyway; I think he may respond to you."

"I don't have much experience with men you know," I said, with a slight half smile and a raised eyebrow.

Chapter Twenty-Two

As soon as I said this however, my memory exploded to those times when my mother would awaken me, and in a voice distorted by fear, she would ask me in a tone somewhere between begging and demanding, to talk to my father downstairs where he was semi-stuporous with alcohol on the living room couch.

I would always respond immediately, momentarily basking in the status bestowed upon me by this request and the suggestion that I had influence with my father at times beyond my mother's. That's where the positive valence of my emotions ended; now the fear began, fear that perhaps my father wouldn't respond to my pleas this time and might just either explode into a continuous tirade, as he had done once before, or more frightening, rebuff my advances and thereby reject me. I felt the sting of this latter possibility more than the former.

A past rebuff still festered in me after burrowing deep inside of my heart when my father called me 'stupid'. This word still daily rises in my mind like a boil. At school I wondered if my teachers knew I was stupid; did my friends know? The layer of shame thickened around me each time I saw my father drunk again. Each time my mother's eyes flashed with terror in the night, I would slink deeper into insecurity that all would not be well, something very bad surely would happen.

The only relief from this emotional chaos came at church. In the ultimate privacy of my prayers, I discovered something steady, stable, unchanging, and utterly accepting.

There were no late-night terrors, no wild eyes, no fear, accusations, names, or stings. There was only peace and benevolence, the way my father was when he wasn't drunk.

Here it is all over again! Nurse Jan playing the part of my mother, and Dr. Renowski the part of my father. The stakes were high when I accepted the role from my mother, but I had no idea that tonight a new chapter of my life would open with stakes even higher.

Nurse Jan hoisted me into a wheelchair. It was a gentle transfer perfected with care by thousands before this one. I adjusted myself with my hands tightly gripping the chair arms. I found I could actually lift my body right off the chair. This was a feat I didn't believe I could do only days before. Yet, here I was, infused with new strength, and strangely, did I dare admit it ... new hope!

Chapter Twenty-Three

Together we crossed the hall into Dr. Renowski's room. He had been quiet since Nurse Jan left him. I had the wisp of a thought that he might be asleep. This thought evaporated as I look up at Dr. Renowski and heard, "So what's this, have you brought in reinforcements?"

"Well, something like that," replied Jan.

I chimed in, "Good evening, Dr. Renowski, I can hear you from my room across the hall and thought you might like some company for a while."

"Oh you did, did you? Well, I don't need a nursemaid, especially one dressed like a nun – are you a nun?"

"I'm no nursemaid, Dr. Renowski, and, yes, I am a nun." I said, "I'm just here to listen."

Fear shot through me again as Renowski's stare of rage captured me. His face was contorted as if he were about to attack me. Instead, he simply snorted and looked away."

"I thought since I'm just across the hall, perhaps we could just talk. Sometimes it helps to get things out, just to let go ... you know what I mean?"

His silence poked at me. But I had been here before. I was back in my childhood living room, my father silent, looking away.

Without moving his eyes to meet mine, Renowski said, "Did that nurse send you in here ... did she put you up to this?"

"She's concerned." I answered. "She wants you to be comfortable here, and right now she knows you're not!"

"Who could be comfortable here, who could be anything but distressed here? This is not exactly my idea of fun, said Dr. Renowski, "Is it yours?"

"No, I couldn't call this fun, but it's not exactly fun that I'm after. Are you?"

"What a stupid question. I'm in a place I never dreamed I'd be, in a position ... in a position ... well, just look at this position, and we're talking about fun! I can't see one thing that remotely resembles anything close to fun here. If you can, then you're a better person than me, and I can't hardly imagine that!"

"Well, thanks for the compliment. What did you like to do for fun?" I asked, changing the thrust of the conversation.

"My life is really none of your business. But if you must know, my fun is my work ... my work ... my work. I live for my work; work is my life; nothing else matters. I do grand things, I save lives; I ... me ... I developed the world's most reliable means of bringing people back from certain death. I not only raised the bar of cardiac surgery, I created an entirely new bar. I did what no one else could do; I perfected surgical procedures so radical and so creative that the world of surgery stands still for me. I am the greatest surgeon ever! Do you get that? Fun is trivial. My work is a monument to human achievement; my work stands above everything else ... nothing else matters to me. Do you understand?"

He sat there, physically helpless, yet verbally potent. His words stopped. I let the silence be.

Finally he said, "You couldn't possibly understand!"

I said a little prayer for him. I realized that he had just made his profession of faith. Surgery was his god. He only trusted himself. He was the center of his world. How tragic!

I felt his emptiness and said, "Your work means a lot to you ... your work is everything for you ... sounds in fact like your work is pretty much your god."

"You have no idea whatever what you're saying. Triumphs like I do everyday require complete, full, and unfettered dedication; every bit of my life is taken up with it. I am committed to surgery, to continuing science, to furthering knowledge, to being the best!"

Again, I simply let the silence linger. I think I see a tear forming in his eye.

"Tell me about your work Dr. Renowski."

"My work ... my work ... my work ... is everything." His rage momentarily submerged to reveal the deep hurt that pervaded him now.

"You seem so hurt Dr. Renowski," I said, not knowing what else to say.

"I can't do this. This isn't real ... this can't be," he blustered.

"You know something, Dr. Renowski, I notice that you're speaking in the present tense, you know, like your work as a surgeon is still going on."

He turned his head and stared at me. "What do you mean?" "Well," I said, "When you speak of your work you always use the present tense as though there's been no interruption in it. I just think this is odd given current circumstances."

"What do you mean?"

"Dr. Renowski, you're still looking at what was; are you looking as intently at what is?"

"I am a surgeon!" he demanded. "The world's best surgeon!"

"Certainly you're a surgeon, but are you a practicing surgeon? You make it sound like you'll be in the operating room tomorrow; this just puzzles me, I guess."

Silence again.

"Do you want to tell me about your accident?" I asked.

Again he threw that stare at me as if I had asked him to fly.

"What's there to tell? It just happened."

"I can tell you about mine if you'd like."

"I don't want to know," he retorted.

"OK."

Silence again.

"It was raining. It was dark and it was raining hard. My wife ... she made me late. I couldn't see ... something must have splashed on my windshield." *Long pause*. "That's all I remember."

"Where is your wife ... how is she?" I asked.

After another long pause, he simply said, "She's gone."

"Oh, I'm so sorry. You must feel terrible," I stammered.

"Feel? I don't know what I feel. I don't feel. Feelings are useless; they just get in the way. Feelings aren't real ... I don't deal in feelings."

"Feelings are the emotional facts of the moment." I replied. "We always have feelings whether we're aware of them or not. Feelings give us the signals of what we need to do next; they kind of emotionally point the way ahead. You must have lots of feelings about your wife."

Silence again.

"I told you, it's useless to feel. In the operating room feelings are dangerous; I can't have feelings. I just focus on my work; my work is all there is."

"You mean, all there *was*, don't you?" I don't mean to be blunt, Dr. Renowski, but you keep talking about work. It seems to me your perspective is a bit unfocused, isn't it? You keep looking back at what was, don't you think that part of why we're here is to begin to learn how to look ahead?"

"What do you mean, look ahead?" he demanded. "There is no ahead, there is no future. My life is over; my life is done! I'm dead, don't you get it?"

"All that 'I get' is that you're stuck. I can tell you that you're not dead, Dr. Renowski, you're just stuck!"

"OK, what do I have to look forward to? All that I am is gone ... just like my wife ... she's gone too. There is no future for me ... it's over."

"Your life isn't over, but your life does need to change. What needs to change is how you view your life. Up till now you've looked outside to define who you were inside, perhaps it's time to shift that perspective. When you look inside yourself, you're apt to discover a whole new world in there."

"I don't know what you're talking about, it sounds like some kind of psycho-babble to me."

"Dr. Renowski, we're both at a turning point in our lives. We can't turn back; our lives will never be the same. We can't keep going around asking why the past isn't the present; we can't use the answer to yesterday's questions to define us anymore. We don't have a choice; we must change. All our bridges to yesterday are broken; we need new bridges to tomorrow. We have to find answers to new questions. If we can't ... we'll simply exist, just survive; we'll never thrive."

"Well, that's not for me. I don't want to live like this, and I won't live like this. I can't live like this!"

"Dr. Renowski, where is your vision? You're only looking back. We need to start looking ahead."

"Look, there is no looking ahead for me, my life is over. There is nothing out there for me anymore. There is no *up ahead* for me."

Silence again.

"I've had enough of you tonight. Why don't you just leave?" he blasted.

"I'm sorry. I said too much; I usually do. I'll go now, but ... I'll be back."

"Don't bother."

Chapter Twenty-Four

I wheeled back across the hall. I rang the buzzer to be transferred back into bed. Nurse Jan arrived quickly. She shut my door.

"Well, how did it go?" asked Jan.

"Oh, not well I'm afraid, he threw me out."

"Oh no," she replied. "He's one tough bird. I just thank you for trying. I'm sorry to have put you in such a position. I promise I won't do it again."

"No, no, he needs someone; I'll go back. He's so afraid but he can't express any of it."

"How do you know that?" asked Jan.

"Oh, I don't know how I know; I just know!"

"OK, but right now it's time for you to get settled."

She lifted me into my bed.

"Need anything else?" she asked.

"No Jan. I'll be fine."

"OK, have a good night."

As she left the room I looked up at the holes in the ceiling tiles and retraced my conversation with Dr. Renowski. He was scared, just like my father was scared. My father was scared that he couldn't measure up, he was scared he wasn't the husband and father that he should be. My father was scared of his job; he was scared of his boss, but most of all he was scared of God. I wondered if Dr. Renowski was scared of God too. Was fear at the base of the existential morass he wallowed in? It was then that I felt the first sensation of care for Dr. Renowski. We were taught compassion and care in our novitiate, but only in the sense of offering mercy. This care I felt now might be different!

I prayed ...

Dear God. Here I am. I'm as confused as ever. You know why I'm here ... but I don't. You know what I'm doing ... but I don't. Help me dear Lord, find the path to you. Give me the strength to go on; give me the understanding to know you better. I know all of this will eventually allow me to be closer to you and consequently closer to the real me as well. Lord, give Dr. Renowski peace. He needs your peace so much. He's floundering Lord; he's confused, he's angry. Let your Spirit rest in his heart and illuminate his vision so he can see ahead. Amen.

Chapter Twenty-Five *Youthfulness*

Five days later I saw Dr. Renowski in the rehab therapy gym for the first time. He was in his wheelchair, together with five other patients, along the wall of the therapy gym as he waited his turn for physical therapy. I couldn't help thinking that they looked somewhat like penguins lined up at the edge of an ice floe that was adrift far from the security of the mother glacier. All of them, except Dr. Renowski, looked eager to get going on their morning regimens of stretching, strengthening, and straightening body, mind, and spirit.

Dr. Renowski's expression reminded me of the way my brother would stare at my father when he came home late from work ... drunk. Dr. Renowski glanced at the man next to him with a sneer as the physical therapist Colleen greeted him and wheeled him to the middle blue exercise mat.

I remembered when I would assist wheelchair-bound passengers onto the aircraft. I always felt a special connection with them along with a light of gratitude that warmed my soul. What must a physical therapist feel as she (probably 70 to 80% were female) manipulates severely impaired individuals day after day here at St. John's rehab center? Since I arrived here I've been impressed by their care, their desire to help, their courage, and their ease of connection with their patients. Certainly they must get tired, their work is physical and emotionally demanding, but they don't seem to show any fatigue. They move from one patient to another as in a well choreographed ballet, effortlessly gliding as though invisible wings propelled them, always poised, always smiling, always up.

Chapter Twenty-Six

Amy, my therapist for today, appeared at my right side.

"Good morning Sister, how are we doing today?" she asked

"Well." I say, "I'm doing well. And how are you Amy?"

"Oh, real well thanks Sister, my 3-year-old started day care yesterday so I'm just a bit unsettled, feeling a little like I've given my baby away."

"Wow, that must be difficult. Your first child?"

"First and only so far, Sister, but number two is on the way."

"Oh wow, how far along are you now?"

"Three and a half months. I'm just over the morning sickness, thank God," she said. "Not as bad as the first one, but still something I could do without."

"Let's get started, shall we?" Amy suggested.

"This is a slide board, some people call it a Beasy board, I guess after the person who invented it. Anyway, it serves as a bridge between your chair and this elevated exercise mat. I'll just slip it here under your right leg and set the other end on the edge of the mat."

"OK," I said timidly.

As Amy crouched down with her legs bent, she wrapped one arm around my back and the other over my shoulder and around my neck.

"Now, I've got a good grasp of you," she said. "I'm going to rock you on three counts. On the third count, I'll pull you a bit along the slide board. At the same time you try to move yourself along with me in any way you can. Are you ready?"

"Yes, I ... I think so."

"All right then, one." Amy rocked my body back and forth. "Two." Again she rocked me back and forth. "And three." This time she pulled me along the board. I probably moved an inch or two along the slide board, but you'd think, from Amy's reaction, that I ran a mile.

"Great Sister, that was great! You moved right with me so well, just like you've done it a thousand times."

"Now. Let's try it again ... "one ... two ... three." Once again we slid an inch or two, and once again Amy exploded with affirmation.

"Wonderful - you're a pro at this! Do you think you can do it again? Do you want to rest a bit?"

"No, I can do it." Her encouragement had found its mark ... she was clearly motivating me.

"Great," she said. "One ... two ...three." Again we moved only inches; and again she showered me with affirmation.

"Wonderful, wonderful; we're almost there. One more time and I think we'll make it."

"OK," I said. "I think I'm ready."

"One ... two ... three. Wow ... great, you made it; you went completely across the slide board. That was just excellent Sister; you are a pro!"

I hadn't felt so good about an accomplishment since I made my profession of perpetual vows.

Amy helped me recline on the mat and said, "One thing I need to tell you, a very important skill you need to learn and practice from now on is pressure release. Your body can't give you signals of discomfort from your waist on down. You need to move your body every ten minutes or so. The simple pressure of you sitting still will gradually cut off circulation without you knowing it if you don't move your body regularly. Before your injury you would move and shift your weight unconsciously, and that's what pressure release will become for you, almost automatic. But, we need to work on this quite intentionally until it becomes a habit ... you know, kind of involuntary you might say; something you do without thinking about it."

"Let's get you on your side," she said. "That's good!"

"Now, move your shoulder over as far as you can, swing your free arm, and on a count of three see if you can move your body onto its other side. I'll help you through this. Any questions?"

"No." I quickly responded, trying to hide my apprehension. Amy's soothing voice and confident demeanor compelled me to try ever harder.

"OK," she said. "One ... two ... three. Now, over we go."

"We did it," I exclaimed.

"Great work," she said smiling. "That was just superb. I can see that you're a natural at this."

"Oh, I'm not so sure."

"This is the movement you'll do in bed as a pressure release."

"I think I need some more practice."

"Let's try again," she said. "We'll move back onto your right side. OK ... one ... two ... three ... and over." She pulled me until I was fully over on my other side, resting on my left shoulder.

"That was so nice. How do you feel? Are you comfortable?"

"I feel fine." Even though I thought the movement would be almost impossible for me to do alone.

As though she knew what I was thinking, Amy said, "Right now, you're probably wondering how you could possibly do this movement on your own. But, believe me, you can and you will."

"So you're a mind reader too,' I blurted.

"No, not a mind reader, just a heart reader." she replied.

Chapter Twenty-Seven

It was true! Amy, this agile, alert, and amiable woman was indeed a heart reader. My anxiety evaporated in the warmth of her care and her confidence. She is obviously well trained, but far beyond her technical ability, I sensed her soul, her desire t help, to care for me, to be a vehicle of empowerment for me. This power in her is not her human power, it's divine; it's God's energy, uniquely compressed into this woman who had found her calling. Amy wasn't just filling a position, working at a job; Amy was living her dream. She had somehow tapped into that vast reservoir of God's energy that's in each of us, each one of us different, and yet the same. Her vitality gave testimony not only to the fact that she was in great physical shape, not only to the fact that she was mentally alert, but probably more to her connection with God within. How lucky I was to be in her care, her hands were like those of an angel on my skin, bringing back to life what could be, and animating the rest.

"How was your night?' she asked.

"Oh, pretty good. Actually I could say it was better than pretty good. I slept well, I even had a good dream."

"Really, what was that?'

"Well, I was on an island. It was a jungle island, and at first I was scared. You know, 'lions and tigers and bears' and such. But something compelled me to go away from the beach and into the interior, into the jungle. I don't know why. But when I did, my fear subsided. Then, when I was deep into the jungle, I found a clearing. There in the clearing was a picnic table under an apple tree full of fruit. I picked an apple, sat on the picnic bench and began to eat. Soon a man appeared, dressed all in white. He sat beside me, put his arm around me, and simply said, 'don't you worry, everything in your life is unfolding as it should.'"

"Wow, what a dream!"

"Yeah, and when I awakened this morning, I just felt that sense of peace and a real feeling that everything really would be all right."

"Do you dream a lot?"

"I dream all the time."

"I wish that I could remember my dreams better, but right now we better get on with our work here, or I won't have much to write on your therapy report today."

All right."

"OK, one ... two ... three. Wonderful!"

Amy grasped my right knee and foot and simply bent my knee for me.

"Can you feel that, I'm moving your leg?"

"No."

Trying the movement again, she asked, "Can you feel a stretch anywhere in your body?"

"A bit in my lower back, but no other place."

"Can you feel my hand on your foot?"

"No."

Again she moved my right leg.

She asked, "Can you feel any stretching, or anything at all in your hip joint?"

"No," I responded. She made no reply.

"This stretching is good for your legs, particularly your hamstring muscles down in here," she said, as she pointed to the back of my right thigh.

"We do stretching every day, it's part of your program, and something we want you to do on your own when your get back home," said Amy.

"Back home? You know, I haven't yet thought about returning to the convent."

"Oh, you will!"

"We need to increase mobility in these joints," said Amy.

Amy proceeded to stretch both my legs. I felt minor sensations in my lower back and stomach area, but only minor ... very minor!

"There is fun in stretching," Amy said.

Chapter Twenty-Eight

I glanced across the gym at Dr. Renowski who was on a blue mat now like me. I couldn't hear what he was saying to his physical therapist, but from the look on his face, and the movement of his head, I could tell that he was trying to direct the session. What was it in Dr. Renowski that pushed him to command the way he did? Was it simply impatience ... the super-intelligent Dr. Renowski just exasperated by the intellectual 'deficiencies' of the rest of us? Was it some sense of entitlement he developed ... from home ...from his successes ... from his medical degree ... from his accomplishments? Or was his demanding and directive personality the product of something deeper, some personal insufficiency that he was trying to cover-up?

"Can you feel that stretch?" Amy asked. "Can you feel the pull? I'm bending your knee farther."

"A little bit," I said, with hopeful anticipation that I just might be feeling something. But in reality, I didn't know for sure.

"I want to be sure that you can tolerate it OK?" she asked. "Is that OK?"

"Oh yes." I replied. I felt I had entered a kind of reverie, as though this was all somehow unreal.

"Let's finish up today with your ankles. I'm pulling your calf muscle here ... is that OK?"

"Oh yes." I said. But I felt nothing.

"OK," she said. "I'll hold it right there for a short time. Are you OK?"

"Oh yes."

"Can you feel any pressure on the bottom of your foot with this stretch."

I had to say no, even though I wanted to say I was feeling great pressure, mostly for Amy's sake, but some for my own.

Amy completed the session and we reversed the slide board procedure getting me back into my wheelchair. She wheeled me over to the penguin line on the other side of the main entrance to the gym from where I started.

"There'll be a transporter for you shortly who'll take you back to your room." Amy said with a thread of tenderness in her voice.

"Thank you! God's grace is in you and even though I can't feel much yet from your hands, your heart messages are loud and clear."

"Thanks, Sister!" Amy replied. "I'll see you tomorrow."

Chapter Twenty-Nine

As I waited for the transporter, I spied Dr. Renowski struggling on the mat. His therapist had called in two reinforcements and the three of them stood next to Renowski's mat, each with their hands behind their backs focused intently on him. It looked like he was reprimanding them.

As I was wheeled from the rehab gym, I took a mental snapshot of a tableau. The three therapists were tangled around Renowski trying to wrestle him into his chair. The look on his face was an emotional composite of anger, sadness, distrust, and disgust. I filed the picture away.

When we arrived at my room, I asked the transporter, "Could you position me so I can see out the window?"

"Oh, of course Sister," she replied.

I guess everyone knew by now that I was a nun, I guess they didn't get too many here ... at least not as patients. When I was in the rehab gym I wore normal "civilian" clothes; my habit was much too bulky for ease of movement. I had been changing back into my habit at all other times, but now this seemed somewhat cumbersome too and so I decided that my new "civilian" look was simply easier for everyone. Except for a small headpiece that I still retained, I put my full habit aside.

I reached for my rosary on the nightstand and began my prayer as I looked out onto God's glory in nature. I ticked off each Hail Mary one-by-one, and ten-by-ten, but as I tried to concentrate on the Glorious mysteries of Christ, my thoughts seemed pulled to Renowski. 'He's so emotionally needy, Lord, how can I help him?' I finished my rosary and entered into contemplation that was interrupted by a voice.

Chapter Thirty

"Sister, here's your lunch," said the voice.

"Oh, thank you," I said. "Would you mind putting it on my stand and rolling it over to me?"

"Oh sure, Sister," said the voice.

The face of the voice startled me, indeed scared me. He must have sensed my surprise and shock.

"Are you OK, Sister?' he asked.

"Oh, ... oh ... yes, I'm fine. I guess you just surprised me, that's all."

I couldn't take my eyes away from this man because he reminded me so much of my father. The bridge of his nose, his bald head, his jowls, his sad eyes, and his rugged skin creased like canyons from years of smoking. His whole presentation was all so much like my father it seemed. I stared at him.

"Are you sure you're OK, Sister?" he asked again.

Awakened from my mesmerism, I said, "Oh yes ... I'm fine, thank you."

"OK then, I'll just leave this here for you. Can I open up your milk carton for you?" he asked.

"Oh, ... no, I'm fine ... I can do it, thank you."

"Well OK then," he said. "I hope to see you next week when I volunteer next."

"Oh, you're a volunteer?"

"Yeah, I've been here about three years I guess, ever since my wife died."

"Oh, I'm sorry"

"No Sister, I'm fine now. I had a rough time for a year or so but her death was something of a blessing ... Alzheimer's you know."

"I'm so sorry," I said again.

"No, not at all," he said. "We had 52 good years. God was good to take her when he did."

As he left my room, he said, "We all have our crosses to bear, and bear them we must."

I was stunned. What was God saying to me? What kind of healing would I find in this place? I had the sense that I was part of a grand play that God was directing, no not directing; maybe God was more like a lifeguard in the play, always watching us with a care-filled eye, ready and able to help us in times of trouble ... if we let him!

Chapter Thirty-One

I had just started eating my lunch when I heard Renowski returning from the rehab gym. He was stabbing his two transporters with verbal barbs.

"Don't ever leave me waiting again. I hate waiting; it's useless and inefficient. Just leave me here and go," he blurted.

I wondered if Renowski possessed a conversational tone of voice. All I'd heard so far from him was demanding, commanding, criticizing, or lecturing.

I ate slowly, listening for the next drama to erupt across the hall. A few moments later it started.

"Hi, Mr. Renowski, I have your lunch for you," I heard a female voice say to Renowski.

"It's not *Mr*. Renowski, it's *Dr*. Renowski; you got that, *Dr*. Renowski, and don't forget it!" he barked.

"Oh, of course, I'm sorry Dr. Renowski," said the female volunteer.

"Just leave the food, I'll eat it later."

"But, Dr. Renowski, I'm here to help you eat. You can't ..." she stopped herself from finishing her sentence, but her meaning was more than clear.

"Just leave it I said!"

"Well, OK I guess," said the volunteer as she left his room.

I imagined Renowski sitting there in his toxic, exclusionary thoughts. I imagined the tray of food sitting there also. The two couldn't come together without help. I swung my wheelchair around and crossed the hall into Renowski's room.

Chapter Thirty-Two

"May I help?" I didn't break my movement as I rolled right up next to him.

"What do you want?"

"I thought maybe you could use some help with your lunch."

"Oh you did, did you," he replied with agitation.

"I think one of the things they're trying to teach us here is to accept help," I said.

"I don't need anyone's help!" he blustered.

"Well, I don't know if that's entirely true," I said. "It looks to me like you could use some help with your lunch."

I wedged a piece of his meatloaf onto his fork and lifted it to his mouth. For a long second he leered at me, and then, like a boy breaking through his tantrum, he quickly denuded the fork of its food.

"Thank you," I said, as though he had done me a favor. In truth, he had done much more.

I forked a dollop of his mashed potatoes and offered it to him.

"Here you go," I said "Meat and potatoes, the staff of life."

He said nothing. I continued feeding him his lunch without conversation. I had the sense that this man was not at all used to being served in any personal way. I felt a certain empowerment simply accomplishing this minimal task. This simple act of giving seemed good to me. But there was something more to this act ... more than performing a task. I was offering me. In offering him bits of food, I was also giving me. The food nourished his body, but I felt myself wanting to nourish more of him. As we began on the Cool Whip topped Jell-O, I broke the silence.

"Have you done any thinking today?' I asked.

"What do you mean?"

"Well, I saw you down in the rehab gym today. You seemed to be struggling a bit with your therapist."

"She doesn't know what she's doing. I can't stand her patronizing tone of voice, her pandering to me; it's insufferable," he snorted.

"I understand that she's one of the best therapists here," I said.

"Well, that doesn't say much for the place."

"Amy was my therapist today; she was great. She's always so positive, so encouraging, so upbeat, and she certainly knows what she's doing."

"Good for you," he said.

"You're not giving an inch, are you?"

"Look, I don't know what you mean," he said.

"Well, don't you think they need our cooperation to move us along?" I asked. "They need our help; without it they can't do much for us."

There was silence for a time.

"Just like I say, you don't give an inch," I said.

"I've given all my life," he retorted. "All I've done is give, give, give! And I've done it all myself. There was no one to pay for my college. I worked full time to pay my own way through. I patched together a scholarship, a work assistantship, and several jobs to get through medical school. I won top honors to get in the best surgery residency there was. I worked, worked, worked. I did it myself. I did everything so I could get to where I got. Nobody helped me; I did it all alone. So don't tell me I don't give an inch; I've given miles and miles."

"Sounds like you were blessed," I said. "Blessed with intelligence and drive."

"Look," he stabbed. "I worked for what I got ... I achieved it; I'm the best!"

"Oh, I remember, that's where we left off in our last talk, you being the best," I said.

Chapter Thirty-Three

I found myself emboldened by his anger. Instead of retreating, I rather uncharacteristically fired right back at him. I wasn't simply trying to win an argument; it was just that in some strange way I saw his fear, his distress, his internal anguish, and I wanted to help him grow beyond it. He had to get beyond it. But how could I help?

With trepidation I asked, "Do you think you might need to change that attitude of yours Dr. Renowski?"

"If you want to stay in here with me, you're the one who had better change her attitude," he blasted.

"Dr. Renowski, maybe you need to find new vistas. You can either stew here in your own toxic juices or you can begin to look inside yourself.

"Oh really! Are your blind? Just look at this body."

"You're not a person in decline. While your body is not the same as it was, your spirit can be on the ascent if you let it. Here is your opportunity to be reborn, as it were, make a new start.

"Are you nuts! What kind of new start might that be?"

"You can't be stuck in your past, as rewarding as it was for you. You've got to find some new integration, some internal cohesion within you, some new synthesis of what you were and what you are, so that you can gain a vision of what you'll become.

"I was living my vision, but now it's gone. There is no more vision for me ... it's all gone. The only vision there is for me now is the reality of what once was," he said in disgust.

"You can't impose the past onto the future, that's an illusion. You've got to accept the impermanence of life and fully recognize the new road in front of you. If you can't, you'll only mire yourself in a restless angst and a perpetual anxiety.

"You said it Sister, restlessness and anxiety, that's all my life is now."

"Dr. Renowski, you need to find God's peace inside of you."

He looked at me with deep disdain, but I saw a shard of light from within him, a hint of agreement. I knew that he couldn't concede his position, nor did I want or need him to ... not yet at least. But I needed to punch through his armor. I needed to let him know I couldn't ever agree with his confusion. I had to keep going ... I was compelled ... I couldn't help myself. A new boldness had overtaken me, and somehow I know that this new power was not from me. I also know in a flash that this bold new power was the only way to get to him.

"You can leave now," he said, as he continued to glare at me.

I gave no response except to retreat from his room and into mine. As I closed my eyes offering myself to sleep, I talked to God.

"Dear Father, what are you doing to me? I've become so brazen with Dr. Renowski; something in me has been unchained. What is your Spirit stirring up in me?"

Chapter Thirty-Four *Contradictions*

I was startled awake by Renowski's verbal assault on Nurse Jan from across the hall.

"Nurse, I've told you and told you, I don't want to go to the rehab gym today, and I'm not going," barked Renowski.

"Dr. Renowski, I can understand your feelings, but I also need to tell you that the therapists are quite strict, they demand patient participation. It's a bedrock policy of St. John's that patients must cooperate with their stated rehab programs. You know that without cooperation from you, they can't help you. You must be fully involved in your therapy," said Nurse Jan.

"I don't care, do you get that? I don't care what they want or need; they can demand all they want, I'm not going ... period!"

"I hear you very clearly Dr. Renowski, but you need to know that some patients are actually asked to leave the hospital if they don't cooperate actively in their therapy."

"And I told you I don't care ... I don't care! Get out of here, leave me alone," shouted Renowski.

"Dr. Renowski, I do hope you'll reconsider. You just can't let yourself go like this; you're only hurting yourself."

"I do what I want to do, and I don't do what I don't want to do. Neither you, nor anyone else can tell me differently! Do you understand that nurse?"

"What I understand, Dr. Renowski is that you're hurt and angry; you're sad and you're confused ... I understand that. I'd like to help you, everyone here wants to help, but they can't do anything without your cooperation and full participation."

"Thank you for your understanding... now can you leave me alone!" stabbed Renowski.

I wanted to do something, but I didn't know what. I had two competing urges; one was to slap him for being so insolent and so ridiculously obtuse; the other was to give him a hug of reassurance to soothe his deep, deep pain. I chose neither!

I ate my breakfast in prayer.

"Dear Father, I need your help. I know I need to concentrate on my own healing. I need to mourn my own losses, and feel my own sorrow at what has happened. But I can't. My mind is filled with Renowski, I can't get away from him ... I'm trapped, dear Father; I'm confronted by him at every turn. What is happening, Father? I don't understand; I want to help him ... but how can I? Please, dear Lord, I need

your strength, I need your vision, I need your steadfastness ... I need you! Please help me!'

Chapter Thirty-Five

"Good morning, Laura. I see your name on your nametag. Are you my transporter today?" I asked.

"Good morning, Sister. Yes, I am; today's my weekly volunteer day at St. John's. I've been doing this for two years now ... and I love it," said Laura.

"You know, I'm curious. What is it that makes you love it so? What do you feel about coming here?"

"Oh that's easy; it's the people," she said. "All these patients are at a crucial juncture in their lives. They're all a little scared and wondering what's next for them. They need to feel a sense of the world outside of St. John's. They all feel so disconnected. Maybe I can be some little reminder of that outside world for them ... you know, Sister, kind of like a messenger."

"I see," I said absentmindedly. But my mind was whirling. She's right, I thought. That word "disconnected" is right on! Did I feel disconnected; certainly Renowski felt disconnected. Metaphorically it was a good word for our situation, our disconnected spinal cord has disconnected us both from our former lives. But he feels disconnected from everything he saw as his life before; while I seem thrust more deeply into mine. His life was the outside world; mine was the inside world. The world he knew is over; mine is still so rich! Yet paradoxically, our individual disconnections have mutually connected us!

"Sister, are you all right?" asked Laura. "Can I help you into your wheelchair? You seemed like you tuned-out there for a moment.

"Oh, I'm sorry, Laura. I just had a little mental reverie, that's all. Yeah, let's get going."

Laura brought me to the penguin line where I surveyed the rehab gym. There was Dan. I met him yesterday down here. He's 27, single, and a farmer from Iowa. He rolled his tractor over and came up like me ... a para. He's already talking about rigging up his John Deere so he can work his fields next spring. He told me he prays everyday, and that his prayer is so much deeper now than ever before. The Holy Spirit works in strange ways ... I guess faith does build on nature, even in ways that I hadn't ever imagined.

Chapter Thirty-Six

Amy appeared. "Good morning, Sister? Ready to begin." Her words seemed to bounce out of her.

"Hey, Amy, good to see you. Oh yes, ready, and as able as I can be."

Once we got me onto the blue elevated work mat via the slide board, we started. I was lying on my back when she said, "I'm gonna put this bolster under your knees ... like this. I want to see if you can squeeze your bottom at all. I'll slip this band under your bottom to help you. I'll pull up on the band as you try to squeeze your bottom muscles and try to thrust up your pelvis. OK? Well, let's see. Go ahead and try to squeeze."

As hard as I tried, nothing happened. I was disconnected.

"Are you trying? Do you feel anything at all, any movement, even any tiny sensation at all?" she asked.

"I'm afraid not, Amy."

"That's perfectly OK. I'll just pull on this band and lift you up. You just might feel something as we proceed. Are you ready? We'll do ten of these."

"OK, Let's start," I said.

"One ... two; feel anything? Three ... four ... good job! Five ... six ... seven ... eight, ... good! Two more now, nine ... and ... ten. Great, that was great!" she said. "Just like I said, 'you're a pro.'"

"Next on our list this morning is this new exercise," said Amy. "I'll raise your left leg straight up with my right hand, so it touches my left hand with your toe. We're gonna do 15 of these. Ready?"

"Oh, sure," I replied.

"One ... two ... three ...four ...five ...six, very good, ... six ... seven ...eight ...nine, good, ... ten ...11 ... 12, three more, ... 13 ... 14, and ... 15. That was great, that was really great, Sister. Now, can we do the same with your right leg?"

"OK," I said.

"Here we go. One ...two ... three ... four ... five, good ... six ... seven ... eight ... nine, great! ... Ten ... 11 ... 12, and three more ...13 ... 14 ...and 15. Wonderful, wonderful!" she said. "How we doin', do you need a break?"

"No, I'm OK." I responded, even though I felt fatigued and wanted this part of the session to be over.

We did several more movements and I was surprised that our hour was up. Together we transferred me back into my wheelchair. Amy wheeled me back to the outgoing penguin line.

"Laura! Oh I'm lucky today, I got you again to bring me back to my room," I said.

"How did it go today, Sister?' she asked.

"Great, Amy is just wonderful."

"She really is!" said Laura. "The patients always gush about Amy."

Chapter Thirty-Seven

Renowski's room was quiet as we rounded the corner from the hall into my room. I wondered what he was doing in there all alone. What was he thinking? What was he feeling? I picked up my prayer book and began reading the psalms for the day: Psalm 143:1-11.

Lord, listen to my prayer:
Turn your ear to my appeal.
You are faithful, you are just; give answer.
Do not call your servant to judgment
For no one is just in your sight.

The enemy pursues my soul,
He has crushed my life to the ground;
He has made me dwell in darkness
Like the dead, long forgotten.
Therefore my spirit fails;
My heart is numb within me.

I remember the days that are past:
I ponder all your works.
I muse on what your hand has wrought
And to you I stretch out my hands.
Like a parched land my soul thirsts for you.

Lord, make haste and answer;
For my spirit fails within me.
Do not hide your face
Lest I become like those in the grave.

In the morning let me know your love
For I put my trust in you.
Make me know the way I should walk:
To you I lift up my soul.

Rescue me, Lord from my enemies;
I have fled to you for refuge.
Teach me to do your will
For you, O Lord, are my God.
Let your good spirit guide me
In ways that are level and smooth.

For your name's sake, Lord, save my life;
In your justice; save my soul from distress.

Chapter Thirty- Eight

"Lunch, Sister," came the voice from my door.

"Oh, thank you. Just leave it on my rolling table, would you?" I asked.

"Sure, here you are, hope you like it!" she responded.

I looked at my lunch and immediately thought how Renowski was doing. It was too quiet over there. Just then I heard Renowski.

"Yeah, leave it on the table," he said.

As if that was my invitation, I swung my wheelchair toward his room. I stopped at his doorway.

"How are you today?" I asked.

He gave no reply.

"Perhaps that's not a good question; perhaps I should just say, 'Good to see you today, Dr. Renowski.'"

He glanced over toward me and I thought I saw a hint of a smile on his face. I felt invited in even though he said nothing.

"Here, let me help you with your lunch. Oh, a hamburger, macaroni and cheese, corn, applesauce, and a piece of cake with pink frosting," I reported. "Let's put this napkin under your chin and straighten out your covers."

He didn't resist, nor did he say anything. Again he ate in silence. I tried to punctuate the silence with little quips about my rehab session, the weather, the nice people here at St. John's, and how festive the pink frosting was. But he gave no reply to any of it. We were down to the cake when I asked him directly...

"You're feeling pretty disconnected aren't you?"

"Disconnected?" he repeated.

"Yeah, you know, cut off, severed, pulled-away," I responded, trying to get him to grab any one of these as a starting point. He simply looked away.

"Here, here's the last bite of your cake," I said. He took it.

There was a long, awkward silence that I didn't try to fill. Finally, with his chin lowered and eyes cocked, he said flatly, "Thank you."

Taking this as a cue to continue, I asked, "Feeling any better today, I mean inside?"

He took a deep nasal inhale and replied, "I don't know what you mean."

"Well," I said. "For me, what I feel inside is very important to me. I've learned to go inside seeking a clearer understanding of what's going on in there. I don't think you've ever learned to do that."

"What's the point?" he quipped.

"The point is that's where God resides and I like to be with God, I like to talk with God, I like to ask God questions. Most of all, I ask for God's help."

"That's much too sloppy for me," he reported.

"Sloppy? Now I don't know what *you* mean, Dr. Renowski."

"God is a sloppy concept. It's just like feelings; they're sloppy, too. There's no data for either, no proof; they're not logical. Reason rules against God, and against feelings, too. Both God and feelings are illusions that simply get in the way."

"You want an orderly world, don't you?" I said. "You crave order, harmony, organization. You want everything predictable. You actually believe that it's possible to achieve control of the human condition through man's work alone, don't you?"

Renowski shot back. "I believe that reason, research, and enough work are the answers to the human condition; if that's what you mean."

"So, you believe that science can fix the world?" I asked.

"It will take a lot more work, but yes. If we could get all the players, the government, the medical community, academia, business, insurance and pharmaceutical companies all working in the same direction ... we could do great things."

"Like what kinds of things?" I asked.

"We could conquer cancer in all its forms. We could eradicate pain entirely ... it is possible! We could do away with autoimmune diseases such as ulcerative colitis, rheumatoid arthritis, lupus, MS and the like. We could even get to the point where we could do elective cardiac surgery making heart attacks all but obsolete."

"That's impressive all right. But, what would we really accomplish? Would we actually have a better world? I'm not lobbying to stop medical research or close the patent office on new drugs, all I'm asking is would our world be better? Would our lives be better? Oh, we would be materially better for sure, and human pain would be eased; but would we be ethically, morally, or spiritually better?"

"Of course we would! It would be the triumph of science over the pathogens of the world," Renowski retorted.

"Haven't we already had many, many medical triumphs, Dr. Renowski? With all of these triumphs; let me ask you, is our world better? Let's put it this way, are people happier?"

"You're asking the wrong questions, Sister. You're asking questions that don't have quantifiable answers. How would we know if people are happier today than 200 years ago?" Renowski snapped.

"Well, I keep hearing that we're in the middle of several epidemics. Take for example obesity; can medical science conquer obesity? And take depression; can medical science conquer depression? What about greed and injustice and crime, and prejudice and war... can medical science conquer these too?" I asked.

"You're way over your head, Sister." Renowski said condescendingly.

"It seems to me that as medical science finds a cure for one disease, three others pop-up," I said. "Maybe our diseases today are more rooted in our affluence, environmental neglect, and out-of-control competition, rather than in the whole biological pathogen, tsetse fly life cycle sources of sickness the medical community is more comfortable with. Again, I'm not saying to stop the march of science. I'm simply pointing out that there are many issues, perhaps the most devastating issues, that are out of the reach of science."

"When we put our minds and pocketbooks to work -- really to work -- we can conquer anything," Renowski slammed.

"Dr. Renowski, it seems that each of us has a different vision. You see science as the redeemer, as our salvation. I see the world as broken, and we ourselves as broken too, right along with it. Our brokenness will always be with us. I see science, as potent and as wonderful, and sometimes even seemingly miraculous. But as it is now it's always playing a catch-up game. As humankind progresses we seem to become ever more susceptible to our own brokenness. We can't help ourselves from finding more brokenness."

"No," said Renowski. "Man's brokenness *can* be repaired. Science *can* catch-up. We *can* be fixed."

"That's where we disagree," I said. "We can never be fixed, at least not here on this earth. We can never find full repair here because we're supposed to learn here. As strange as it sounds, we learn best through our brokenness."

"You're illogical, Sister." Renowski interjected.

"Let me ask you this, Dr. Renowski, will the world be fixed when you die?"

"No, of course not. Silly question!" he retorted.

"Perhaps not so silly. What you seem to be saying is that for your whole life, you will live in a world that's broken. Isn't that right?" I asked.

"Of course."

"Well then, I only have one question. How do you deal with the brokenness of the world?"

"By doing all that I can to solve the brokenness," said Renowski.

"But you can only work on one small piece of brokenness; in your case, that small piece is heart disease. What about all the rest of the brokenness?" I asked.

"Other scientists and researchers will work on those."

"OK, but that still leaves you in an untenable position given your attitudes," I said.

"And what position is that?" asked Renowski.

"You must deal with all the other brokenness. You need to make some accommodation with it. You need to recognize the brokenness and make some sort of peace with it ... all of it. Have you made peace with the brokenness of the world?" I asked.

"Look, I can do and think what I want," he said.

"Well of course you can -- naturally. But, what if your thoughts are hurting you? Don't toxic thoughts bring toxic feelings, feelings that eventually make you depressed, or perhaps just angry?" I asked.

"Only if you let them," he answered.

Chapter Thirty-Nine

"Well, what about this; did you see incompetence in your operating room, your OR?"

"Did I? It's there all the time," said Renowski.

"Well, how did you deal with it?"

"I always pointed it out. I always let people know when they did wrong. I developed something of a reputation in that department Sister," said Renowski proudly.

"Is that incompetence caused by insufficient training, or is it due to human foible? What if one or your assisting nurses was recently divorced and was trying to raise three kids as a single parent. She was stressed way beyond herself, and she forgot to count the surgical sponges correctly. How would you deal with a situation like that?"

"There are no excuses, Sister, the job is either done perfectly, or it's done wrong; there is no in-between. It's black and white, open and shut," Renowski answered.

"So how do you fix that brokenness? Will science do it, or does this human condition, human foible and brokenness require another form of help?" I queried.

"She's gonna need a lot of help because she's gonna be out of a job!" Renowski retorted.

"That's my point. Does that really solve the problem?"

"It does for me. I'll just hire someone who can do the job."

"Well, you're making some assumptions here aren't you? Aren't you assuming that the nursing schools are doing good work? Aren't you assuming that sufficient numbers of people will choose nursing as a career and will be happy enough with it to stay for their career? And what about the nurse you let go; what will she do with her life, and what about her children?"

"You're carrying on a bit, aren't you Sister," said Renowski.

"All I'm trying to say, Dr. Renowski is, to what degree have you made accommodation, made peace with the brokenness in the world, because apparently it's all around you, even in your OR!" I said.

"I guess it doesn't make any difference now, does it, Sister? I don't think I'll be darkening the door of any surgical suites anytime soon."

"Dr. Renowski, that's where you're wrong. The fact is that you're broken, your body is certainly broken, and how will you make peace with that fact? It sounds like you haven't dealt real well with brokenness in the world so far, so you don't seem to have much patience in making peace with your own brokenness. I'm worried about you, Dr. Renowski. You don't know how to deal with brokenness, and you're broken! This doesn't bode well for your recovery."

"I'll get along, and I'll do it my way, I always have," he answered.

"You won't be able to deal with your brokenness in any positive way until you integrate the tragedy into your life. You need to let the good in you mix with the not so good in you," I said.

"And just what does that mean?" Renowski asked.

"It means that you need to see the reality of the world in clearer focus. Regardless of how hard you try, you can't make the world 'right' in your sense of right. The world is the way it is and you, or any other human can't change it. There's wondrous good in the world and there's terrible bad. You can't simply eradicate the one for the other."

"And why not?" interjected Renowski.

"Because it's all interconnected, it's all innervated. These polarities exist in opposition to each other inside us. These opposites are paradoxically dependent upon each other; in some strange way, one supports the other. Can you have a north pole without the south? Can you have leaves without roots? Can hope exist without despair? Can we understand the concept of good without knowing something about bad? How about in your profession, can you work with disease without knowing health? One defines the other."

"So what's that got to do with me right now?" he asked.

"You want the world to exist without the poles, without the opposites. You want to eradicate one and hold up the other. You don't deal in integration, or wholeness. I'm simply saying that's impossible and the degree to which you believe that, is the degree to which you live in unreality.

"So if I were to go with your thinking what would I do?" he asked.

Was he finally starting to soften? This was the first time, I think, that he asked such a personal question. Was I actually making some headway with him?

"Well, for one thing you'd learn to accept. I know that must be a hard word for you. You see acceptance as resignation or submission. I see acceptance as spiritual grit, a steadfast realization that we're broken, we'll always be broken, and the only resolution, if I can put it that way, is our salvation."

"And what does salvation mean, floating on clouds in heaven?" he asked.

"No, salvation means we're saved from ourselves. We're saved from our omnipotent, egotistical beliefs that we can achieve perfection somehow on our own merits. Salvation means that we let go of false beliefs about who and what we are, and adopt the true reality."

"And what's the true reality?" he asked.

"The true reality of our situation is that we're both broken. Your belief is that your life is over, but that's not reality. The reality is that you're being asked to live your life differently, and so am I. But the changes I have to make are minimal as compared to the changes you're being asked to make. You have the bigger job here. If you keep demanding that science has the solution, that research can somehow fix you, and that if they can't, the only alternative is to end it all yourself, then you have resigned, you have submitted but you haven't moved up to acceptance, not by a long shot."

"You know, Sister, you speak in riddles."

"No, Dr. Renowski, what I do speak in is paradox."

"Paradox! What the hell are you talking about?"

"Perhaps the best known paradox is one attributed to Saint Paul when he said: 'It's in my weakness where I find my strength.'"

"That's nonsense," Renowski blurted.

"Is it?" I retorted.

"Yes it is. Strength is a power to overcome, weakness is the opposite of strength; weakness cannot overcome anything," he said.

"There you go with your battle terms. When you think like that you can't go beyond the material level; you're stuck!"

"Life is a battle, Sister, in case you haven't seen it. But, then again how could you know about real life when you've penned yourself up in that cloister of yours. You're here telling me about reality, how paradoxical is that? How would you or could you know reality when you don't even see it."

"Dr. Renowski you have said it, living in a cloister is a paradox. A paradox is an apparent contradiction that points up a truth. Have you ever heard, 'you can't see the forest through the trees,' that's a paradox? Its meaning is that when you're so embroiled or enmeshed in a situation you can't objectively see it's true reality. When you're embroiled in the world, can you see it more, or less clearly? It's not until you remove yourself from the world that you can possibly come to see it more accurately. I like to think it's that way with the cloister."

"Sister, your life is a mystery to me!"

"Right again! That's what I try to do is live the mystery. You want everything understandable, everything explainable, measurable, and quantifiable. That's not the world where I live, Dr. Renowski. I seek to live the mystery as well as I can. Another paradox, I seek to walk more by faith and less by sight."

"Sister we have to stop. I don't see any possible way I can ever agree with your illogical logic. I'm tired, I need to rest."

With that he simply closed his eyes and turned his head. I felt alone.

Chapter Forty

Had I come on too hard? Was I attacking him, and me the one who chastised him for his military mentality? He did seem to shift a bit, perhaps not in his thinking, but perhaps in his view of me. I had the impression he may at least respect me more ... not that I needed his respect. Or did I? What was I trying to do with Dr. Renowski? Where was I going with him?

I retreated to my room and to my prayers hoping to find some clarity.

"Dear Lord, I'm back! And I'm more confused than before. I'm not being me with Dr. Renowski - why not? I come on like I'm a steamroller. Am I trying to teach him something? Am I trying to overpower him? These logic-based monologues I offer don't prove anything. I don't understand what and who I become when I'm with him. It's not my usual nature to be confrontational, to stand toe-to-toe with anyone. But with him I turn into someone else, it's like there's another me that emerges. I need your help Lord ... or is this the help you're sending?"

Chapter Forty-One *Shift in Focus*

"Why do you always make me reach for my food?" Renowski bellowed. "Why can't you bring it to my mouth? I want someone else to help me eat."

Renowski's words echoed across the hall and boomed into my room where I was saying my morning rosary. I was meditating on the fourth sorrowful mystery, *Carrying of the Cross...carrying the cross by Himself, He went out to what is called the Place of the Skull (in Hebrew, Golgotha)*. I turned my wheelchair around to discover that my breakfast tray lay on my rolling table. I hadn't even heard the aide deliver it. I silently blessed her respect for me, and for my prayer time. How did she know, I wondered?

I hadn't spoken with Dr. Renowski in several days. I ruminated over our last conversation and felt embarrassed by the presumptive posture I took with him then. I've prayed that my words hadn't damaged our relationship and yet I sorely wanted the Holy Spirit to use my words to stir up Dr. Renowski's spirit. Was it my right to steer the Holy Spirit in this way? Was this respectful, or was I simply being pompous and egotistical? I've always felt this way about my prayer, so self-centered of me to ask for something so specific. Surely God knows the needs of his children. Who am I to be so directive as though I commanded the Holy Spirit? How prideful I am. Would I ever grow beyond this human foible and achieve a higher spiritual awareness so I could pray with more respect, with less of me and more of God? And yet, was it my ego or the power of the Holy Spirit that had moved me beyond my usual personality and emboldened me to speak with such authority? I do believe that when we speak for the Lord, the Holy Spirit animates us; we are inspirited! Am I being inspirited with Dr. Renowski?

Chapter Forty-Two

Nurse Jan glanced down the hall from the nurse's station and once again noticed the faint glow spilling out of Sister's room into the hallway. What was that she wondered?

"Look down the hall. Do you see anything different down there?" Jan asked Sam, the custodian on this floor of the hospital. She'd known Sam from the first day she arrived here at St. John's. She'd grown fond of his gentle, unassuming manner. She'd been surprised many times by Sam's wise insight into human nature and by his unwavering faith in God.

"I think I know why you're asking," replied Sam. "I've wondered if anyone else saw the light that I see in sister's room. There's something powerful going on in there."

"I saw it the very first day she arrived. I thought it was my imagination. Sometimes it's there and other times it's not. But when sister is in her room the light is there sometimes a bit stronger than other times, but always there," Jan said.

As both Nurse Jan and Sam looked down the hall, the aide came out of Dr. Renowski's room and with her head tucked down, she made her way to the nurse's station. Jan could see the tear that was making its way down her left cheek.

"What's wrong, Cindy?" Jan asked the aide.

"Dr. Renowski is sometimes so difficult," she blurted.

"Oh, Cindy, what did he do now?"

"He said I don't feed him right."

"That's ridiculous!" said Jan. "I know how well and how carefully you fed the patients. He's just angry. Don't pay any attention to him!"

"But that's just it; he's probably right!" confessed Cindy. "I'm scared of him. I'm afraid he's gonna yell at me and so I don't think I'm doing my best. I'm just so nervous when I'm with him."

"I know, Cindy, I know. Dr. Renowski makes everybody on edge. Please don't think you're the only one who feels this way. We're all walking on eggshells around him."

I need to talk with Dr. Renowski, Jan thought. He just can't keep intimidating our staff. He's so arrogant, so pompous, so self-centered. He thinks everyone else has to kowtow to his needs and wants, like he's the only patient on the floor. I think I'll talk with Sister.

Chapter Forty-Three

"Well, Sister, I'm back again for your counsel," Jan said.

"Hey, good to see you, Jan," I replied.

"Everything going OK, Sister?" Jan asked.

"Yes, I think so. My therapy progresses well. The therapists are just angels ... I mean it, just angels. I only hope I can keep up with God's grace."

"From what I see this room simply glows with God's grace."

"Oh, I have no doubt about that, my only doubt is whether I'll be able to catch all that God sends me," I said.

"Sister, I need your help again. Dr. Renowski is just getting a bit much for some of the staff. Just now, one of my best aides, Cindy Ramirez came to me in tears. She's scared of Dr. Renowski, says she can't do her best work with him because she's so nervous around him. I don't know what do. I could talk with him, but I think he'll just dismiss me because I'm 'just' a nurse. Somehow I think you'd have more success than I would. I hate to ask you again, but what do you think? Do you think you could make a dent in his armor somehow?"

"Wow, I don't know Jan. My last conversation with him was a bit strained. I'm afraid he'd dismiss me as well. Although, I'm not so sure that I wouldn't deserve it, I did come on a bit hard with him. I don't think he's used to people talking to him so directly, especially about God. I don't know how he'll react to me."

"Well, Sister, I'm stumped. You know, I'm also afraid that if Dr. Renowski doesn't begin to cooperate with the rehab program here at St. John's, they just might decide that he's not good therapy material; you know, that he's really not ready yet to get the full benefit out of the program here," said Jan. "It's a wonderful program here, but it does require the full participation of the patient. I've seen them ask people to leave for less than what he's done already, or should I say, what he's not done already."

"I know, one rehab therapist said as much to me yesterday when I remarked to her that Dr. Renowski seemed somewhat slow, shall we say, in his progress."

"I shouldn't tell you this, you being a patient and all, but I know you can keep a confidence; his name has already come up in our staff meeting as a possible candidate for transition. Transition is the word we use to say that we might have to ask him to leave. I hate to see that happen to anyone, but especially Dr. Renowski. From what I understand, he has no family; his wife was killed in the accident that injured him; he has no children, no siblings, and his parents are gone. Sister, I think he's completely alone in the world."

"I know, I know. I keep thinking that he trips over his own blustery personality. I'm not criticizing him, quite the contrary, but it's like he's never learned to walk in someone else's shoes, look through their eyes; he seems stuck in his own perspective."

"Sister, I'll be frank, if the staff doesn't see some improvement in his attitude, I'm afraid his time here at St. John's will be very short indeed."

"OK, Jan, I'll try. Let me pray first for a while, I'm not due in the rehab gym for another hour. I can't go into Dr. Renowski's room alone, I need the Holy Spirit with me. What's the phrase; I need God 'big time.'"

"Thanks so much, Sister. I'll just hang loose until I hear from you. Good luck."

Chapter Forty-Four

As Jan left my room I felt a weight pressing on me. What if my little talk with Dr. Renowski backfired? What if he reacted like he did last time? I felt so responsible, and yet that's not all I felt. There was something beginning to ache in me. The ache was more compelling than it was painful. I realized that on the one hand I felt repulsed by Dr. Renowski's inexcusable behavior, while on the other hand I was strangely drawn toward him in a way that I had felt only one time before.

I prayed. *"Dear Lord, I offer myself to this task through you. I need your strength Lord; I need your stamina, your courage, your mercy, and your empathy. Help me, dear Lord, examine my motives and find them clean. I want to approach Dr. Renowski in your name. Help me quell these feelings I have toward him, help me keep my distance emotionally, but, dear Lord, touch his spirit. Use me, dear Lord, to speak what he needs to hear. Oh Lord, I pray in Jesus' name. Amen."*

I meditated with a vision of an angel of God touching Dr. Renowski's spirit. The tip of her finger glowed, just like in the movie ET, as it moved toward his heart. As it extended closer and closer to Dr. Renowski, a faint glow appeared on his heart as the angel's finger closed in on him. The glowing spot widened and brightened more and more, brighter and brighter until his entire heart was enveloped in the angelic glow; it shone like a star. I remained in meditation for some time fixated by this heavenly scene, feeling almost a part of it. Suddenly, my meditative reverie was invaded!

"Sister ... Sister, it's time to go to the gym," came the voice of the transporter.

"Oh, it's that time already, is it? OK, let me see; do I have what I need?" I asked, as though I was preparing for a cross-country trip.

"I don't think you'll need more than just yourself," said the transporter.

Chapter Forty-Five

The penguin line was very short this morning. In fact, I made it a line by anchoring the second spot. Soon I was on my way.

"Good morning, Sister," said Justine. "It's my turn to have the best patient in the hospital. I guess I could say that your reputation precedes you."

"That doesn't sound very good at all!" I said.

"Oh no," said Justine, "just the opposite. You're the buzz of the therapists, why you practically were the singular topic of discussion at lunch yesterday.

"Oh my, you all must be suffering from indigestion today," I responded.

"You're funny, Sister. Why don't we get started?"

We went through the same stretches in much the same way that Amy had done with me all week. Justine however pushed and pulled a bit harder. She was as gentle as Amy but she put a bit more oomph into it. How strange it was, I didn't feel any actual sensation, but I still knew somehow that my body was under more pressure. It must be the muscles and nerves on the edge of my paralysis that pick up the echoes of feelings and transmit them to my brain as sensations heretofore unknown to me. Justine and I worked together in relative silence. She continuously told me what she was doing but somehow she realized that my focus was elsewhere. She didn't pry, or even make notice of my unresponsiveness; I just hoped she didn't interpret it as indifference.

"I'm sorry Justine, my mind seems to be preoccupied today." I said words to this effect several times during our session.

"Oh sister, it's perfectly OK, we all have days when we like to huddle down a bit in silence," Justine said.

"'Huddle down in silence,' what a unique phrase I thought, what a different way of putting it."

"You know, Justine, I think you just hit the nail on the head ... 'huddle down in silence' describes it just right. Thank you, that somehow makes it better just knowing that another human being understands."

"Sure thing, Sister, I just wish my husband could do it for me once in a while." Justine said.

"I'm sure you can teach him," I responded.

"I'm trying, Sister."

"Go girl," I said.

"Well, that pretty much does it for today, Sister. I won't be here tomorrow; I'm working Saturday so I get a mid-week day off. Have a great day today and tomorrow too."

"You too, Justine, and thank you for what you do, and thank you mostly for who you are; you're a beautiful child of God. Bless you."

Chapter Forty-Six

The elevator door opened onto my floor and, as we rounded the corner by the nurse's station and headed down the hall, I could hear Dr. Renowski yelling.

"And where did you get your diploma from, Know-Nothing Tech?"

"I asked the transporter to leave me right outside Dr. Renowski's room. For several minutes I listened to the expanding interchange.

"I'm sorry, Dr. Renowski, how can I do this better for you?" I heard the aide's voice.

"I'm uncomfortable. You didn't bring the bed angle up high enough. You dropped soup on me already. I don't know why they insist on soup anyway. What are they trying to do, torture me at mealtime, too! You're not bringing the food close enough to my mouth. You make me stretch for it, like a bird stretching for a worm. If I were giving you a grade, you'd flunk!" asserted Renowski.

That's enough, I thought. I can't let this continue. I need to save this poor aide, and Dr. Renowski needs to learn a lesson. I wheeled myself into his room and announced.

"It's OK, Cindy, I can take it from here."

"Oh, it's you," said Renowski. "I thought you gave up on me."

"Oh no, I just thought you needed a bit of a respite from me. I was too hard on you in our last conversation. I was something less than fully respectful of you and what you're going though."

"You, too hard on me? I doubt it! I can take whatever you might have to blow at me," he grumbled.

"I know how strong you are, I'm sure you had to be very strong being a surgeon and all. It's just that this is an entirely different situation for you now; it takes a very different kind of strength to confront what's happening now. I know the struggle I'm having; you must feel it ten times more."

"Sister, let me tell you, even if it was 100 times more difficult, I'd rise to the occasion," Renowski said.

"Well, it's great to know that, Dr. Renowski, because I'd like to know when you're planning to start?"

"What do you mean by that?" he snapped.

"To tell you the truth, I haven't seen much of this strength that you speak of. All I've seen is bluster, fumes, and tirades. I've seen more inner strength in fifth-grade boys than I see in you. Forgive me for saying this, but you do make a lot of noise, you do a lot of commanding, but it doesn't tell me what's really inside of you."

"Sister, what's inside of me isn't relevant here; you don't have X-ray eyes do you? How do you know what is or isn't inside of me?" He stared at me.

"Of course not," I replied, "but behavior is a pretty good gauge of what's inside a person. As Jesus said, 'You can tell them by their fruits.' If you ask me, there's only two explanations for your noxious behavior, either you're scared or you have a very low self-regard."

"Oh is that so, low regard for self is it? I want you to know whom you're talking to. I was awarded the National

Cardiac Surgery Award, not once but twice. I also was awarded the International Cardiac Surgery Award. Sister, you don't get that with a low self regard."

"Well, here's where we differ, Dr. Renowski. You just described the 'what' of Dr. Stanley Renowski, not the 'who' of Dr. Stanley Renowski. I'm not talking about the professional, I'm talking about the man."

I think if he weren't paralyzed he would have physically pounced on me.

"What the hell are you talking about?" he blasted. "You have no idea what it takes inside to achieve what I have achieved. How could you know, you haven't achieved anything, all you've done is hide from the world in a cloister locked behind walls. I've confronted the pain of the world; I've taken on the demon of sickness; I've done battle day after day with the forces that tear us down. What have you done, Sister?"

He crashed his head down onto his pillow and looked away. This seemed his standard defense, I'd seen it before and knew that this was his signal that the conversation was over. But it couldn't be over, it mustn't. We have a lot of ground to cover and beyond the practical necessity for our continuing interchange, I knew, I just knew, with some compassionate compulsion; no, with sure loving longing that I must somehow resurrect our intercourse. It needed to be so! I reached within; I scoured my heart for a word, a thought, a something that could give life to what threatened to be lost. Finally I asked God!

Dear Lord, place your words on my tongue. Let me give voice to your will for this tormented man. Let me listen deeply to your word and translate it into our words so that your child Stanley may hear and respond.

Chapter Forty-Seven

Without realizing at all what I was about to say, I blurted, "Stanley, I love you."

I almost gulped my words back fearing that they would repulse him, and if not that, they would scare him deeper into his conflicted self. But they could not be contained. Again, I said these words that I had said to only one other man in my entire life. "Stanley, I love you."

I went on, "Stanley, the love I have for you now is not the erotic love of the carnal type, but the love of one human being who sees the pain in another and wishes to surrender whatever is necessary to ease that pain, because the pain is so much bigger than you can carry alone. You need a partner, Stanley; you need someone who can put her shoulder to the task along with you so that the burden becomes a weight not of pain, but of togetherness. You need someone to help, and I need someone to help me. Stanley, I believe we need each other in this time of terrible transition; we need each other for sharing, for laughing, for caring, and for mentoring. Stanley, please don't move away now, I depend upon you to be with me as I take this painful course. Stanley, I'd be on my knees if I could with this request for love."

His silence deepened my resolve somehow; I knew in my heart that he was moved by what God gave me to say. The words were genuine, they flew from my heart with joy, and yet I know they were God's words, not mine. My surrender to

God's will have paradoxically given me license, a new freedom to say what was on my heart in a way I couldn't have done only yesterday.

He raised his right eyebrow, opened his eyes and looked at me; he simply stared at me. At first I wasn't sure what he was feeling, what he might be thinking. Then some relaxing of muscles in his forehead told me that he had softened, that some scales of protection had loosened and might at any moment crash to the floor. He was moved, how much I couldn't tell, but he was moved. I awaited some response.

Finally he said, "Sister, you indeed are a special person. Your heart is pure, made of a substance I haven't seen before. You are not like the world I know. You speak simple words, but your speak them with a power that is beyond what I've known. You speak of love at a time like this. You speak of laughing when my heart feels no lightness at all. I don't know how you can say such things ... but ... nonetheless I like your words."

"Oh, thank God you have a heart ... you do have a heart and you can express it. I feared that your heart had hardened so that it had turned to stone, never to be retrieved. But you do have a heart, and you can access its tenderness. I thank God for this. Stanley, thank you; thank you for renewing the spirit in me."

But even though I couched my words in agape love I could feel that a different type of love had once again appeared on the doorway of my heart. It was a love that was at once so reassuring and at the same time so threatening. Had I passed the point of no return as the Phantom had once sung to Christy when he wooed her into the bowels of the Opera House sub-basement?

A long silence ensued that I broke saying, "Stanley, I must talk to you about something very important. It's a touchy topic, but it must be addressed. Please do listen to my words and know they come from deep within me, a place that knows no criticism, no blame, no judging. Stanley, for my sake if not your own, I'd like you to listen to me. May I proceed?" I asked.

"Proceed." was his singular response.

"Stanley, your attitude toward this place, toward everyone who works here, and what they're attempting to do for you, must, Stanley, it must change! Whether you realize it or not, and whether you care or not, you are in danger of being asked to leave St. John's; you're in danger of being kicked out! Stanley, I don't want that to happen, neither for you nor for me. Up until now your attitude and behavior have been resistive at best, callous, self-centered, even arrogant; the staff can't take it anymore, they don't deserve it.

He made no reply, but he kept his gaze steadily on me. I thought I saw a slight softening of his eyes. I continued.

"Stanley, you need to recognize how much they want to help you. I don't understand you completely, perhaps I never will, but I do think that your behavior is a buffer, a very effective buffer you use to show anger and keep people away from you. You've intimidated so many of them; they're scared of you. I need to ask you to please shift your attitude. Whatever anger resides in you needs healing; your entire personality has been contorted in service of this demon that roams your soul."

His facial muscles seemed to quiver a bit, and yet still he said nothing.

"Stanley, you need a new way of looking at yourself, a way that can express the real you, not this puffed-up, cutout version that shows only the 'what' of you. Stanley, I'm interested in what's underneath all this bravado, all this show ... I want to get to know the real you. But, I can't if you don't know him."

Again, the silence surfaced, the blank silence like a slab of concrete in the midday sun — blank. Then I saw it, a tear, a single tear burst out of the corner of his right eye and slowly slid down his face.

Stanley said, "Sister, I don't know who I am. I never have known who I am. I don't know where to start."

"Stanley," I said, "we can take this road together. You can let go of the absurd selfishness that keeps you in your internal prison. You can let go Stanley. You've been trying to overpower your basic human powerlessness through your accomplishments. Even though your achievements are magnificent in human terms, your achievements alone can never give you peace."

"Sister, I know no other way."

"God doesn't want your 'doings' Stanley as much as God wants your loving ... your being. It's time Stanley; it's time to start anew. This tragedy that has come upon you is only an assault on 'what' you are. When you let go of the 'what' of you, your injury can become the greatest opportunity for you to discover the beautiful 'whom' of you."

"It's still not fair Sister. God doesn't play by his own rules. If he expects peace and justice, care and compassion, goodwill and fair play from us, what about him? Is this analysis his idea of care and compassion, his notion of peace and justice?"

"Stanley, that's precisely the point. Jesus said, 'My kingdom is not of this world.' And you're trying to make it so. Don't confuse your human sense of justice with God's. We don't know the rules of God's kingdom, but let me ask you this: does God love you any less now in your current physical state you're in than he did when you were at the pinnacle of your surgical career? Of course not!"

"It's not fair, Sister."

"Stanley, your egotism has prevented you from seeing clearly ... from growing into a fuller awareness of who you really are. Spiritually you haven't graduated from sixth grade, that's about where your spiritual maturity stopped. You need a crash course on living and loving. I am here, and I'm a willing teacher."

"But God should be different."

"Stanley it's this simple: either you learn to do God's work or you continue to be the embittered, self-centered person you've become. You've always focused on yourself Stanley; yes, I know what you did was for other people but it was first for you. You were always on center stage. It's time now to turn this around, to become a new person, to see new light. Won't you come along with me?"

"I don't know, Sister, I just don't know if I can, nor if I want to."

I could see he'd had enough. He was beyond fatigue. He closed his eyes. After a time I wheeled out of his room into mine. I spent the rest of the day in prayer.

"Dear Lord, be with Stanley. Stir up his spirit, Lord, give him a new heart. Please Lord, let the seed you planted in his soul today germinate and grow quickly."

I only wondered what tomorrow would bring.

Chapter Forty-Eight *The Turning Point*

It was restless sleep most of the night. I re-ran my conversation with Stanley over and over. I know something wonderful had occurred, but I wasn't sure about the consequence of it all. Did I see only what I wanted to see? Did Stanley really open up a bit, or was it my desire that he would that may have distorted my perception? And, if he truly did make a breakthrough, could he sustain it? Or, would he, in the new light of day, look at himself and conclude once again that he had nothing to live for? Would he merely step back to his previous veiled self? I prayed like a nun, and worried like a woman.

What was it about Stanley that pushed and pulled me so? In the mystery of the deep night, when reality seems so distant, I reminisce. In my reverie I remember Jay. I see him smiling at me as I walk down the concourse, after the flight crew had secured the plane following the LA to NYC flight. We embrace and walk hand-in-hand. We dine, have wine, and find ourselves back at my shared NY apartment where we make love before he has to go home ... to his wife.

How many times have I asked God, pleaded with God for forgiveness? I look back at this broken time in my life and connect feelings now with feeling then. As I lay in bed now, paralyzed physically, I connect with my paralysis then, not physical, but emotional. What anchor secured me to Jay in sin? What compulsion pulled me back to him again and again? What force pulls me toward Stanley now? His tortured, frightened, and arrogant interior seduces me so that I'm powerless to leave him.

Am I compelled to help Stanley, like the Good Samaritan was compelled to help the man beaten and abandoned on the side of the road to Jericho, as Stanley has been beaten and broken? But this lofty motivation would be easy to hide behind, and there's something fraudulent about attributing my motivation to pure altruism, my compulsion is more an ambition, a primal desire bubbling up from a part of me I supposed I had left behind when I entered the cloister, the day I surrendered my life to become the bride of Christ. Was it back?

Had this man Renowski, by his anguish, brought some shadow back to life by his visceral contempt for others, by his worldliness, by his arrogance? All of this is so alien to the cloister. Was I so mesmerized by nature so contrary to what I espoused? Was this very contrary personality so compelling to me because it somehow made a whole personality when added to my own? Where was this brokenness within me?

As the questions swirled, the morning light began its magical metamorphosis, bringing on the day by overpowering the night. Blackness became shades of gray, and the gray gradually offered more visual contrast to my abode until the first color crept in to arouse, articulate, and animate the fearful starkness with life and love. I emerged from my mind of doubt and now rested on more sensible ground. My fear was overpowered by gratitude.

Chapter Forty-Nine

Breakfast arrived trailing a volunteer whom I didn't know. When she gave no eye contact, I followed suit in an uncharacteristic silence. I heard no stirring across the hall. I waited and listened, straining, even holding my breath. Soon, the angels sang. Then I heard a faint sound; I couldn't discern it, if in fact it was anything at all. But then I heard it again, a bit louder and this time unmistakable.

"Sister ... Sister, can you come over?" It was Stanley.

Had I really heard what I thought I did? Then again, "Sister, Sister, can you come over?" asked the voice.

I wheeled around and headed across the hall into Stanley's room. His eyes fixed on mine as he asked, "Could you help me with my breakfast?"

I wanted to hug him. His simple request unburdened me and provided the answer to my sleepless self-queries.

"Of course, Stanley, I'd be happy to."

As if to couch his request in functional rather than emotional terms, he added, "You're so much better than those clumsy volunteers."

I deflected the remark, preferring to bask in the glow of the apparent sea change I was feeling.

"Certainly, I'm honored that you asked, Stanley."

I positioned us both for the task and started. I wanted to shower him with questions about last night, but deferred instead into a poised and careful concentration on his breakfast. He seemed bright, alert, and even buoyant, yet he too preferred to focus on the job at hand. I guess I had hoped for more because as we finished I felt a slight deflation of affect. Yet, I sensed he didn't want to risk disturbing the emotional residue of last night by chancing words that might not find their desired mark. Perhaps he simply didn't trust that he could find the words to convey his feelings from last night and so instead remained in silent safety. After all, he was unpracticed in the language of intimacy, as he was likewise unpracticed in the relationship essentials of togetherness and respect. He was acquainted with these only conceptually, not behaviorally. This was alien terrain to him that he could traverse only awkwardly, if at all. Even this logical insight couldn't contain my emotional curiosity. I found myself blurting out what must have seemed inane.

"So, Stanley, how are you feeling this morning?"

"No change," he quipped.

How stupid of me to be so generic in my question. I tried again.

"Did you sleep well?"

"No change there either," he answered.

This was not unfolding as I hoped. Let me try another approach.

"Are you having feelings this morning that are different for you?"

"Ah ... no," he replied.

I was frustrating myself. "Dear Lord," I asked. "What can I do here? Where can I go with him? I want to know him better; I want to understand." I tried once more.

"Stanley, did you enjoy our conversation last night?"

After a pause, he simply said, "Yes."

It wasn't much, but there was certain definiteness in his voice, a surety, and even an accommodating anticipation of something more to come. Still, it was paltry, and I decided to just let it be. We sat in silence for several minutes, until a transporter appeared at the door.

Chapter Fifty

"Dr. Renowski, it's time for your morning rehab session."

"OK ...OK," he responded.

"Let's just get the Hoyer lift all set for you," said the transporter.

I observed the transfer into his wheelchair that took a good 10 minutes. Both Stanley and the transporter seemed exhausted upon completion.

Soon my transporter arrived and I found myself on the penguin line once again. My eyes fixated on Stanley. His therapist, Colleen, was using the Hoyer lift to bring him to a semi-upright position. I hadn't seen them try this before and Stanley was struggling.

Amy came for me and we started on the hand bike, a mechanism that looks like a bicycle drive sprocket, but it's mounted on a stand. I turn the pedals not with my feet, but with my hands. The hand bike stand was close to where Colleen and Stanley were working.

Colleen had a new electric wheelchair for him today. Evidently he had some slight potential muscle movement in his right shoulder that just might be trained to move his right arm enough so that Stanley would be able to work the joystick, as they called it, on his wheelchair. If they could accomplish this, Stanley could operate his own wheelchair.

Stanley was visibly perplexed. His face squeezed-out determination as Colleen strapped him in the Hoyer and began the transfer to the electric wheelchair. Stanley craned his neck to see the new chair that was his target. Colleen gently guided him into position, His back seemed straight and with his head against the headrest on the chair, Stanley looked more in control of himself and his predicament that I had ever seen him.

Amy prodded me along as I evidently slowed my hand bike action. I watched Stanley take obvious delight with this new advance in his therapy, savoring the possibility of regaining some measure of self-sufficiency.

Once Colleen had him positioned, she demonstrated a new feature. "Dr. Renowski, I want to show you something pretty spectacular about this chair, it's called *power-tilt* and *power-recline*. It's important that you periodically move your body if only slightly. When you had feeling in your body you would do this unconsciously. When a point on your body began to give you sensations that it was becoming numb, that is a point of pressure from sitting, you would move your body to relieve the pressure without ever realizing it. This movement must now be done quite intentionally and this chair will help you. You will learn how to do this yourself, but right now I'd like to demonstrate how the tilt and recline features on this chair work. "Are you ready?"

Yes, I'm ready," responded Stanley.

"OK, I'll go slowly," said Colleen.

Very slowly the entire back of the chair began moving backward to a point where Stanley was almost completely reclined.

"How do you feel down there Dr. Renowski?" asked Colleen.

"OK ... I guess."

"Any pressure in your head?" she asked.

"No, I feel fine," said Stanley.

"OK, we'll start our way back up. We need to go particularly slowly because I don't want you experiencing any orthostatic hypotension, you know Dr. Renowski, lightheadedness. Ready?" she asked.

"OK, let's roll," said Stanley.

Colleen reversed the procedure bringing Stanley back to a fully upright position.

"Well, what do you think, Dr. Renowski, pretty clever huh? How do you feel?"

"Fine, I feel fine," said Stanley.

"Are you sure, Dr. Renowski? You look a little pale," said Colleen.

With that, Stanley lost consciousness. Almost immediately Colleen produced smelling salts and roused Stanley by passing it under his nose.

"Wow, you gave us a little scare there, Dr. Renowski. Let's rest a bit before we try it again," said Colleen.

I kept my hand bike going, but with only minimal attention, my main focus was on Stanley.

After giving Stanley time to rest, Colleen once again used the power recline on Stanley's electric wheelchair, but much slower this time.

"How was that Dr. Renowski?" Colleen asked.

"Good ... very good, thank you," Stanley said.

I was astonished; this was only the second time I heard the words "thank you" from Stanley. It was obvious that for Stanley these words were not uttered casually, certainly not instinctively. What forces had worked on this man to forge the inelastic character he had developed, a character that found the simple words "thank you" so difficult?

"OK, Dr. Renowski, time to come back up with the rest of us," said Colleen. "Are you all set?"

"I think so, I feel OK," he responded.

"Let's go real, real slowly here, Dr. Renowski; I don't want to lose you again. I think we'll bring you up a bit at a time. Maybe you could talk to me as we go up, just so I know you're still with us," she suggested.

"What shall I say, 'Mary had a little lamb?'"

"Say whatever you want, maybe you could tell me about your work as a surgeon."

Immediately Stanley became very serious, even somber. He furrowed his brow and pursed his lips. Then, he exploded. "I am a great surgeon. I am a world-renowned surgeon. What am I doing here? What happened to me? I can't stand this! Don't you all see that things like this happen to other people ... not to the most celebrated surgeon on Earth? Get me out of here, get me out of here, get me out of here!"

Chapter Fifty-One

Stanley's anger cracked into tears. He cried deeply. He flailed his head from side to side with his torso at a forty-five degree angle in his new electric wheelchair.

"Dr. Renowski, oh, I'm so sorry; I didn't at all mean to upset you!" said Colleen.

Other therapists rushed over, but nothing constructive could be done. I wheeled to him. Even though my heart was breaking for him, my logical side was jubilant. He had finally given himself permission to show his pain. Now that all his former defenses of competence, power, status, fame and possessions were gone, all the security devices he had put in place and to which he had grown so attached had no meaning; he was left with only his immense pain inside, a pain that now overflowed out of him in raucous tears.

I positioned my wheelchair right next to his and instinctively found myself stroking his head. "It's OK, Stanley, everything is OK; all will be well. You can handle this. I'm here for you. I won't leave you. I'm here to stay with you." I said over and over.

I cradled his head in my arms and moved as close to him as I could. I whispered in his ear.

"Stanley, I'm here with you, I won't let you go. You are all right. All these people here want only the best for you. Stanley they love you. Stanley ... I love you!"

With this -- he simply started sobbing.

Without conscious intent, I kissed his cheek. I tasted his tears, they were bitter. I kissed his forehead; I kissed his hair; I kissed his chin; I kissed his tears one by one as they burst from his depths.

"Stanley, you are so beautiful. God loves you so," I whispered.

I kissed him more as I wrapped my arms around his head and neck. My lips were wet and hot. I wanted so much to comfort him, to ease his pain, to kiss away the layers of hurt I knew he was now penetrating. He sobbed; he gushed with pain!

"Stanley, go ahead, cry it all out! Cry it all out; empty yourself of those toxins from the past, these poisons within you ... let them go! You are so beautiful, and God loves you. Stanley, I love you."

My kisses continued. They felt so natural, so spontaneous; they felt "so right." I meshed my face with his. His tears lubricated our touch making our contact smooth and wet and wholesome. I told myself I was kissing the sorrowful face of Christ at his passion. Yet, I knew that the woman in me was ignited in a way I hadn't felt for more than 25 years. Stanley couldn't stop his tears; I couldn't stop my kisses.

I have no idea how long we clung together, it could have been minutes or it could have been hours. The spectacle of pain and passion unfolded in the gym with fifty pairs of eyes in audience. All actions outside the tangled knot we made stopped to witness a scene of the nun and the doctor together. The St. John's gym itself, the scene of so much healing, had never sheltered such healing passion as Stanley's tears and my kissing embrace, yet healing it was for us both, for it was not only Stanley who was penetrating the layers of pain deep inside.

Chapter Fifty-Two *Brokenness*

I must have blacked-out or suffered some form of temporary disconnection from reality because I was somehow back in my room with no recall of how I got there. I heard Dr. Renowski arriving in his room as well. After the encounter in rehab I need rest, I needed peace. Yet perhaps more than physical rest I needed time to reflect, to let my mind and being assimilate the morning. What happened?

My mind throbbed with excitement over the apparent breakthrough, yet my soul feared a rising tide of attraction to Stanley. Lights were flashing and bells ringing, but I couldn't decide whether these were signs of celebration or signals of caution. My emotions tossed me over myself and into an unknown arena where I felt an internal tension as if opposing forces each had one hand of me. I wondered if I might fracture myself. I was flummoxed by it all, and yet I sensed a new opportunity, not so much for me as for Stanley.

How was Stanley? I heard nothing more from across the hall except the footfalls of the regular monitors looking in on him. The footfalls walked in and out of his room in silence. They also found my room. Preferring my reverie, I simply waved and smiled to signal my presence and exterior peace. My internal monitor however registered no such peace.

I prayed all afternoon.

"*Dear Lord, make me an instrument of your peace. Guide me to do your will. Use my stirred-up being to come ever closer to you. Extend your healing hand so I may receive your power. Let me be the bridge that Stanley can cross to you dear Lord, the bridge to his most noble parts and away from the personal fragmentation he has lived for so long. Lord, hold Stanley in your hand; give him your strength, your patience, your perseverance so he can move his soul if not his body. Amen.*"

I don't know whether my meditation took me so deep, or whether I simply slipped into slumber and dream, but I saw myself walking through a hospital. I was on the orthopedic floor where every patient had broken bones. I had a gaggle of medical residents following after me; I was their teacher. As we came to each bed, one of the residents recited all the vital medical data about the patient. I listened with reverence to the residents' assessment of each patient. Following each recitation I said exactly the same thing: "This patient has experienced broken bones, and she/he will experience healing when she/he invites God into their life." I then asked the patient in a private whisper if they wanted to receive God's power. Each patient nodded affirmatively, at which point I laid my hands on their cast at the site of the break and said, "Father, this your child asks for healing. Focus your power and offer the healing that is needed." Then I miraculously lifted off their cast to expose healed skin and bones. Patients immediately got up, packed up their belongings and walked out of the hospital. The residents stood in awe.

Chapter Fifty-Three

I was awakened from my altered state by the food service tech.

"Sister, here's your lunch," she said.

"Oh, thank you," I replied. "Has Dr. Renowski received his lunch yet?"

"No, not yet, but it will be coming up very soon."

"Would you tell them not to send up an aide with his meal, I'll take care of feeding him myself."

"OK, sister, I'll tell them."

I quickly ate what I could of my meal until I heard the tech enter Stanley's room. I dropped my utensils, transferred myself into my wheelchair, and went over.

"May I come in?" I asked, at his doorway.

"Ah ...sure," he said after an uncertain pause.

I wheeled over to him and without hesitation I laid my hand on the side of his face so that my palm was over his ear, my left thumb touched his right cheek, and my fingers nestled in his hair.

"How was your afternoon?" I asked.

"Well ... ah ... all right. And yours?"

"It was very good, I prayed and meditated and thought about this morning."

"I'm glad that's over," he replied, with his eyes averted away from me.

"Why Stanley, it's just the beginning."

"What do you mean just the beginning? I want whatever happened this morning to be well over ... never again. I lost control, I felt so naked. I can never face all those people again. I never lose control."

"Stanley, what happened this morning was an act of God; it was so beautiful, your true emotions welled up from your very core. You were magnificent. I was thrilled; I was exhausted by it all but Stanley, it was exhilarating. You gave so much, you gave yourself, the real you ... the authentic you."

"Sister, I can't go through that again, I won't," he said.

"No, no Stanley, like I said, this is the beginning. The dam has burst and now we can carefully deal with all that comes out. It will be tedious, it will try us both, but I want to be with you as you unburden yourself of all your brokenness."

"Brokenness?" he asked, "what is brokenness?"

"Brokenness is what we are Stanley ... all of us. I'm not referring here to our broken bodies; I'm talking about broken minds, and broken hearts, and broken souls. Do you feel any of your brokenness, Stanley?"

"I can't say that I do."

"Look at it this way, Stanley. What came out of you this morning?"

"Tears, a lot of tears, and I don't want them."

"Yes, I know tears, but what was it your tears were saying? If you gave your tears voice and listened closely, what words would you hear from them?"

"I don't know, and I don't care to know."

"Stanley, tears are a marvelous form of emotional expression, they speak from the very center of you; your tears can say things that you can't say in words, they speak so eloquently."

"Sister, I can't remember the last time I cried."

"I'm not surprised, that's why it's so important to understand them now. You have your emotions so tightly shutdown, and you have for years is my guess, that you've lost touch with them. It's like you said the other day, 'Feelings are sloppy.' The fact is, Stanley, you don't deal in feelings, you don't know your feelings; you're out of touch with them. This may be one of the ways that you're broken ... a big way."

"But feelings *are* sloppy. Not only that, feelings can get you in trouble. When I'm in surgery ... well, when I was in surgery, I couldn't focus on my feelings. I needed to be 100% focused on the patient's heart. I couldn't think about anything else."

"There it is Stanley, you just said it.'

"Said what?"

"Of course you couldn't focus on feelings in surgery, but listen to what you just said, 'I need to focus 100% on the patient's heart.' Stanley, that's how you live your life; you focus on things, on tasks, on performance. You submerge your feelings into all your activities and interests, mostly into your profession. You're broken because you're only living half a life; you're fragmented."

"What was I supposed to do, feel sorry for my patients because they had heart disease? I couldn't live like that; it wouldn't be good for them, or for me. Eventually I'd loose my edge, I'd simply loose myself in a sea of emotion and become ineffective. I couldn't let that happen."

"Stanley, listen, I'm not saying you needed to feel sorry for your patients, but you didn't let any feelings emerge. Your attitude about feelings in general consistently pushed them under the surface; the primary tool you used to accomplish this was your work. Stanley, you didn't lead a life, you let your work lead your life for you ... that's broken."

"Well, I guess I won't need to worry about all that now. I can't see myself in surgery anytime soon."

"Stanley no, you do need to be concerned about your life now, concerned about living a fuller life. Your injury has given you the life change you needed so you can learn how to live differently, live more fully and become whole."

"Sister, you talk about this injury as though it's some kind of salvation, like I've been waiting all my life for this to happen."

"You have!" I responded.

"Sister, I want you to know that I was living a very full life before this damn accident. I had everything possible. I had a worthy profession that gave me respect ... even fame; it gave me wealth and status, it gave me my wife. Sister, I had it all ... everything. I was envied, the world applauded me, I didn't need it of course, but it's true ... so don't talk to me about the opportunity of my injury. My injury took everything from me, Sister, everything!"

"You're right, Stanley, it did take everything, but things, even *everything* isn't real."

"Well then Sister, you just tell me what is real."

"All right, I will. There's only one true reality, Stanley, and that reality is love."

"Is that so? Love is the only reality. Wow, that's a little deep for me. You're gonna have to unpack that one for this feeble-minded know-nothing, Sister."

"Stanley, you know you're not feeble-minded, it's just that you haven't dealt much in love, you've been too busy working."

"So, Sister, how do you 'do' love?"

"One doesn't do love Stanley, one simply lets the love that God has planted in your soul find expression. It would actually be more accurate to say that you find your being in love, rather than you 'do' love."

"My 'being' in love? I don't understand," Stanley strained.

"Yes, your true being, that which is most real, and rich, and noble in you. When you can live your life there, in these deep, real parts of your soul, you are then living in love; you are in love, your life is centered in love."

"That's still pretty deep Sister, I don't get it fully, but what about this, what if I said that I was in love with Anne? How does that square with what you're saying?"

"Well OK, to say it most accurately, Anne was the focus of the love that's inside of you. You expressed this love onto Anne, so Anne was the vehicle so-to-speak for you to find your deep, true parts and let them come out of you. You were *in* love when you were with Anne, connected with her in more than a simple physical or even emotional way. Does that make any sense?"

"It's all pretty spongy Sister."

"Stanley, can I ask you a question, a somewhat personal question?"

"Sure, you will anyway."

"Were you in love with Anne? You mention her so infrequently. I've wondered about that, you know, especially since Anne is no longer with us. You've never talked about your accident."

"Sister, don't push."

"Stanley, I'm not trying to push. I wouldn't ever want to push you. But whenever you're ready I'd like to help you walk through all of that... agreed?"

"No comment Sister."

"All right Stanley, all right."

"Can we get back to the brokenness issue then?" I asked.

"Sure, why not."

"OK, what about this? Could you conceive of your belief that your life is over because of your accident as an example of brokenness?"

"No, I see that belief as true." Stanley responded.

"But what if that belief keeps you stuck, what if it prevents you from moving forward?"

"What if your idea of moving forward is nothing I'm interested in, nothing I want?" Stanley quipped.

"Then I'd say that proves my point. Isn't your belief that your life is over the very barrier that blocks you from ever considering any new motivation for change?"

"Sister, I don't think you get it. You evidently don't think much of my life as it was, but I liked it; it was my life and I liked it. I don't want another life, I want my life back, not some new one based on a love concept I don't even understand."

"Stanley, I know you're angry, and believe me, I do understand your anger. You feel as though you've been robbed of the most valuable thing you had – your profession. You feel that God has snatched it away from you in some sort of vengeful act."

Chapter Fifty-Four

Stanley was taking those long nasal breaths again. He looked away from me, out the window. He seemed lost, empty and very angry. I wheeled closer to him and gently brushed his cheek. It was hard to remain silent but more words right now would only serve to harden his heart; I just kept stroking. Then I saw it, a single tear puddle in his eye and then burst out, it raced down his cheek and onto my finger.

He looked at me just as I kissed his tear off my finger. With this, he started to sob. I gathered up all my strength and pulled his body closer to me, close enough so I could kiss his face. I held his face in my hands forcing him to look in my eyes. I moved my face very slowly closer to him and instinctively my lips pressed onto his.

I pulled back, surprised at my action. This shouldn't be happening, this couldn't be happening. I sat upright in my chair and stared at Stanley. He was likewise stunned, yet I sensed that even though our emotional reactions were very similar, they were for far different reasons.

"I'm sorry, Stanley."

"Don't be."

I swung my chair around and retreated to my room. For the first time since being here at St. John's, God's place for transformation, I shut my door. I wanted to be alone with God. I just wanted to be with him, not even to talk with him, just be with him. I felt restless though, I couldn't settle down.

"What's happening to me? Why did I kiss him ... on the lips?" Kissing his tears away was an act of mercy, but kissing his lips was passion.

Then it struck me, the way I held Stanley's face between my hands was the same way I would hold Jay's face. Just like then, this face holding and eyes meeting sequence was preliminary to a kiss of passion. What I had just done with Stanley was exactly the same as what I did with Jay. Stanley was stirring up old feelings, old passions long ago buried and forgotten, but now finding resurrection into a new drama. These feelings didn't end well then; would they not end well now? When viewed from a more transcendent perspective however, the passion I experienced with Jay provided the paradoxical push I needed to finally respond to the vocation God had given me.

Often I'd asked myself over the years in the convent if I had simply retreated there because my intimate relationship didn't grow. But I resolved this dilemma long ago. I didn't need the convent to get away from a failed life; rather, I needed the failed life to wake me to the reality of my vocation. I was clear about this. I saw God's hand in my life all along, just as I saw God's hand in Stanley's life. No, I didn't believe that God caused Stanley's accident, any more than God caused mine. But, I do believe that God's hand is in the fact that we were here together. The Holy Spirit always brought out the good from any tragedy.

I reached for my rosary and started praying. Today I meditated on the luminous mysteries as I prayed. My mind needed the illumination.

"*Dear Lord, light up my soul. Allow me the vision to see where to go with Stanley. I'm adrift in a stormy sea. I'm scared, my feelings wash over me threatening to swamp my little dinghy and throw me into a perilous ocean. Be my lighthouse Lord, let me regain my bearings on you. I'm being tossed by the waves that I ride from crest to trough. Let me seek only your light, only your wisdom. Help me, Lord."*

Chapter Fifty-Five

I wheeled down to the chapel. There I focused on the vigil candle as my steadfast light in the storm. I felt more settled and more at peace after my meditation. As the elevator doors opened onto my floor I saw that the evening meal was just being distributed. I found my meal waiting for me on my rolling table. I placed it on my lap and with care I balanced it there as I wheeled over to Stanley's room.

I entered his room and was confronted by his stare. His eyes were serious, yet they were fluid, questioning, wanting. He said nothing.

I regained my composure and asked, "Are you all right?"

"I don't know," he replied. "I've just been thinking about what you said earlier, you know, about brokenness, and about Anne."

"Oh," I said, hoping he would continue. Instead he fell silent. After a time, I said, "Where did your thoughts bring you?"

"Anne was a good person, she cared ... she truly cared for people. She wanted to help people, that's why she originally went into law."

"She was an attorney?"

"Yes, she was a good attorney. Her motivation, at least in the beginning, was to defend inner city kids who got into trouble."

"Did she do that?"

"I guess she did a little *pro bono* work along the way, but her own success in law school probably took that dream away. The way she told it, her professors didn't want their #1 student defending car jockeys and minor drug dealers; they steered her toward the most prestigious law firm in the city.

"Why did she do that?" I asked.

As smart and as hard-working as Anne was, she just couldn't disappoint anyone; she couldn't say no to her professors, after all she was their star, it was almost like she had no choice. In the end, the firm courted her, and again, when they offered her the job with all the perks, she simply couldn't say no.

"I guess I still don't fully understand," I said with furrowed brow.

Anne was the classiest lady I ever met, but she came from a tough family. Her father was a loser. Anne went 180 degrees the other way. I guess trying to distance herself from her family, or maybe trying to make them respectable. In any event, she took the position with the prestigious firm and naturally started making big bucks. She told me once that she felt like she had sold out. Maybe she thought the same about her marriage."

"What do you mean?" I asked.

"Well, you know, maybe I came on to her like the big law firm – I made her an offer she just couldn't refuse. Maybe Anne was just seduced by intelligence and power. Maybe because her father couldn't get it together, she had to be the best, and be associated with the best. Maybe that was her brokenness, Sister."

"Could very well be, the seeds of our brokenness are often sown by our own reaction to what we experienced as wrong or lacking early in life. But what about you, Stanley, what about your brokenness?" I asked.

"I should have treated her better, she was really such a good person. I took her for granted, she was always there for me ... always did what I wanted."

"Did you love her?"

"I must have because I did think about her. I always looked forward to taking her to dinner. I liked what she did to our house. I liked how she looked - she was pretty."

"But Stanley, did you love her?"

"I don't know, Sister. What is love anyway? I don't know, do you?"

"Yes Stanley, I do. Love is when you want to be with her. Love is when your respect her so much that you honor even what you don't like about her; it's when the best time of the day is talking with her. Love is sharing yourself bodily, psychologically, emotionally, every way; it's trusting her without doubt ... putting it all on the line ... total commitment."

"Is that all? How do you know so much about love?"

"Stanley, right now this isn't about me, sometime later we can talk about me, but not now. Now the focus is on you and on Anne and about your brokenness. Did you love Anne like that?"

After a long pause and several nasal breathes, Stanley said, "Probably not, Sister ... probably not."

I let the silence seep into every corner of the room.

"I didn't love her, not like you just described. I just wanted her and I needed to have her," Stanley said.

"You mean, wanted and needed her almost like you wanted and needed to have nice car?"

"Sister I never *wanted* a nice car; I *had to have* the best car. I had to have the best address, the best watch, the best vacation, the best nurses, the best department ... the best ... the best ... the best. There is no such thing as second best for me."

"Stanley, what kind of brokenness is that?" I asked almost laughing.

"I don't know, Sister, the best brokenness?" he retorted with a glint of humor.

"Stanley, what kind of person needs to have the best of everything?"

"Tell me sister, I'm clueless ... maybe a demanding person?"

"And what kind of person demands, not just sometimes, but all the time, with everything, and everybody?"

"I guess a person who has to have his own way."

"Right," I said.

"But, Sister, that's because my way *is* the best way."

"Oh, is that so? I guess we should all just draft you to become the benevolent dictator of the world. If you know what's the best way for everyone and everything, you would be perfect. But that's not what this is about, is it Stanley? It's not about your perception of you. No, it's about your perception of others and your relationship with others. The fact is Stanley you don't like people; no Stanley, you use people. You use people to prop yourself up because underneath that haughty exterior of yours you really don't love yourself. Stanley doesn't love Stanley."

"Sister that sounds pretty profound, but to me it is like you're talking in circles; 'Stanley doesn't love Stanley?'"

"Stanley the first great commandment says that you must love the Lord your God with your whole heart, your whole mind, and your whole soul. Number two is that you love your neighbor as yourself. It sounds like Stanley's commandment is to use everyone to make you look good ... to cover up the fact that you're not so sure. Stanley, can't you see that this is the crux of your personal brokenness?"

"Sister, I don't see what the big deal is here. I'm a good person, I do good things for society, and I pay my taxes. If more people were like me, I'll tell you, this world would be a much better place."

"Stanley, I'll tell you the big deal. The big deal is that as good as your life appears from the outside, you, in your inner core, are unhappy. You keep trying to fill up this deep hole of dissatisfaction. You're not happy because you're living a fraudulent life. You won't let the real Stanley express himself, you're all bound up in this image of who you think you should be, rather than doing the hard work to discover who you authentically are."

"Oh, now I'm a fraud. I guess I shouldn't have gone to medical school, I shouldn't have become a surgeon, and I shouldn't have become the top cardiac surgeon in the country. I should have just worked on an auto assembly line and womanized around. I should have done as little as possible, never do anything of significance, never achieve, never learn, never create, never help anyone. Is that what I should have done Sister ... just be a bum?"

He started sobbing once again, but when I moved toward him, he looked at me in disgust and said, "Get out ... get out ... get out."

"Stanley, can't I just ..."

"Get out, just get out." He cut me off.

I heeded his demand.

Back in my room, once again I felt alone. Once again I felt guilty for my aggressive behavior. What was I doing? Why was I coming on so hard at him? Who was this person masquerading around in my body?

Chapter Fifty-Six *Desolation--Consolation*

I had hurt him. I threw my ideas at him with such force that he simply backed away ... he retreated. I have to remember the depth of his despair; I have to remember his emotional pain. Stanley's well-constructed and well-defended identity as a surgeon is gone - never again will he hold a scalpel, never again will he command an OR as the undisputed captain of the warship steaming directly into the enemy, never again will he feel the glow of personal satisfaction after saving yet another life.

I can't lose sight of this tragedy that he's encountered, not even for a second. My life, by comparison remains pretty much intact. I can continue to live my life for God without interruption, save cleaning fans that is. Certainly I feel a deep loss, but this loss allows me to join with Jesus and his passion so much more closely. In a strange way I have gained from this loss, and I hope to grow spiritually more and more. I feel God's consolation. Stanley, at least at this point, feels nothing but desolation.

> *Dear Lord help me find a new way to help Stanley. Help me be ever mindful of his pain, help me join with his anguish; help me bring him your consolation as you have given this gift to me. Forgive me for my terrible bluntness, forgive me my perfectionism, and forgive me of my neglect of Stanley's true needs right now – he needs compassion not logic, he needs understanding not bullying, he needs my tenderness not my opinions. Amen.*

Chapter Fifty-Seven

I heard a new voice across the hall in Stanley's room.

"Good morning, Dr. Renowski, it's good to meet you. My name is Debbie. I'm your water therapist. Today we start your therapy in the pool. My assistant Jim and I will use the Hoyer lift to get you in your wheelchair and then we'll all go down to the pool. What do you think of that?"

"What am I supposed to think?"

"Well, most patients really like the pool, they say it gives them a new sense of freedom. I'd like to start working on that right shoulder of yours. They tell me that you have some movement there and we want to start strengthening it."

"Will it hurt?"

"Oh no! You might feel a twinge here or there but that's good, that means you have some feeling, some sensation, and that's good — very, very good."

"I'd rather stay here."

"Well, I can understand that, some days are better than others; maybe this isn't one of your better days. You know our motto here at St. John's: Success is one-third on us, one-third on Mother Nature, and one-third on you. From my experience, that final third is certainly the biggest."

"Don't expect any big third from me."

"I know, it's hard, all your energy is being used up just trying to adjust, but just for today try to reorder yourself from where you've been to where you're going."

"I don't care to be going where I think I'm going."

"The future is unknown to all of us Dr. Renowski."

"Yeah, but your future may be a little different than mine."

"Of course, mine probably won't involve the adjustment that yours will."

"You're right there," snapped Renowski.

"But whatever happens, your inside has to change before your outside can change."

They finished the transfer. I heard them wheel Stanley down the hall. I sent a little prayer after him. A piece of my heart seemed to go with him. My feelings welled-up from deep within me; the conflict inside was palpable. One part of me screamed for expression, pushed me toward Stanley, wanted to hold him, to kiss him, and simply to be with him. Another part of me held my heart in compassion for him, it wanted to give him comfort. A third part wanted to bring his faith, his relationship with God, into sharper focus. Finally, there was the part of me that feared him; this was the curious part. Like a coiled snake Stanley was always ready to strike out at me. I was mesmerized by the snake's rattle, its texture, shape, and color; I was strangely drawn to it, and yet repulsed at the same time.

Chapter Fifty-Eight

"Hi, Sister," said Martha, "it's time for therapy."

"Oh, good morning, Martha, it's good to see you again."

"Is there anything I can help you with before we get started down?"

"Let's see, just let me brush my hair a bit."

It had been a long time since I brushed my hair. In the monastery we kept our hair so short under our veil that we never needed a brush. I'm surprised how fast my hair grows.

"Martha, do you think we could swing by the therapy pool on our way down to the gym?"

"I suppose that will be OK Sister, just for a minute. I can't leave you there though."

"Oh, I know Martha. I just want to see how Dr. Renowski is doing, it's his first time in the pool you know."

"The first time can be great, or it can be a little rough. Some patients just love letting themselves relax in the water; others, the ones who always need to be in control, hate the pool."

"Why is that?"

"In the pool you need to rely on others, you need to let go of controlling yourself and allow the therapists to work with you. If you're too tight with yourself, the pool isn't your thing."

We arrived at the pool. Martha held the door so I could peer in.

Chapter Fifty-Nine

"What are you doing? Don't do that. No, no, get me out, get me out of here," screamed Stanley.

"It's OK, Dr. Renowski, we won't let anything happen to you. We've got complete control of you," said Debbie.

"No, I want control, I don't want you to have control; I need control myself."

"Now, Dr Renowski, we do this all the time. Just relax in the water, you're securely attached to this chair; there's no way you can fall out. Just try to relax, it's really quite OK."

"No, no, it's not OK. You'll make a mistake, and I'll just sink to the bottom of this pool."

"That's quite impossible Dr. Renowski, this chair you're in is supported from the bottom; you can't sink."

"That's less than reassuring."

"It's OK, Dr. Renowski, maybe we'll just try again tomorrow, perhaps now that you know what is expected, you'll do a whole lot better."

I felt Stanley's anxiety in the pit of my stomach. "OK, Martha, I guess we can go now. Thanks so much for coming here with me; I appreciate it," I said. As I said this to Martha,

I wondered if Stanley had any inclination at all that I was spying on him ... I doubted it!

"Sister, you're most welcome; I can see how concerned you are about Dr. Renowski."

Chapter Sixty

I didn't wait at all on the penguin line. Amy greeted me as Martha and I arrived at the gym.

"Good morning, Sister, how we doin' today?" asked Amy.

"Oh ... oh ... good ... I guess ... yeah, good."

"Not quite sure about that yet, huh Sister?"

"Oh, I'm sure, I'm just worried a bit about Dr. Renowski. He had a rough first session in the pool just now."

"That happens fairly commonly Sister. Give him a day or two; he'll come around," said Martha.

As we got started I glanced over and spotted a new patient. He looked so strong and handsome, flowing jet-black hair, muscular arms each with a tattoo, and a determined look. I overheard the conversation between him and his therapist.

"So, you've been sitting with your legs out straight – not a good position for you," said Colleen.

"Hey, I like watching TV," he responded.

"That TV isn't as important as your legs."

"Yeah, I know, I know, but I like watching those faith healers – I might even go to one of their sessions."

"Oh yeah, what makes you want to do that?"

"Hey, I want to be healed. Every time I watch the show on TV a lot of people get healed."

"That's just it ... most of it is just a show."

"It may be, but people who couldn't walk in can actually walk out ... all on their own."

"I'll tell you what troubles me. I'm concerned you'll go there and come back all depressed. You've been doing so well," said Colleen.

"I still wanna go!"

"Well, I'll still be here when you get back."

"I wanna get back in my rig. Driving long-haul tractor trucks is all I know, it's all I've done since I got out of the Marines."

"I know you do Frank," said Colleen.

"That's my life, and I want to get back into that tractor again."

"Well, you can, at least you can get behind the wheel again."

"I don't want to use my condition as an excuse. I may not be able to use my legs, but the rest of me is just fine."

"You'll be able to drive again, that's if you work at it."

"That's what I intend to do, you know the Marine's motto: 'You never look back, you always look forward.'"

"I thought the Marine motto was '*semper fi*'. What does that mean anyway?"

"Always faithful. That's another motto."

"Oh, there's more than one?"

"Yeah, there's a bunch of them. There oughta have been one about not driving your semi into a tree. Maybe I wouldn't be here at St. John's today if there were. Not that this isn't a great place and all, but if I had my druthers I sure wouldn't choose to come here. No offense."

"No offense taken Frank, believe me, I understand completely."

"One thing the Marines did teach me was how to get back up after a fall. That's what I intend to do here ... get back up!"

"Good attitude, Frank. Keep thinking that way."

"I still have my mind, and I still have my mouth, that's what I'm in command of – my mind and my mouth. Nobody's takin' that from me."

"That's it, Frank, that attitude is your ticket."

"I have a lot more of my life to live, and I intend to live it."

"Frank, I wish I could bottle your positive attitude and have everybody take a long drink of it."

"Well, I know, Colleen, it rains on the just and the unjust alike. I can't blame God for what's happened to me. The only person I can blame is me – but that's crazy too. Blaming anybody is crazy. What's happened has happened ... and that's that."

"Good for you, Frank."

"The only question is will I be able to fully accept the grace of the Lord and go on?"

"Faith is a big part of your success in therapy Frank. How many times have I seen that the patients who have faith are the ones who seem to do the best?"

"I may be physically paralyzed but I'm not gonna be emotionally paralyzed. This will not get me, no way!"

"No one can rattle your cage, Frank ... that's great!"

"I'm not gonna live out of a shadow, I intend to live fully in the light. I just want to know what I can do to be all that I am."

Wow, what an attitude, I thought. Frank is inspired! What factors and forces have come together to give this man this courage, this mentality of challenge rather than doom, of self-respect, even honor, as opposed to self-degradation? How has he been able to take on a new identity of himself so soon after his accident? He's only just arrived! What power of grace is working in him? He hasn't a tenth of the education that Stanley has; yet he's light years beyond Stanley in his perception of who he is. Perhaps his positive attitude comes from the fact that Frank does have a chance to drive again and Stanley has no hope of ever doing surgery again. Yet, Stanley still has command over his mind and his mouth, as Frank says.

"Sister, are you with me today?" asked Amy.

"Oh ... yes, I'm sorry Amy, I'm just day dreaming I guess."

"That's OK Sister, I do it all the time. But knowing you, it's my guess that your thoughts are more than daydreams."

"Well, you're right this time. I was just overhearing that new patient Frank, talking with Colleen. What a great attitude he seems to have."

"I know, I worked with him yesterday and I was more than surprised by his positive and forward-looking way. To tell you the truth, Sister, I talked to my husband about Frank all last night. I've never seen any patient like him before."

"What do you think it is that allows someone to have what Frank has?"

"Sister, I can tell you one thing, whatever he's got, it's not of this world. Frank must be tapped into something a whole lot bigger than he is. That's your department more than mine. Sister."

"Amy, it's all of ours."

Chapter Sixty-One

I was back in my room again, and lunch had come and gone. I heard the aide helping Stanley, but I just couldn't bring myself to go across the hall; I just didn't feel ready. I guess I was still feeling guilty about hurting Stanley. In light of his difficulty in the pool today, somehow I thought he might need some private time. I decided to write letters to my sisters back at the convent; I'm sure they're always eager for news - they do love me!

I was tired after writing four letters. For some reason I struggled to transfer into my bed, but after she did, I was asleep in a minute. Once again I was dreaming.

I was at a circus and Stanley was the circus barker. He was dressed so strangely. He had a bowler hat and a parasol, spats over his high shoes, a bow tie, and a morning suit. He looked so out of place. As he began addressing the audience they immediately began booing him. He tried to yell over them, but they just booed him louder. He became angry and started reprimanding them saying they weren't acting as they should. One man stood up and threw a tomato that splattered over Stanley's chest. Stanley looked up horrified. Others joined in throwing tomatoes that found their mark all over Stanley.

Stanley didn't move, he simply raised his face and arms up and began transforming right there in the middle of the circus center ring. He glowed slightly as his morning suit became a clown outfit. Stanley had become a clown, a happy, smiling clown. Without a word he began doing back flips and somersaults; he walked on his hands, and he skipped around the ring with glee, all the while holding his little parasol. The audience began to clap; they were delighted, they were all on their feet now and their applause filled the circus tent to a deafening pitch.

Soon Stanley went back to the microphone. The audience hushed as Stanley once again raised his arms. After a pause, he glanced around the entire big top, bowed his head into the microphone and simply said, "I'm so sorry, please forgive me." The crowd erupted into enthusiastic applause. The spotlights illuminated Stanley in columns of light. He raised his arms again, took a deep bow, and walked backwards out of the center ring.

When I awakened I felt light, and pure, and clean – my guilt was gone. Excited to tell Stanley, I wheeled across the hall to find him watching TV. This was a change in itself; I hadn't seen this before. I paused at the door and asked his permission to enter.

"Come in," he said.

"How was your time at the pool this morning?"

"Fine," he muttered. His denial was deep.

"Oh, that's good," I said, playing his game. I thought it best to steer away from the pool episode.

"I have to tell you about the dream I just had, it was so vivid. I'm eager to hear what you think of it."

I described my dream as clearly as I could, giving detail after detail.

When I was finished, he said, "I never dream."

"You probably do Stanley, you just don't remember them. But anyway, what do you think my dream means?"

"I have no idea whatever. Dreams are just silly."

"Oh Stanley, I don't think dreams are silly at all, neither the dreams we have while asleep, nor the dreams we have when we're awake."

"What do you mean, dreams while you're awake?"

"Well, for example, I have a dream about you. My dream is that you find yourself anew, that you discover a whole new Stanley Renowski. This new Stanley is happy, and simple in a most positive way; he's friendly and caring, he's quiet and respectful, he's interested and interesting, but most of all this new Stanley loves!"

"Sounds a bit boring to me," said Stanley.

"Not at all, Stanley, he'd probably be the most stimulating man I know. This new Stanley knows himself well and is at peace with himself; he's patient, and he's very, very wise."

"What do you mean wise?"

"To be wise goes way beyond having good common sense, it means you have excellent uncommon sense. To be wise is to see true value in others, in life, and in oneself. To be wise is to recognize the wonderful connections that exist between and among us all, and all that God has created. To be wise is to love deeply, so deeply that you realize that life isn't about you, it's about others, helping others. A wise person knows he or she is first a servant to others."

Chapter Sixty-Two

Stanley looked at me; he just looked at me blandly, until ever so slowly his face gradually deepened into pain. His cheeks tightened, his brow furrowed, his eyes squeezed shut, and all the lines on his face became canyons. He erupted into tears again – violent tears!

My heart broke for this man in torment.

"Stanley, oh Stanley," I said as I wheeled close to him and took his head into my hands. "Stanley, let me take your pain away." I washed his face with his tears. I combed his hair with my fingers. He continued in tears.

"Let me help you Stanley, let me be your bridge. Rest in me, in my heart dear Stanley ... find yourself in something new."

I brought his face toward mine. I kissed his tears. I kissed his brow, I kissed his hair, his ears, his cheeks – I kissed his lips. Over and over I kissed him. The more he sobbed, the more I kissed him. I couldn't contain myself. All the tension and turmoil in me for him flowed from me as his tears flowed from him. I wanted to caress him – all over. I wanted to touch every part of him. I wanted –him! Something was emerging from me that I had buried long ago. I was out of my control. I became excited and expectant; my desire overtook me. I began caressing his chest, his shoulders, his arms and hands. I knew there was no physical feeling for him but I sensed a release from him as though something had burst out. Something had exploded from within me too!

Slowly, his tears receded. His violent sobs subsided. He gradually came to peace. He lay there, eyes closed, face placid but somber. He opened his eyes to slits, but from the corners I could sense his emotion. Something had shifted in him. After a time, I said, "Stanley do you feel better now?"

"Thank you. Yes. You're too good to me."

"No, Stanley, I'm not too good to you. You just haven't yet discovered the good, the deep good in you, that's all."

"I don't know what good there is in me."

"Stanley you just haven't learned yet how to give words to the goodness in you, you've been too busy trying to win in life that you've overshadowed your innate goodness, the places where the true Stanley resides. It's that Stanley that needs to rise from the deadened place it's been in up till now."

"Sister, if there's any good in me, please help me find it." "Stanley, all of your wonderful achievements, your personal accomplishments, all your medical credentials and awards cannot satisfy your true heart's desire. You need a new wellspring of personal OKness."

"Sister, where ... where is it?"

"You've been walking a desert inside, an arid place of lifelessness, a bitter place where you had no room for God."

"Sister, I have no idea about God."

"I know Stanley, and you've suffered the ache of being alone long enough. You haven't been abandoned Stanley."

"Sister, I don't know what else to call what's happened to me."

"Stanley, you've been so forlorn and angry because you've lost the grip on God' hand."

"Sister, I don't know where or how to find it again. You're the closest thing I know to God. God is present in you, I can see that, but you've dedicated your life to God, even if it is in a way I don't understand."

"You need to feel God's love too Stanley, your heart aches for it, so much more than you know. I know, Stanley. I once walked a desert inside of me and completely overlooked the garden that God had given me. I was fragmented and I was so, so sad. I looked to fill up my cold emptiness with a forbidden love.

"What do you mean a forbidden love?" he asked.

I fell in love with a married man, long before I entered the convent. I tried so hard to make it all work. I tried to be what he wanted, what I thought the world wanted me to be. I tried to be cool, but found it just made my life colder. I tried and tried, but in the end, I became hardened; I became a shell of a person. The world thought I was terrific, but inside I knew I was badly broken. I see that brokenness in you Stanley – I recognize it!"

"Sister, I grew up trusting only myself. I don't know another way. I know it causes problems, like today in the pool; I couldn't trust the therapist. She was trying her hardest but the more she talked the more I became afraid."

"That's just it Stanley, fear is always the result when we try to go it alone, when we try to live without God. Trust is not something we can manufacture like plastic toys. Trust comes only from God. We need to find God, Stanley – then we can gradually learn to trust."

"OK sister, but how do I find God?"

"It's a paradox Stanley because God is right inside us signaling us in so many ways to find him."

"You think that your accomplishments in medicine are the result of your hard work. Did you ever ask where the desire and the means to work so hard came from? Did you manufacture them?"

"No, but I used a lot of self-discipline. When everyone else was out playing ball or watching TV, or just hanging out, I was inside studying. I knew at a very young age that my future was in my head, I invested in my mental capacity. I know I had an intellect and that's what set me apart."

"Yes Stanley, you do have an intellect and you still have command of that mind, don't you? You still have command of what comes out of your mouth. Do you think that might point to your future today as it did so many years ago?"

"What do you mean?"

"The most precious parts of you Stanley are unaffected by your accident; isn't that your true earthly treasure? Isn't it in your heart and soul where your eternal treasures lie?"

"But what is my mind without my hands?"

"Your hands only did what your mind directed Stanley. Your mind can go in any direction you choose. Certainly there are new directions for you. Where does one go with an excellent mind and the voice of experience? You have so much to share Stanley. Find these new avenues."

"How can I do that in my condition? What does it take?"

"Stanley, it takes faith, a trust in something bigger than you Stanley – it takes God! Let God enter your life in a new way. Feel God's love for you, let God console you as no mortal can. The ball is in your court Stanley, and your mind is holding the racket."

Chapter Sixty-Three *On Purpose*

I left Stanley without saying good night; I thought it best to leave him with these new thoughts – and even if they weren't entirely new thoughts, perhaps my actually giving voice to the possibility that Stanley could have a new life beyond his old one may jog him sufficiently so he can consider it with more objectivity. At the very least my assertion of a new life awaiting him may move his thinking away from his awful negativism – even for only a brief period.

I felt better now. Stanley was still in deep pain, and a curtain still shrouded his vision of the future. Yet the most meager hope was beginning to advance onto the stage of Stanley's life – a hope that had been banished from his life for such a long time, if it had ever been there before at all.

Maybe I felt better because I had jettisoned the guilt that I felt from our previous discussion, if that's what it was, when I so severely invaded his comfort zone. Our last talk was consoling for me; I hope it was for him as well. Even though my guilt was gone I still felt in a vortex , trapped in a torrent of emotion sucking me somewhere, I didn't know where. I feared that these emotions I had for Stanley stood in direct contradiction to my promise of full surrender to God. Yet, what I wanted most was for Stanley to find God for himself – to have him invite God into his heart. How could this be contradictory to my promise of obedience to God? What nagged at me was not my desire for Stanley's conversion; what nagged at me more was my desire for Stanley. This desire tore me away from intimacy with God and from myself.

Chapter Sixty-Four

Back in the rehab gym I looked around at all the familiar faces. Amy had me stretching – both the ones that I could do alone as well as the ones where she did most, if not all, of the work.

"That's good Sister," said Amy. "Keep going."

"OK, I'm trying ... somehow it seems a bit harder today for some reason."

"Some days are better than others. Wasn't it the same way before your accident?"

"I guess it was."

This was certainly true; being a "card carrying" migraine sufferer I knew well that some days were a whole lot better than others. I often wondered exactly what brought on my migraine attacks. What had I done, thought, felt, ate, discussed, etc. that lit the fuse that would eventually explode in my brain sending my entire being into a migraine shock? I never figured it out completely, except that there were an amalgam of forces and factors that converged together in ways that pushed me into my migraine vulnerability. How much of this I had any control over and how much was simply a bio-emotional proclivity, I guess I'll never know. But, yes, some days are definitely better than others. I need to accept this more fully not only for myself, but also for Stanley.

After a half an hour Amy ended our shorter stretching and strengthening routine and said, "Well, Sister that about does it for today. You did a great job!"

"Thanks Amy, so did you. And thanks for the reminder that some days are better than others."

Amy wheeled me over to the penguin line where another transporter, Marge, was ready to transport me upstairs to my room.

"Hey, Marge, good to see you; you're looking well today."

"Well, thank you very much, Sister ... that made my day."

"You're too kind, Marge. Say, do you have any time to swing me by the therapy pool?"

"Are you starting pool therapy Sister?"

"Oh no, Marge, I just want to see how Dr. Renowski is doing with his therapy."

"Well, I guess so, there aren't any patients waiting to go up right now ... so ... maybe just for a minute."

"Thanks so much Marge."

We arrived at the pool to find Stanley immersed in his pool chair with a therapist on each side of him.

"You're doin' great today, Dr. Renowski. How does it feel?" asked Debbie.

"All right!" said Stanley. "I told myself last night that I was not going to let this pool get to me again. I'm in control of my emotions, not the other way around."

"That-a-way. Doctor. I've seen lots of people pretty apprehensive about the pool at first, just like you were yesterday; but I gotta tell you that I never saw anyone regroup as quickly as you did. You're a new person today."

"In some ways you're absolutely right, Debbie."

My heart jumped in glee; his words were like an ice cube on a bug bite – immediate relief. Stanley's self-discipline is potent indeed. Can he keep this rolling I wondered?

Chapter Sixty-Five

After lunch both Stanley and I took a nap. Strange how fast one can get used to naps. When I awoke I listened for him – nothing. Perhaps we could go to the solarium today. I'd been there several times, but I'd never seen Stanley there. On any given afternoon you could always find two or three patients in the solarium just talking. I transferred myself into my chair and rolled across the hall to Stanley's room. His eyes were closed and I thought him asleep, but just as I wheeled around to leave his room, I heard ...

"Sister stay, why don't you?

"Oh, you're awake, I thought ..."

"No, no, no, I'm awake, just resting that's all!"

His words "stay, why don't you," heralded a new attitude in Stanley. They were like balm on parched skin, tender and calm, yet strong and assured without the arrogance that had given an edge to everything he said before. My heart shuddered as I took in his invitation to come closer.

"Thank you," was all I could say.

"How was your morning in the gym?" he asked.

I didn't know that he followed, or even cared at all about my therapy schedule, or about how I was progressing.

"Oh, very well."

Now it was I, not Stanley, who could only give short responses.

"Whom did you have?" he asked.

"What?" I responded.

"Which therapist worked with you?"

"Oh ... um ... Amy." I stammered, not used to this solicitous manner in him.

"I like her, she's competent and very caring."

Where in him was this coming from? He was disarmingly charming, not as much in his words as in his manner. He was actually tender!

"How was your morning?" I managed to ask.

"Very good! Debbie said she had never seen such a quick regrouping as I did; that's the word she used ... regroup."

"What did she mean?"

"Well, yesterday was a bit difficult for her. Actually, I made it difficult for her. When I first got in the water I didn't like it. I felt naked and without any control. But after our talk last night I simply resolved that I'd conquer that pool today. I think I did."

"Stanley, I'm so very proud of you! That was a giant step. Oh, sorry, that was a poor choice of words on my part. That showed your true inner strength."

Stanley gave me a curious look that I couldn't quite decipher. Then he said ... "You know, Sister, I can't remember anyone saying that they were proud of me."

"Stanley, that can't be true, surely your mother told you she was proud of you. And what about Anne? She must have told you she was proud of you."

"No, never; my mother was too busy being depressed because of my father. And Anne, no ... she didn't have room in her heart to be proud of me, not genuine pride. She complimented me, but only when I'd prompt her. I would give her a cue that I wanted some sort of praise and she would respond in kind. It was a little game we'd play; I gave her all she wanted and in turn she praised me."

"I hear your words but it's so hard for me to put it together. I can't imagine being married, especially to you, and not being proud of you all the time."

"I'm sure I was a bit of a challenge to live with. Maybe she really was proud of me but couldn't bring herself to give words of genuine praise because she'd have to surmount her growing resentment of me; her husband who was bent on controlling everything."

"Surely you could talk things out with Anne."

"Not really, Sister. The moment I started getting closer to her she'd pull away like she was afraid of me."

"Maybe she was Stanley; fear is the shadow side of love."

"What do you mean?"

Chapter Sixty-Six

"If love is a force, a very, very positive energy, something we obviously can't manufacture on earth, what state would you call the complete absence of love?"

"Hate, if you don't love then you hate."

"Not really, hate may eventually emerge, but what springs up first is fear."

"Let me think about that," he said.

"Stanley, haven't you ever heard, 'Perfect love casts out fear'?"

"I guess so, but what about the idea that we're supposed to fear God?"

"What fear means there is that we have a healthy regard for God by living our lives with the knowledge of God's presence."

"So, do you think that Anne feared me?"

"It's a good bet. When two people love each other they can be honest; they can reveal all of who they are, the good, the bad, and, well you know -- warts and all. It's called intimacy – sharing one's total self with another. I've vowed my total self to God, that's why sisters can't give themselves fully in physical terms, in other words no sex because that would be a violation of the intimate state they have with God; that way they can maintain their total commitment to God."

"I never saw it that way, I had no idea why nuns couldn't marry."

"Well good, I'm glad we straightened that out. But, what about Anne and you ... what about your relationship? If Anne did fear you, even a small amount, what did that mean for your intimacy? Wherever there is fear it signals an absence of love."

"I often wondered if Anne loved me or whether she stayed with me to live the kind of lifestyle she wanted."

"That could be to some degree, but intimate relationships usually aren't so black and white as that. More often there's a mix of many things and feeling going on all at once that all change day by day. You know this; togetherness is mixed with a little self-centeredness, respect and honor can be tainted with indifference, good communication can be infected by criticism, trust can be doubted, and commitment can be betrayed. It can get pretty confusing after a while if the couple can't be honest with each other."

"How do you know so much about intimate relationships?"

"Stanley, I didn't go into the convent out of grade school you know. I worked for 10 years as a flight attendant and I met a guy or two along the way."

"Really, did you have any serious relationships?"

"One, but I'd rather not discuss it."

"OK Sister, I respect your privacy."

"Thank you Stanley."

I felt a blush of embarrassment that surprised me. Here I was prompting Stanley to be honest and I drew a line in my life that he couldn't cross. Perhaps it's because my relationship with Jay was forbidden then for one reason, and any intimacy with Stanley now would be forbidden for another reason. Yet I felt I was already in an emotional relationship with him and it's any guess that he felt the same toward me. I didn't know where this is going.

"Stanley, let's go down to the solarium, it's a nice sunny day and the view from there is so pretty."

"I don't know, I don't think I'm a solarium-type guy."

"How would you know, have you ever been there?"

"No, I haven't, I'm just remembering from the hospitals where I've worked. Solariums are just chit-chat places; I spent as little time in them as possible."

"We both need a change of scenery, so I'll give you a choice: the solarium or the chapel."

"Since you put it like that I guess you just forced me to the solarium."

Chapter Sixty-Seven

I called for transfer assistance and after 15 minutes we were on our way to the solarium. I felt elated that I was able to motivate Stanley this far. The solarium was empty when we arrived."

"You see the sunlight in here, Stanley? Isn't it great, and what do you think of the view?"

The generous grounds around St. John's are populated with gigantic oak trees all strong and full. The lawns roll; they undulate, and all of this is bordered by woods. Paved pathways traverse the park-like setting with benches at measured intervals. The view from the solarium could be a postcard.

"Very nice," is all Stanley could say.

The sun felt so gentle and warm on my arms. I caught myself just before I asked Stanley how the sun felt on his arms.

"Doesn't the sun feel good on your face, Stanley?"

"Yeah," he said.

Something was upsetting him, pushing him out of the more casual, upbeat mood he sported in his room. I wondered if taking even this tiny step out of his room unnerved him. He obviously felt less secure here. I was just about to suggest that we leave when Frank rolled into the solarium.

"Well, Sister, nice to see you here this afternoon," said Frank.

"Yes, it's so nice in here. Have you met Dr. Renowski yet Frank?"

"Ah, no, not yet."

"Frank Sileo, this is Dr. Stanley Renowski."

Instantly Frank offered Stanley a handshake. Stanley's look at Frank could have burned toast.

"Oh, I'm so sorry," said Frank, "I should have known."

Stanley just stared at Frank without saying anything.

"It's a beautiful day," I said.

"Sure is," Frank said. "Just look at that sun starting to set, it's beautiful ... God's glory all right."

I could almost see Stanley deflating into himself.

"It's days like this that make living worthwhile," said Frank.

I didn't respond. Stanley retreated deeper.

"When I see a sunset, I see God's words written all over it. 'I'm giving you this so that you know who's in charge,'" said Frank.

Again, neither Stanley nor I reacted.

"Somehow just peering out these windows reminds me there's a wide world out there and I can't wait to be back in it again," said Frank.

Another silence. Stanley was getting more perturbed by Frank's optimism; it's alien to Stanley, he didn't know what to do with it; perhaps he was afraid of it?

"I can almost smell the sweetness of just-mowed grass, and breathe in that fresh air. Makes you feel like a million bucks, doesn't it," remarked Frank.

"It sure is nice," I said, knowing that Stanley's ire was rising.

"I remember on real long hauls when I got to the mountains out West, driving into that setting sun, that glow, that orange glow washin' everything was just so gorgeous. I could almost cry when I'd see that. Fact is, I did cry a time or two, but they were tears of gratitude that God would give us such sights, such wonders as these. Just talking about it makes me anxious to get out there again ... and I will too! I'm working just as hard as I can down there in that gym and I'm gonna learn how to get back out there on that open road. My legs may be dead, but me ... I'm very much alive and rarin to go. What about you doctor, oh ... what did you say your name was?

"Stanley ... Dr. Stanley Renowski," I answered for him.

"Oh thanks, Sister. What about it, Stanley, what kind of plans are you makin' for when you get out of here? Great place though it is, I'll still be one happy man to leave, won't you?"

Stanley stared at Frank again. To me his face said something like, "You have no right to ask me anything; how could you be so stupidly presumptuous?"

Frank was obtuse to Stanley's emotions.

"So what do you think doctor?" Frank pressed.

"I think it's time to go," said Stanley.

Silence pervaded the room. My pounding heart kept time until Frank said, "You know what Doctor, I think you're right, it is time to go."

With that Frank slowly swung his wheelchair around and rolled out of the solarium without saying another word. I was immediately angry with Stanley but felt I couldn't express it because I had coaxed him into the solarium against his protest. Nonetheless I was angry because he was so rude to Frank without any reason.

Chapter Sixty-Eight

"Stanley, what's the matter?"

"That guy is a jerk."

"And what makes him a jerk?"

"Sunsets and grass and mountains and all that ridiculous talk about God. He wouldn't know an education if he fell over it."

"Stanley, he was just expressing his feelings; what harm did he do?"

"He's stupid that's all, couldn't you see that from the way he talked. He's just an uneducated truck driver."

"And aren't uneducated truck drivers supposed to talk to Dr. Stanley Renowski?"

"I'm not descending down to his level, if that's what you mean."

"Stanley, why do you look for things that separate you from others? There's a lot more about you and Frank that's quite alike than there is that's not."

"Sister, what does he know?"

"Well Stanley, for one thing he knows where he's going."

"He's *never* getting behind the wheel of a cross country tractor trailer. What company would hire him?"

"He seems pretty determined to me. I have little doubt that he'll find himself doing something productive."

"Yeah, maybe making rosary beads."

"Stanley, not only is that a low blow, it's also hurtful to me. I happen to place great faith in the rosary."

"OK, OK but this guy is just blowing smoke, he's blue-skying this whole thing. He's not in reality, Sister!"

"You mean he's not in your reality. The fact is that Frank has a goal; he has a vision of where he's going. He is putting his energies to work for this vision. Frank is motivated by his vision; he needs his vision." I gathered my strength, and with some consideration said, "Stanley ... you need a vision."

He knew that I meant what I said and since he was starting to trust me, he couldn't simply dismiss my words as he would anyone else's.

"I don't see any visions," said Stanley.

"Stanley, you need one ... you need a vision; you can't get on with your life without one. Everybody needs to have some idea about the purpose of their life."

"I had a purpose, Sister, but it's gone."

"Yes, I know you had a profession, and I know you had great success in it. It's the particular way you practiced your profession that's gone Stanley. But that's not what purpose is; purpose is a lot bigger than that."

"What do you mean? Are you saying my life had no purpose before?"

"Of course not, cardiac surgery has great purpose; to save lives of men and women who have heart disease. But, is that purpose your purpose now?"

"I don't know what you're talking about."

"Look, do you want to live a meaningful life?"

"I did, before this damned accident."

"No Stanley, I'm talking about now ... do you want to live a meaningful life now?"

No response...

"You see, you can't answer that can you," I said. "You know what, Frank can answer that question – does that make him stupid?"

"Oh, we're back on him."

"No ... no, we're on you. Experiencing meaning only comes from pursuing purpose. If you have no purpose then you can't experience meaning. You think your life is over because you don't have a vision of what will give you meaning again. Your thinking is stuck on surgery as the only path to meaning; surgery is your only vision, the only purpose you see for yourself. Until you formulate a vision for what's next in your life, you'll want to end it."

Stanley seemed to consider this solemnly. His face grimaced; he stretched his neck back as far as he could. Finally, he said, "So what's my vision, smelling grass and watching sunsets?"

"Your vision probably has something to do with your profession, or perhaps the science and art of medicine in some way, but not actually doing surgery. Purpose has to do with helping others in some way."

"OK, go on."

"Well, I've gotten the sense from you that maybe you were getting a little bored with surgery anyway. You've already won all the honors there are to receive, so what's next for you in surgery? My sense is that you might have already been thinking along these lines, even before your accident."

"Well, one or two thoughts might have crossed my mind, but there were no specifics at all."

"There, you see, I knew it. You *were* starting to get bored. You needed a new vision even before the accident; now it's imperative."

"I don't know."

"What kind of thoughts crossed your mind, Stanley; come on, out with it."

"The only thing that made any sense at all was teaching."

"Teaching who ... what?"

"Surgical residents of course. But I can't do that because I can't do surgery."

"Do you need to do surgery to teach?"

"Of course, you can't demonstrate technique without actually doing surgery."

"You have so much knowledge and experience and creativity, there must be a way to share this with students."

"I haven't seen it."

"You'll just need use the creativity God gave you to come up with something new."

"Fat chance," said Stanley.

"That brings me to what really needs to be said here Stanley."

"What's that?"

"Purpose is not just about worldly utility, it goes way beyond that. The world, that is the secular world, sees little utility in my vocation of prayer; yet, my purpose is immense.

I'm following my purpose because I'm following what God wants me to do. That's the question I need to pose to you. Stanley, what does God want you to do?"

"Well, how would I know?"

"The way you know, Stanley, is to ask him ... ask God. If you don't get an answer at first, just keep asking God. When you ask, and you listen deeply, you will get an answer."

Chapter Sixty-Nine *Change*

My mind wandered far from my conversation with Stanley. As I was considering possible options for Stanley's life purpose after he was released from the hospital, an image flashed on the screen of my mind that disturbed me so that it almost forced me out of Stanley's room.

The vision was of Stanley maneuvering himself in his wheelchair down the ramp that led from the front door, through the white picket fence and out to the sidewalk. The little cottage complete with blooming roses was straight out of a Norman Rockwell painting. What scared me so was seeing myself; I was waving good-bye to Stanley from the front door. Whether I was just his caregiver, or his wife I didn't know, but either way I wasn't in the convent. It was more than shocking that this new image of Stanley's future included me! From what part of me did this image arise?

Once back in my room I searched my soul looking for that part of me that served up this image. I know that I'm invested in Stanley's well being; I know that I want the best for this man who has seen so much of the world and yet has realized so little about himself. I probably understand him in deeper ways than anyone has, even his wife, Anne. Yet I don't want my compassion and empathy to morph into something more intimate, I don't want my heart to become so involved in Stanley's life that I lose it. I'm intimate with Stanley to the degree that he has shared, such as it is, with me some of the vulnerable parts he has never had the courage to expose before. I cannot allow myself to be seduced by his need, as I once was so many years ago. Yet what can I do?

Dear Lord, help me remain so close to you that I could never share that closeness in a human way. Help me to respect my vows to you, as I surrender all that I am. Help me, dear Lord; to talk with you often and share my most intimate me with you. Help me trust the you in me and remain steadfast in your love. Amen.

I said a rosary and my Liturgy of the Hours prayers. After that I felt more internal coherence, yet I knew that I remained shaken by the image of Stanley and me together. I didn't want to distort the power of kindness that God has given in me into a form of self-forfeiture that promised only to separate me from the most noble parts of my being. Stanley, I knew was fighting the terrible tension that results from cutting himself from the core of his being, that part of him that is transcendent, and searching for security only in that which is transient ... only in the world.

After my nightly hygiene needs, I transferred myself into bed and lapsed in dream. Stanley and I were walking hand-in-hand through a meadow flush with flowers. Snow-covered mountains provided the majestic backdrop. We talked and laughed; we skipped and hopped over meadow boulders. Sunlight graced us, the picture of everything good about being human.

A brook sprang out of the tree line bordering the meadow and we began to follow it into the forest. We hiked for several miles into the wood that thickened as we did. Soon no sunlight penetrated through the canopies of the forest. The brook ended at a pool. Without a word Stanley plunged in. He surfaced once and waved to me flashing an immense grin. It spoke of grand health and pure heart, clean soul and strong faith. As quickly as he surfaced, he once again submerged. I somehow knew that he wouldn't surface again. I watched the surface of the pool settle itself to the undisturbed sheen it had been when we first came upon it. I repressed an impulse to dive in after Stanley, restrained by some celestial prudence that gave me the strength and direction to turn away.

I walked slowly out of the wood, back in the flower carpeted meadow. But storm clouds and claps of thunder had replaced the sunlight that momentarily scared me. To my surprise however it didn't rain, instead the gentlest snow began wafting its way in millions of delicate snowflakes. Soon the ground was white with innumerable flowers poking through the white blanket that offered a background and a frame for the meadow flowers. I reveled in the gentle snow, raising my hands to heaven and thanking God for the beauty that surrounded and enveloped me. Stanley, I now knew was quite all right, secure in God's grace and buoyed by the fruits of the Spirit.

Chapter Seventy

I awakened in the morning feeling fully refreshed and recuperated from the shutter I felt the night before of the image of Stanley and me together at the cottage.

"Good morning, Sister, here's your breakfast," said Cindy Ramirez.

"Cindy, good morning back to you, and a fine morning it is."

"Sister, how can you awaken so cheery, it takes me at least several cups of coffee to feel even half normal."

"I could always awaken easily, I guess it's from all the practice in the convent, getting up in the middle of the night for prayers."

"Sister, I'm really curious, how did you make the decision to become a nun? How did you know it was right for you, especially a cloistered nun? I have to be honest, I couldn't do it ... maybe for a week or even two I'd love it, but for a lifetime ... no ... never could I do it!"

"Cindy, it wasn't a snap decision. When I first felt the nudge of God toward the convent I resisted with everything in me. I couldn't believe ... I didn't want to believe that God could be calling me. I was nobody special ... for sure! But, as much as I pushed away from God, the more he pursued me it seemed. More than once I wrestled with God; once or twice I even relented and negotiated with God to go in, but I always managed to put it off. Finally I had no place to go, had no place to hide; I simply had to go ... and I did."

"Did you ever regret it?" Cindy asked.

"I certainly questioned my vocation. Several times I thought about leaving, but each time God somehow reminded me that I was where I belonged. Now I can say I don't question God's choice at all. That's not to say there aren't times when I become impatient with the life, I long to taste this or that in the world, but these are rare times indeed. I simply remind myself that there is no perfect life anywhere ... at least not on this earth. Now I feel nothing but blessed by God's call and his powerful grace that enabled me to surrender to him. It's a privilege to live this life."

"Sister, you make it sound so beautiful, but I know it must be tough too. If I volunteered for a couple of weeks do you think they'd let me come? I'm just kidding of course, I could never leave my three kids, and what would my husband do?"

"No Cindy, it sounds like you're where God wants you."

"Thanks, Sister. You know, you're my favorite patient."

"Well, thank you indeed, Cindy, I do more than appreciate that, but be assured it's me who is honored to be with you."

Cindy blushed and cast her eyes away in humility.

"How are things going with Dr. Renowski?" I asked.

"Oh, he's changed a lot; why only yesterday he told me that he's going to a better place when he leaves St. John's. I thanked him for sharing, but beyond that I didn't know what to say."

"A better place? I wonder what that meant?"

"I just thought he had found a new hospital, or maybe some residential setting for spinal cord injured doctors."

"Huh, that's strange, he's never mentioned a word about plans after St. John's ... I'll have to ask him about this," I said.

Chapter Seventy-One

I took my breakfast across the hall. Stanley looked asleep, until I wheeled over to his bedside and whispered.

""How's the world famous patient this morning?"

"Oh ... ah ... hi," said Stanley as he arched his right eyebrow and cracked his eye open a slit. He wet his lips and opened his other eye. He feigned awakening, but I could tell he was already awake.

"What were you thinking?" I said.

"Ah ... I don't know. Nothing I guess."

"Are you hungry? They're serving breakfast now."

Before he could answer, his breakfast tray arrived.

"Thank you Marsha," I said to the aide. "Just put it down on the table; I'll take care of it."

I positioned the table so I could feed Stanley.

"Here you go; one of your favorites, pancakes and sausage."

He accepted the first few bites and even took a sip of his coffee.

"You just looked like you were thinking when I came in, that's why I asked you the question."

"No, nothing in particular."

He took more food and gulped it down. Then he said, "What do you plan ... you know ... when your time here at St. John's is over?"

"Oh, I'll go back to the convent. I'll have plenty of caregivers there. What about you? What plans are you formulating?"

"Well, that's what I was thinking about when you came in. Up till now I had a real simple plan; find a way to make all this go away ... find an opportunity to end it all. Now I'm trying to come up with other options."

"That's a relief. Does anything look good?"

"Nothing, nothing looks good. Everything I think of is just dismal."

"Stanley, you know you're depressed, you have been since your trauma; you're still not thinking straight. I have no doubt there is an option that will allow you an entirely new life."

"You know, you keep saying that; it's been your theme to me from the very first day. But sister, I've got to be honest; I can't see it. There's nothing that would or could satisfy me now, not after the life I've lived."

"Stanley, that's just not true."

"Sister, you've got to get the picture here. What can I do? Where can I go? Who will care for me? I killed the only person who might have cared for me. Anne is gone - and I killed her. Sister, it should have been me; I should have died in that accident, not her. Anne didn't deserve to die; she did nothing! I'm the fool whose arrogance caused that accident. I deserve to die. But Anne is in a better place now, and the only choice I see for myself is to find a way to join her."

"Stanley, I cherish the confession you just made. I honor the insight you just showed about yourself. I can see that your heart is contrite, and I do celebrate that you believe in life after death. All of that is wonderful. But Stanley, your conclusion is totally illogical and to me utterly unacceptable."

"Sister it's not your choice to make."

"Of course not, but Stanley, I'm here and I can't simply agree to what I see as your depressive thinking. Stanley, you're still so regressive in the way you see all this. You're still stuck on bringing things back to the way they were. Stanley, it's a new day, and the new day, as much as you don't like it, demands that we see things through new eyes, eyes that see clearly and accurately. Stanley, I can tell you that you haven't gotten there yet; no, I'm afraid you're still far from it. Stanley we need change; you're still fixated in the past and we need change in the present."

"Sister, I'm afraid that would take a miracle."

"Stanley, in the world where I live miracles happen everyday. I expect miracles."

With that my transporter darkened the door.

"Sister, time for your morning stretching program at the gym."

"OK, let me just finish a thought with Dr. Renowski and I'll be right over to my room to freshen up before I'm ready. Can you give me a minute?"

"Sure, I'll be back in a couple of minutes," she replied.

"Stanley, this is very, very important. We need to continue this conversation. Let's get back together later, OK?"

All right sister ... all right."

Chapter Seventy-Two

After a pause when each of us stared into each other's eyes, a stare that was completely devoid of any of the contempt that formerly defined Stanley's interaction, I was handed off from the transporter to Colleen, the head rehab therapist in the gym.

"Hi, Sister, how's everything today?" Colleen asked.

"Colleen, how common is it for patients to want to end their life?"

"Whoa, Sister ... where's this coming from? Are you having thoughts about hurting yourself?"

"Oh no, not me, I could never do that; I'd never want to do that. God has given life and only God can take it away. No, I'm just curious, that's all."

"Well, they say that at any given time some 5% of the general population can be diagnosed as at least mildly depressed. Over the course of a lifetime some 15 to 20% get clinically depressed. So when you figure that almost one in five people can get depressed anyway, what happens to those people who have a natural tendency toward depression, when they experience a high-level trauma that brings them here to St. John's?"

"Wow, I guess when you look at it that way, at least 20% are depressed at any given time."

"Yes, and we've noticed, as one would think, that as the severity of their physical disability increases so does the likelihood of depression."

"Well, I guess that's logical, but what keeps some other people together and depression-free who also have severe disabilities? What forces and factors keep body and soul in good working order even under the most dire circumstances?"

"Sister, you've just asked a question that's more in your field than mine. I should be asking you that question. I don't think that medical science has the data to answer that one ... please tell *me* if you have any thoughts."

"Oh, Colleen, I have plenty of thoughts and they all start with faith."

"I'm sure you're right Sister, but right now I'm sorry I have to bring you down to this worldly level. We need to go through our morning stretches."

"Of course, let's get at it."

"Actually, I wanted to assess how you're doing these movements on your own. First I'd like to see you transfer from your chair onto the exercise table by yourself. Do you think you can do that?"

"OK, I'll try. Larry, the exercise physiologist and I have been working hard on my upper extremities strength training so I think I can transfer on my own ... let's see."

Sister seems to glide from her wheelchair to the raised therapy mat with ease.

"Great, Sister, very smooth and clean ... no wobbles, really good."

"Thanks Colleen."

"Now that you're on the mat, can you demonstrate your morning stretches for me?"

I went through the latest program that I'd been taught right along.

"Good, Sister, now you know we encourage you to do these religiously. Oh, I guess you already know how to do things religiously, don't you?"

"I think I do."

"Could you show me your pressure relief movements?"

"You mean this ... and this ... and this ... and this?" I said to Colleen as I demonstrated the various pressure release techniques.

"Yes ... great ... really wonderful. You're really on top of this Sister, I'm gonna have to give you the gold star."

"Thanks."

"Now, can you transfer back to your chair without using the slide board?"

"Oh, I can be a show-off on that move."

"Great, Sister. Now for the higher-level wheelchair moves. I want you to be able to do a wheelie so you can go up and down curbs and such if you need to."

"Colleen, that's my absolute favorite." I then delighted in showing her how I could raise the front wheels of my wheelchair to clear curbs. I did it several times just to show off.

"Wow, nice job Sister ... that was really nice. I think you're a candidate for the wheelchair Olympics all right."

"Anything else today?" I asked.

"No, you've mastered what you need. You know you're pretty advanced and we can start think about a discharge date for you. What do you think?"

"Well Colleen, I'll tell you, I have some items on my discharge plan that still are a ways from completion."

"What do you mean?" she asked.

My answer was a nod of my head toward Stanley who had just entered the gym with his transporter.

"Oh, I see. You've got some unfinished business there?"

"He's still struggling and I don't think he can open up to anyone else here. I know the counselors from the psych. department are wonderful, but Dr. Renowski can't or won't share anything with them."

"Sister, Dr. Renowski has a lot more work to do. I have no doubt that you'll be ready for discharge ahead of him."

"I know, and frankly I'm worried about that. I don't know what he'll do ... I don't think he's made any plans. His wife is gone, and he has no other family that I know of. I don't know how he'll ever manage."

"Sister, he's gonna need help ... a lot of help."

Chapter Seventy-Three

I asked the transporter if she would take me to the chapel. I needed to pray.

Lord, we need you. We need a miracle. Help me gather up all the grace you have bestowed upon me, and the gifts that give me your power. Help me, dear Lord, to focus all of this so that Stanley can move closer to you. You are what he needs Lord; you are the source of all and the end of all. Stir-up in Stanley what you have given him from the first so that he may be able to see his situation, and his entire life, more clearly. Help him use your power of vision to catch a glimpse of a plan that can bring him to you. I need you too, Lord. Help me do what I can and to get out of your way as you work your will through me to Stanley. Amen

I sat in the chapel for some time aligning my will with God's as best I could. Time passed faster than I realized. When I arrived back in my room my lunch was already on my table. I ate, and took a short nap. When I awakened I felt a strange sensation of heat in my body. My brow was clammy and my face flushed. I rang for the nurse.

"Hi, Sister, what's seems to be the problem?" asked nurse Jan.

"I don't know, suddenly I feel warm."

"Well, let's give a feel here," said Jan as she placed her palm on my forehead. "Oh yeah, you're warm all right. Let me take your temp, Sister."

The new electronic thermometers take only a minute to register. Jan studied the digital display. "One-0-one point six. Yes, just as I thought, you'll need an exam. I'll ask Dr. Pollack to come up. Right now just rest and I'll send down some fluids for you."

I must have dozed off again. I was awakened by the sound of someone entering my room.

"So, here's the hot nun," said Dr. Pollack in jest.

Nurse Jan shot him a surprised half-stare. His return look at Jan said he might have thought twice about his remark.

"The nun may be hot but she feels pretty flat," I said.

Dr. Pollack relaxed noticeably.

"Well. Let's take a look. Could you open your mouth, Sister?' asked Dr. Pollack.

I did as he instructed.

"Pretty clean in there. Let's listen to your chest." He unfurled his stethoscope from around his neck and listened to my lungs.

"Lungs are clear too. Sister, have you noticed any vaginal discharge?"

"Well, maybe a bit."

"In that case I need to do a vaginal exam and that needs to be done in my exam room." He turned to Jan, "Jan can you arrange to have Sister Theresa brought down within the hour?"

"Sure, Dr. Pollack, we'll have her right down."

"I'll need a female in the room, too," he said.

"Sure, I'll come myself."

"Thanks Jan, I appreciate that," said Dr. Pollack.

Within minutes we were on our way to Dr. Pollack's exam room. He took us right in and proceeded with his exam.

"Pretty much what I thought. Sister, you have a UTI, a urinary tract infection," he said.

"I do? How did I get that?" I asked.

"It's pretty common. Your body is still adjusting to your new life; your regular movements have changed. You may be a bit more susceptible to UTIs now, especially if you've had any history of them. You'll have to visually check yourself regularly since you can't feel the burning sensation anymore that accompanies UTIs," said Dr. Pollack.

"What do we do now?" I asked.

"I'll put you on an antibiotic, and I'd like nurse Jan to keep close watch on its progress. I'd like to see you again in two days."

Jan and I put me back together and started back to my room. We moved in silence, until Jan said, "You know, Sister, this UTI might extend your stay here a bit. As a matter of fact you can probably plan on it.

"You're kidding," I said.

"No, any infection is more serious for you now, and we have to make absolutely sure that you're infection-free before you can be discharged."

Jan gave me the antibiotic, and also a Tylenol for my fever. I went to bed and right to sleep.

Chapter Seventy-Four

I could eat only my soup and other liquids for supper, otherwise I felt pretty good. I heard Stanley and decided to scoot over to his room for just a short visit.

"Hi, Stanley, how'd your sessions go today?"

"OK," he said. He seemed dispirited.

"Anything wrong?" I asked.

"I don't know. I don't know anything anymore."

"Ouch," I said. "You're feeling pretty down aren't you?"

"Well Sister, I still can't see anything positive here at all. You have this otherworldly attitude that totally escapes me. I wish I could grasp even a little of what you've got Sister, but I can't. I'm not like you; you've been anointed or something with a different oil than me."

"Stanley, we've all been blessed equally. We've all been given what we need to rise up and face whatever life throws at us."

"Yeah, and this is quite a wad that's been thrown at me."

"Stanley, do you know what? The fact that you're asking these questions, these penetrating questions, and the fact that you're asking them with such care and respect is so refreshing to hear. Only last week you were still hiding behind your anger and bitterness; today you've got a whole new attitude."

"How's this new attitude supposed to help me?" he asked with some sarcasm.

"Actually Stanley, that's a great question, its power can catapult you to the next level of interior growth."

"Oh yeah, and what can that be?"

"I can say it in one word Stanley ... *change*."

"Change? Sister, as much as I'd like to, I can't change what's happening here; God do I wish I could!"

"I know Stanley, we don't have any power over what happens to us, we can't change that, but what we can change is how it affects us."

"Oh sure, I'm supposed to be happy about all this."

"No, Stanley, not happy. Change is hard; change may not and probably will not make you happier, at least not right away. But that's not the purpose of change; the purpose of change is to make you healthier."

"What I need to make me healthier is one of two things, either this whole thing never happened, or two, that it ends as quickly as possible."

"Stanley, that's exactly the point. The opposite of change is being stuck. Your remedy for your life still revolves around changing external reality, that's not change, that's plain fixation. That's it Stanley, you have a fixation on changing what you can't change. You also seem to be blind to two things: one, what truly needs to be changed, and two, your God-given internal power of making those changes."

"I've got a fixation?"

"Yes, you're trapped in old thought patterns like a fly caught in a spider's web. You want physical reality to change so that *you* don't have to. You've got it backwards Stanley."

"I hear your words Sister, but there's no meaning there for me."

"Stanley look, we're not going to find the answer to predicaments in physical terms. St. John's hospital has assembled the best minds and the most understanding hearts available, yet even with all this they are powerless to cure your spinal cord. Our security, our peace, our happiness doesn't come from the outside in, but the other way around. Stanley, we've already been over this."

"So what do I need to change?"

"Good question! First ... your attitude needs to change. You need to shift your notions about what happened to you. I know this isn't easy but you need to change your basic beliefs. Your ingrained medical attitude that sickness is to be attacked and conquered won't work here Stanley. You need a new attitude, an attitude that in some paradoxical way allows you to see your injury and its impact on your life as a call for change, a call not simply to live differently, but to literally *think* differently. All of your assumptions about what makes you a man that formed the foundation of your life before, need to be replaced so you can set a new foundation ... something more solid and more lasting, so that you can begin again."

"And what might that be?"

"Well, Stanley, I can tell you it's not here on this earth."

I suddenly felt faint. I broke into a cold sweat. I couldn't feel my grasp on the wheelchair arms. My sight narrowed and was about to extinguish altogether.

"Sister, what's wrong?" demanded Stanley.

I couldn't answer. I felt removed from the conversation, even from the room. I seemed to know rather than hear Stanley's cries.

"Nurse, nurse, nurse get down here fast ... now nurse, now!" yelled Stanley.

I saw him moving his mouth and looking scared, but strangely I couldn't hear him.

Chapter Seventy-Five

When I next opened my eyes, I was back in my bed, and Nurse Jan was over me taking my pulse.

"Well, Sister, who told you that you could get out of bed? You scared us all," said Jan.

"What happened?" I asked.

"What happened was, you fainted. Dr. Renowski's screams brought us running to find you all slumped over in your wheelchair; you were pretty out-of-it, but you came around quickly," said Jan.

"Whew!"

"How do you feel now?" Jan asked.

"Tired, very tired."

"Yeah, I'll bet you do. Well, it's time for rest. Now that you're horizontal I think you'll be OK. Your pulse is back up so you're good for now," Jan said.

I fell asleep without any coaxing. I don't think I got to the second *Hail Mary*.

Chapter Seventy-Six *Enrichment*

In deep sleep, a dream bursts onto my internal screen, a dream that I had dreamed many times before. I'm back on the plane as a flight attendant; it's an evening flight from LA to NYC. As the passengers amble on preparing for sleep on the "red eye", I spot a man who reminds me of my father. I can't figure out what it is about him that reminds me, but I'm drawn to him.

"May I help you, sir? Is there anything you need?" I ask. His facial reaction to me seems a mix of annoyance and disdain, as if he is too important to be bothered by a somewhat forward and clumsy flight attendant. At first he says, "No, I need nothing, thank you." I've seldom heard such a condescending tone from anyone.

He catches himself and says, "Well, if you need to get me something, get me a scotch and water." Dutifully, I get him the drink and I hover over him as he takes his first sip. He winces and turns his head as he exclaims, "This is totally unacceptable; get me a better one!" I hurry back with a second, to which he reacts much the same as the first. Again, I serve him a third drink, which he again rejects. He does the same with numbers four and five.

Finally, in deep exasperation, he says "Obviously you can't measure up. In my attaché case in the storage bin above you'll find good scotch; make me a drink from that." I do as he instructs. His first sip brings a contented half smile to his face. All he says to me is, "Thank you for your trouble, you may now be dismissed."

I awakened and checked the time. It's 3:14 a.m., and I felt very warm ... no, not warm ... I was hot. I rang the bell for assistance. I was surprised, even through my delirium I saw nurse Jan appear over me.

"Sister, how are you feeling?"

"Oh Jan, I'm so hot, can I take anything?"

"Oh sure, Sister, let me bring you some Tylenol, that should lower the fever."

She returned and I took the Tylenol with some difficulty, still feeling a bit disoriented either by dream or my fever ... probably both. I fell back to sleep and seemed to pick up the dream again.

I fumble through the entire flight unable to focus on my duties; my thoughts are preoccupied with the scotch and water man who reminds me of my dad. I don't approach him again; I even hold my breath as I pass his seat. As we're preparing for landing in NYC, he calls for me.

"What are you doing tomorrow?" he asks. "I need a secretary for a meeting; I'd like you to accompany me."

I'm flabbergasted; no one has ever asked me for anything like this. Yet, I feel compelled to accept.

"OK," he says. "Be at the Waldorf restaurant at noon tomorrow."

"You mean noon today; that's only seven hours from now," I respond.

"Yes." With this remark he seems to dispatch me.

As he's deplaning he gives me his card with a phone number hand written on the back.

"Don't be late," he says, "noon at the Waldorf."

"OK," I respond.

His card reads, *Pontius Pilate, Governor of Judea.* I know how the dream ends, as though I'm both spectator and main character at the same time, but I'm still startled and scared as I glance down at his card and read his name.

I awakened in distress and realized again that I was not feeling well. The dream puzzled me more now than when I first dreamed it. My father was a kind man; his job was to keep as much harmony in the house as possible, to buffer the kids from my mother who, although a loving woman, could be mean. Somehow this dream encapsulated the confusion I felt for those ten years of flying, but I still didn't' know exactly how.

I opened my eyes to sunshine making angled splashes across the wall of my room. I felt better, the fever seemed broken, if not gone, and I felt hungry. I rang the assistance bell. Cindy arrived almost immediately.

"Well Sister, good morning. I could almost say good afternoon; it's already 11:15. You slept well last night," said Cindy.

"Wow, I did sleep long, but I'm not so sure about sleeping well. Have you got anything around for breakfast?"

"I'm sure I can dig up something. I'll be right back."

Soon Cindy arrived with oatmeal, toast, coffee and juice.

"Thanks so much ... I could eat a horse."

"No horses today Sister, I might be able to rustle up a steer for supper though."

"That's great Cindy. I really appreciate your kindness; thank you so much."

"No problem Sister; see you soon."

As Cindy left, I called after her. She turned back to the room.

"Cindy, what's Dr. Renowski doing today?"

"I think he's in the pool Sister; shall I check?"

"No, that's OK, I'm sure he'll be up for lunch soon."

"No doubt," Cindy responded.

I ate my food in absent-minded reverie. Somehow there was a connection between Stanley and the man on the plane in my dream. Certainly the man was commanding, as is Stanley; or is it demanding? The man on the plane also needed my help, as does Stanley. Like the man on the plane, Stanley can't be vulnerable even enough to ask for help directly; his requests are couched as demands to be obeyed rather than as pleas for help.

Chapter Seventy-Seven

Just then I heard Stanley's voice from down the hall.

"Come on, hurry-up, you're too slow. What's your name so I'll be sure to never get you again."

This doesn't sound good. When the transporter had finished getting Stanley settled in his bed, I wheeled over to his room.

"Stanley, what alcoholic drink do you like best?"

"Well when I'm at home I like a Manhattan, but when I'm out I always drink scotch and water."

"Somehow I knew that," I replied.

"What do you mean?"

"I had a dream last night and I think you were in it, but it wasn't you of course, it's just that I think the character represented you ... or something."

"Tell me about it." This time his request seemed genuine, as though he wanted to not only hear about my dream, but wanted to show me that he was interested in me. Stanley's emotional development had advanced!

I related the dream to him and got all the way to the Waldorf restaurant, when Stanley asked, "Well, did you go? Did you meet him at the Waldorf?"

"I don't know; the dream always ends with him giving me his card."

"Well, that's no fun; it's all up in the air, there's no resolution," he said with disappointment.

"I know, and yet I'd never go with Pontius Pilate. He was a lost man, a man who had forfeited himself to power and authority. Pilate wasn't living an authentic life; he was simply playing a role. He played his role very well, but nonetheless, his role, or his attachment to it, blinded him to the fact that the savior of mankind was right in front of him. He acted out of fear, not out of love. He didn't want to upset the crowd, so he acted against his wife's warning not to kill Jesus, and against his own better judgment. He gave Jesus up to be crucified. Pilate couldn't realize that Jesus was his opportunity to become truly wonderful, truly grand, and completely himself; he couldn't see that Jesus was his road to true happiness. It's true that Pilate would need to completely turn his life around; all that he stood for would need to be jettisoned and he would need to take on an entirely new way of seeing himself and seeing the world. Pilate would need to become a new man."

"That would be impossible," retorted Stanley.

"What do you mean?"

"People can't change like that, especially people who have power, influence, money, and all that. They become trapped in who they are, they become something they're not. It's just like Nietzsche said, 'Power corrupts, and absolute power corrupts absolutely.'"

"Now I never heard that before, but I have to disagree. Not only *can* we change, but we *must* change ... we must become new. Take you for instance, don't you need to become new?" Conversion is not only always possible; it is also always necessary.

"Why didn't I see this coming? Of course you'd make your dream about me. Sister, you have a one-track mind; all you see is changing me."

"That's not all I see Stanley, but I can visualize a new Stanley, someone who knows who he is, not simply what he is; a person who takes his identity more from within than from without."

"Sister, you never give up."

"No Stanley, I don't, and I won't, because I can't."

"Well, Sister, I'll tell you what I can't do is take any more of this right now. Please don't push me to be rude by asking you to leave."

I took this as my cue to retreat ... a noble retreat to be sure. I thought it time to visit the chapel.

Chapter Seventy-Eight

In front of the Lord, certainly feeling more proximate to him, I prayed not a formal prayer, but a free-form conversation with my Lord... *I keep thinking that for so many years I lived according to the immediate desires of the senses and according to my own whims. Now, my good God, you are allowing me the opportunity to make-up for my gross selfishness and at the same time help Stanley turn to you through my own discomfort and inconvenience. If I had not fallen that day in the public chapel I would not be here today ministering to Stanley. His soul was lost in the dazzle of the world. While the Holy Spirit focused Stanley's work for the benefit of mankind, Stanley himself was drowning in his own ego, his own sense of self-importance. He believed, and perhaps in some ways he still believes, that he is the source, the cause of his own worldly success. Please dear Lord unleash your power upon Stanley. Convert his heart, turn his mind around, and let it find you dear Lord. Let Stanley remember who he really is, not a world-renowned surgeon. Please Lord let him remember that he is first and foremost your child, and that you love him the same, with your immense love, whether he practices surgery or whether he is simply with you in his heart. Help Stanley realize that you love him beyond all his human understanding, that you will never abandon him – and that you are more with him now in his hour of need. Help him, dear Lord, open himself to you completely; he wants to believe in your power of conversion so much ... grant his unspoken and unconscious wish dear Lord. I ask this in your son's name, our Lord and savior Jesus Christ. Amen.*

I finished my prayer and waited ... listening; I've talked enough, I asked enough, now it was time to listen. After so many years I shuttered at my distorted life before the monastery when I blithely followed only my own will rather than God's. But back then I could not have cared less about God, let alone his will. This only points out to me all the more, just how much he loved me then, and loves me now. It's amazing! Now that God has taken hold of my heart -- or should I say more accurately, I cooperated with his grace by giving over my will to him -- I saw God's word more clearly and heard it more dearly everywhere. Now I was simply called to listen ... listen ... listen.

I need to learn much more patience and try not to rely solely on my own agenda. I need to be available to Stanley, and be of service to him. The Franciscans call their superiors "servants", i.e., "sister servant" or "father servant." The superior general of the Franciscan congregation in Rome is the "servant general". It's very apt I think, I must learn this, then my life will be more peaceful. If I don't want things or situations, then I won't be upset or stressed when I don't get them.

Lord, I'm back again requesting. I feel there isn't much time left for Stanley. I've worked and prayed for him as much as I can. My spiritual therapy through you has been at least as intense as has Stanley's physical therapy here at St. John's. I feel he's out of my hands Lord, I can only entrust him to you. I am powerless to change him and yet he needs change so very much. Lord, give me the strength to persevere with Stanley. I do love him Lord, I can truly say that I have never loved a man like I love him. But Lord, my love for him could never eclipse my love for you. Stanley has taught me so much about me; he has opened me up to the interior me, the holy me that you God have planted inside. I've been opened in ways I thought were long lost. But Lord, my desire is clearly and absolutely to serve you, now and for always. Amen.

Again I listened ... listened ... listened. *Teach me Lord.*

As I left the chapel I noticed the confessional. *Lord how I need the sacrament now. I know that my ways here have not been completely with you. I know that my own desires and thoughts have invaded my soul and caused me to forget my spiritual identity. I must fly to confession and lay my sins before you Lord in a formal way so that I can feel the intimacy with you hat you expect from me. Stanley also needs the sacrament ... is it possible?*

I rolled onto my floor and glanced at the clock to find it was well past the evening mealtime. I wasn't really hungry, but I knew I should eat.

I greeted the night nurse's aide. "Hi Mary, I'm afraid I've missed supper, is there any food to be had?"

"Oh sure, Sister. I think we saved your meal. Let me check; if not, I'll bring something down. Can you get yourself settled in your room? I should be right down."

I wheeled down the hall and peeked into Stanley's room. For some reason the room looked a bit different, it seemed to have a warmer feeling about it. Stanley appeared asleep, but as I rolled in, he said, "Who's there? What do you want?"

"Oh, Stanley, it's only me; I was just checking on you – are you all right?"

"Sister, come in, I have something to tell you."

"What is it?" I asked, not at all ready for the shift I detected in Stanley. He sounded like he was using my words, the way I would say them – even down to a new tone of voice. What had happened? What had forged this change? Something new had entered into him; something quite profound had occurred. I was both startled and delighted by it.

"This afternoon was incredible," he started. "After you left I felt alone, I thought I had offended you. Gradually, the more I thought about you and how you've tried so hard to help me these months, the more I felt calm -- even at peace. I experienced a warm feeling kind of envelope me, a feeling I've never had before. I was quite content to remain right here in my room, not because there wasn't any other place to go, but because I was at peace here – I felt good!"

"Content is not a word that you often use Stanley."

He continued. "I thought at first it was some drug-induced euphoria, like they gave me morphine by mistake. But then I realized this wasn't a drug-induced high, this was a genuine sense of well-being. I tried to figure out rationally what had caused this. Was I simply thinking thoughts that positively influenced my feelings? Did I stumble upon a new perspective on my condition that got me a bit closer to the real me?"

"Stanley, that's wonderful."

"What I was able to figure out was that I no longer wanted to die. Somehow all thoughts of ending my life had evaporated; they were replaced by an anticipation of the future. I wasn't afraid anymore. I felt strong and confident, stable and sure for the first time in many years. It was like a gift from God."

"I am so pleased."

"Then I realized that I had a future and that future included you. I realized that I could have a life with you. You have such a therapeutic effect on me. At first, as you know, I fought you and everything you stand for. I minimized you, even trivialized you as a simple-minded and clearly misguided, naive woman who had retreated from the world out of fear."

"I know you did Stanley."

"Now I know all of that was my own fear, fear of giving myself to another human. I've learned so much from you Sister, but more than anything, you've given me hope in the midst of my despair; you've given me mercy when all I saw was neglect; kindness when all I could feel was indifference ... you've given me life."

"Well Stanley, you know it's not me that gives you life ... it's God."

"Oh I know, I know, but dear Sister, this very afternoon, right here in this room I feel love and life. I now believe that I have a future ... a future with you. I've thought about this all afternoon, I know this seems quick to you, but I've been moving in this direction since the first day I met you even though I didn't know it. Sister, I love you and I want you to be with me the rest of my life. I feel like a kid asking you like this, in this way, but, Sister ... will you marry me?"

I sat in stunned silence. He couldn't be serious! I couldn't speak! All I could do was stare at Stanley, incredulous of what I just heard. How could this be? I couldn't move, and

I couldn't talk. Suddenly a rush of tears burst from me. Somehow this unlocked me. I turned around and pushed myself down the hall. I slipped onto the elevator just as the door closed behind me.

Chapter Seventy-Nine

"Where are you going Sister, which floor?" asked the nurse who was already in the elevator.

"Oh ... ah ... I don't know ... anywhere, anywhere."

"Are you all right?" she asked.

"Yes ... yes ... I'm fine; I just need to get out."

I found myself in the rehab gym ... no one was there. I raced around and around between and among the therapy tables, the walking bridges, the hand bikes, the universal gym, the exercycles, the weights, and the steps. My wheelchair bounced off the occupational therapy room tub, the toilet, and the kitchen, even the old Cadillac used as a teaching aid.

My thoughts were racing at a pace with my wheelchair. I was panting, frantic, and so confused. I was frightened, angry, and more confused. I didn't know where to go or what to do. I trundled down the hall past the psych department and administration. I raced through the employee cafeteria and banged into the door to the outside patio. I swung around and spotted Henry the security guard, who asked ... "Sister, is anything wrong?"

"No, no Henry, I'll be OK. I just need to keep moving."

I made my way around him and turned left then right, then left again. Miraculously I was at the entrance to the chapel. Yes, this is where I needed to be.

I opened the door and very slowly made my way down the aisle to the foot of the altar. There I broke into a rainfall of tears. I cried for a long time, sobbing, weeping, and wiping my wet face over and over until my face felt raw and my eyes became bloated and bloodshot like orbs of sorrow.

What were my tears saying? Lord, was this your answer? Did my surrender lead to this? Could you want me to serve you best by being with Stanley? Why couldn't I simply tell him "no" and be done with it? Why this intense reaction? Why the deep tears ... the fear ... the anguish? Could it be that at some interior level in me I wanted Stanley, I wanted to be married, to live as husband and wife, to be secure in a relationship with a man? Was I now supposed to shift my vocation? I am very sure that my vocation, my choice to be a nun was not influenced by fear of any sort! I have no doubt at all that God called me to this life and that my "yes" was not in the least bit grounded in fear.

What now? What could or should I tell him? Have I reconstituted myself enough to approach him? I don't want to hurt him: I don't want to hurt myself either. Oh, what shall I do Lord? I have no practice at this.

When Stanley would ridicule me or simply disagree with me, at those times I was fine, cool, and calm, quite emotionally together. There was no threat when he would attack me verbally, no threat at all because his contrary posture kept me at arms length from him. But now he has broken through. He doesn't want my thoughts, or even the teachings of Jesus; what he wants is me!

Look what he did to his last wife ... his trophy wife, Anne. I can't be his spiritual trophy wife. I am Christ's bride; I cannot be the bride of man. I made my vows; I need to be obedient and faithful to what and who I am. This offer is flattering, but, I can't let my ego carry me off, away from my spiritual center; Christ cannot be displaced in my heart. I can't give my heart to Stanley ... I already gave it to Christ. I pray...

Lord, be my guide. Help me discern what's true and real and pure inside of me, and separate all this, these most noble parts of me, from all that is not from you, but which is only illusion that my ego constructs out of nothing. Lord, I need your help. What can I say to Stanley? He has found a new hope for living, a new reason to go on; I don't want to take this from him ... I mustn't! Yet, his hope for his life can't be me, it must be you. Help me Lord say what needs to be said, but in a way that can illuminate Stanley's mind and not extinguish this new spark of hope he's kindled in his soul. Put the words in my mouth, dear Lord, give me the ideas and the phrases that will convey these ideas in such a way that can elevate Stanley beyond himself and eventually toward you, Lord. Buttress my heart and soul, steady my mind, and loosen my tongue so I can be your loving witness in all that I do, especially with Stanley. I trust only in you, Lord. Amen.

I wheeled out of the chapel very slowly. I had no idea of how much time had elapsed since his question: "Will you marry me?" I never dreamed I would hear this question; it still stuck like a spear in my heart. I gripped the hand wheels on my chair with determination lest I lost faith in myself. I made my way to the elevator and pushed the "up" button. The floor was still and quiet; low lights at the nurse's station gave it an ethereal look as though some benevolent force had pervaded the entire setting. It all seemed welcoming and secure, yet I was scared in a way that was foreign to me.

Suddenly I realized that I was cold. My hands shook with the cold. I forced myself to grip ever tighter, hard and fast until my knuckles became white. I made my way down the hall and carefully turned the corner into Stanley's room. He heard me and raises his head.

Chapter Eighty

"Sister, where did you go?"

"Just around, Stanley, just around."

"But I don't understand. I know my question may have seemed strange, but you must have sensed how I felt about you. I can't hide how I feel; it's written all over my face."

"Stanley, I truly had no idea, I simply thought that you perceived me as silly. You have so much worldly education and experience; I thought you dismissed me as a religious zealot of little consequence in your world."

"Sister no, all along you've been educating me bit by bit. You have given me more to think about than anyone ever has before. You brought your thoughts to bear with a power and a passion I've never experienced. You confronted me again and again; you pounded me with salvos of new thinking so different from my own that I had to push them and you away because they were so unsettling."

"I'm sorry," I said. "I never meant to hurt you, if I did. I only meant to crack through your toughness because I could see beyond the hard shell you had created around yourself."

"Don't be sorry," he said. "I think it's great. I had given up on me, but you never did; you persevered like no one else could. I realized all this just this afternoon. If I believed in miracles I'd say this was surely one because in a flash all the heaviness I felt was lifted from me; for the first time in decades I feel free. Isn't that absurd, here I am trapped in bed and strapped to a wheelchair, absolutely constrained and I'm feeling freer than I ever have."

"Stanley, I do believe in miracles; as I said before I even expect miracles. I have no doubt that you experienced a miracle this afternoon, but Stanley, this miracle of freedom was not from me ... it came from God."

"But, Sister, you brought it to me, you made it happen ... you are my angel."

"I may be the messenger of God's grace. If that's so then I thank God, but I didn't cause this miracle. When a hardened man softens his heart; when an unbeliever turns around, when the blind regain sight like you did on a spiritual way, then we know proof positive that God's holy spirit is at work. God works through us humans. I'm sure the Holy Spirit worked through you many times to bring healing; it was Gods' hand in your surgical glove that created so many miracles of healing. How wonderful!"

"Well, whatever, Sister, but the fact remains that I need you. I want to marry you, Sister. I want you with me ... I have to have you with me always!"

"Stanley, I'll always be with you, in your heart, but I cannot be your wife ... I'm already married."

"What do you mean already married? I thought you were a nun!"

"I am, and what does being a nun mean? It means that I'm married to Christ; I'm Christ's bride."

"That's silly, you can't be married to Christ."

"Indeed I can, and I am! I can't not be who I am, and neither can you."

"Who am I, Sister? Without you I'm lost, I have no *who*, I've lost my *what*, and without you I can't hope to retrieve whatever who of me there may be left. You're my key to the future, Sister. Don't you see that I need you, I can't go on living without you; you're my only hope."

"Stanley, you won't be without me, I'm always with you in spirit. You will always be in my prayers, I can promise you that, but I cannot ever be with you in the flesh. I do God's work, that's what I'm called to do."

"Wouldn't it be God's work loving me, caring for me, arguing with me like you have been right along? Sister, you care for me in a very special way when you confront me, especially in that fearless way you've always done here at St. John's. That kind of confrontation is exactly what I need."

"It's God's work being with you Stanley, it can even be God's work being married to you, but it is not *my* God work. My God work is waiting for me back at the monastery. My sisters are there; my earthly life waits for me there. I belong there, picking up where I left off before my accident."

"But what do you do there all day, every day, enclosed from the outside world? What good do you do there? It seems to me that you're just divorcing yourself from the world – a world that needs you. I dedicated myself to help the world, and look what happened to me!"

"No Stanley, forgive me but you dedicated yourself to yourself. But let's get to your first point. You're right I did divorce myself from the world, from the secular world. God chose me to live apart from the contradictory parts of the world that clash with God's ways."

"What contradictory parts?" he asked.

"The world sees happiness in terms of wealth, fame, power, consumerism, and competition. Jesus sees happiness entirely differently in terms of peace, purity, surrender, sanctity of life, and detachment."

"But you could accomplish all that and still be my wife; you could do all of that and more."

"No Stanley, I couldn't. My life is not something I accomplish. Oh, I want to be the best cloistered nun that I can, but it's not about doing things, it's about being in relationship with God."

"I don't understand."

"What I do in the monastery is pray. My sisters and I pray in order to have the closest possible union with Christ, first of all. Then we pray for so many who need our prayers and that includes praying and sacrificing in reparation for the sins of the world. We pray that man's ways become God's ways, and that mankind can make the reach outside of itself and find God."

"So you pray ... that's doing something."

"Yes and no. We don't measure our performance in terms of the number of prayers we say each day. We remove ourselves from the world so we have no distractions from being in constant prayer, in constant communion with God."

"Can't you be in constant communion with God and be with me at the same time?"

"A person who has the vocation of being married can I suppose, but I can't. God hasn't called me to the vocation of marriage; God has invited me to follow a different path. If I didn't accept his invitation then I wouldn't be true to myself ... I wouldn't be authentic, and eventually I'd become very unhappy."

"A person can change, you've been preaching change to me since I met you."

"Yes, we all are called by God to grow toward our authentic selves, but we can't genuinely grow by simply going through the paces of a life that isn't our own. Each of us has to live the life that God desires for us, a life plan that is written on our hearts; we have no choice but to follow it – to surrender to it. If we want to be happy we can only live our own life, the life we're supposed to live."

"So you're saying that you can change, but you choose not to."

"Stanley, I always hope to change until the day God takes me home, but the change I'm talking about is internal growth, growth of my inner life, growing closer to God. As I grow closer to God by accepting God's grace more fully, I become more who I really am, that unique *who* that God made me."

"Well, God made me too and my need to be the who that I'm supposed to be is to be with you."

"You see Stanley, that's just it, you can't do the choosing, only God can do that. We can only surrender to his will, and so when we progressively do that, then we eventually find our true heart's desire."

"My true heart's desire is to have you with me always."

"Right now you think that's what you need, but Stanley realistically, would you want a woman who isn't following her heart's desire?"

"You'd learn, the human condition is flexible – we all need to be malleable ... you would adapt."

"My promise is that I only adapt to God. I must follow what's fundamentally enriching for me, not in an egotistical sense like 'I'll do it my way,' but in a Christ sense, knowing that Christ is *the* way."

"I always think you're talking in circles."

"No Stanley, I'm trying to talk as straight as I can. If I were married to you, I'd be unhappy, not because you're a bad man at all, but because I would be trapped in what I could probably call idle busyness. I'm sure I'd be busy caring for you and for my own needs as well, but if my time and mind and heart were consumed with just that I'd be idle in my busyness because I wouldn't be living the life I'm supposed to live. I'd feel empty, I'd feel idle because I'd be barred from being who I must be; I'd have busy hands but an idle heart and an empty soul. Would you want a wife like that?"

"But I can't find my heart's desire without you. All I know is that I need you. I have money; we'd live a comfortable life. We could hire helpers in the house; you could even have your own private chapel in the house where you could pray all you wanted."

"Stanley, you're so kind, I always knew you had a kind heart underneath all that bravado. But no, I must be in the cloister, I must be with my sisters. The community is life giving for me, it's my life because it's my conduit to God. Our measured life of detachment enriches my soul, it's what I crave, and it's what God wants for me. If I walked away from that, I'd be walking away from God. I can't do that Stanley ... I simply can't do that!"

"But I love you!"

"Stanley, that's beautiful and I can say that I love you too, not in a romantic sense, but in a Christian fraternal sense; I love the spirit of Christ in you. Don't you see if I married you, you would have to become my primary focus? In one way that wouldn't be hard because God has given me an insight to see you accurately, to see the truth, beauty, and goodness that resides in you. But I'm not supposed to go through another human in love to find God in love. I'm called to go directly, straight to God unencumbered by a human intimate relationship. It's a different calling, a different vocation entirely from marriage; that's the way that God has made me ... I can be no other."

"Can't you get a new map so you can love me as a husband and find God at the same time?"

"No, it simply wouldn't work!"

"Am I that terrible?"

"It has nothing to do with you. I couldn't marry a living saint. The human side of me is drawn to you certainly, but I've spent many years cultivating my inner life, the truth that resides in me. I've detached from the human side as the primary source of my motivation and the center of my happiness. I've come a long way toward being *in* the world but not *of* the world."

"Come on, Sister, we're all of the world, we're flesh and bone, sinew and blood; all that's physical worldly stuff. You can't deny that reality."

"Of course not, like I say, I am in the world, so I have all the physical stuff as you call it. But the difference is that my physical being does not decide the course of the real me, the real me is beyond the confines of my physical nature and needs, and it's the real me that I want to lead me, to motivate me, and bring me to God."

"Sister, you have an answer for everything. Isn't it enough for me to simply say that I love you, I want you, and I need you? If I could get on my knees I would. I've never thought or felt so close to anyone in my life. You can't leave me, I don't know what I'll do."

"Stanley, you are strong. You know many things now that you didn't know when you arrived here. Your education is progressing well; it's almost complete, but not quite. You still have some big lessons to learn, but that will come in time. For now, it's bedtime for us both, so I must say good night. If Dr. Pollack ever knew I was up so late, he'd have a few words for me I'm sure!"

My statement wasn't designed to be curt even though Stanley may have thought it was. My comment was designed to be final; I wanted him to know that I was unavailable – and that's that!

I wheeled backwards out of his room, as he stared at me incredulously. I didn't know how I felt, I only knew that I needed to get out of there – it wasn't safe for me anymore.

Later that night I prayed hard. *Lord, thank you for being with me this evening. Thank you for giving me the words necessary to convey my own and your desire for my life. Give him insight, dear Lord, into the core of his soul where he will find his true heart's delight.*

Chapter Eighty-One *Self-Ownership*

I awakened in the morning refreshed and at peace greeting this new day. I thanked the Lord. My mind was clearer than it was. I felt more in control, more "on top" of the situation; what was formerly tangled was now straightened. I was tied in an impossible knot that had to unravel before I could find peace. I felt balanced, right and good and true. My mind was unfettered and my heart unburdened. Direction was in my heart all along; I just needed to talk it out, to coax it out of its hiding place into the light. Of course I couldn't do this alone, the Holy Spirit inspired me and activated God's gifts in me so I could take deeper ownership of that which was truly me. I thanked God again and again.

I prayed.

Dear Lord, Stanley needs this peace too; he's tangled, he has been for such a long time. Stanley forfeited himself long ago to the forces and factors that entice us away from our true selves, he gave himself up completely; his world became a frantic chase of so many things outside himself. As he stacked up more and more trophies that propped up his false self, the true Stanley was descending into emotional and spiritual poverty. Dear Lord, save us from this compulsion.

Chapter Eighty-Two

"Good morning Sister," said Jan.

"Oh, good morning to you, Jan, how are you today?"

"Oh me? I'm fine, but I wish I could say the same for Dr. Renowski across the hall. He looks terrible today; did anything happen?"

"Yes, something did happen, but I can't go into it in specifics. Let's just say that the eggs finally got cracked, and it's time for Dr. Renowski to make the omelet. I only pray that he can."

"Well, you're the only one around here who seems to be able to help him do that."

"Not this time Jan. Dr. Renowski is in God's hands now. I think I need to take a step or two back away from him. He needs some time and space away from me I think."

"Wow, it sounds like something did happen all right. Tell me more."

"I'm afraid not, I'd be invading something very private and I think very precious for him. No offense, but I have to stay mum on this one."

"The plot thickens. I always thought he had a thing for you Sister, you know, underneath the crusty exterior of his."

"No comment," I said.

"You're pretty serious about this, Sister. Is there anything I can do to help?"

"No, I don't think so, not right now at least, perhaps there might be in time though."

"Well, I'll stay tuned of course. To change the subject, Dr. Pollack asked about you in morning report. I said I'd check your physical status. How are you feeling?"

"Oh, I guess the antibiotics are working. I do feel better, especially after a great night's sleep."

"Let me feel your head. Yeah, only a slight temp; let me take it."

With the electronic thermometer in my mouth I always felt something between dependent and pampered. This morning I simply relished the later; it was that kind of day.

"Ninety-nine point four. Just as I thought, not gone but certainly in the right direction."

"Good," I said.

"You know, like I said before, this UTI will probably extend your stay here. They can't release you without a completely clean bill of health."

"I know. That's OK. I do want to get back to the monastery, but I think the next week will be a big one for Dr. Renowski. Somehow I know I'm supposed to be here, I couldn't leave ... not just now."

"My curiosity rises with every word since you won't let me in on this."

"No dice ... I really can't."

"All right then. Dr. Pollack said you needed to be in bed as long as you have a temp. Want me to turn on your TV, it looks like you'll be here all day?"

"No thanks, I'm not much for TV. I might turn on EWTN later, but right now I'll just be at peace."

"Sister, I envy you. When you say 'peace' I just get this wonderful warm and stable feeling, like everything is all right."

"Jan, everything *is* all right, at least it's unfolding as it should. Thanks for your help."

"No problem, Sister, no problem at all. I'll be back later to check on you."

"Thanks, Jan."

Chapter Eighty-Three

Jan's curiosity drew her dignity to Stanley's room. She had to check him periodically anyway, but today she made especially sure she saw him very soon.

"Good morning, Dr. Renowski," said Jan.

"Oh, it's you Jan," said Stanley.

"How are you feeling today?"

"I guess I'm OK," he said without enthusiasm.

"Let me feel your head, there's a bug going around that we have to watch for. No, you feel OK. Appetite, sleep, everything OK?"

"As well as I can expect under the circumstances."

"How are things across the hall, you know with Sister?"

"I don't know; you'll have to ask her."

"Well, that was a little crisp ... anything wrong?"

"I don't know what it is with Sister; she's hot and cold. I never know what she's thinking."

"Well that's the mystery of a woman I guess."

"I don't even know why I'm so attracted to her."

"She's got a lot going for her, that's for sure."

"She's not pretty, certainly not like my wife was. She's got no money, no relevant education, no position or career ... what is it that pulls at me so about her?"

"But she's got so much more than that doesn't she," said Jan.

"She does have spunk. I like the way she comes back at me."

"She knows how to do that -- for sure!"

"At first I wanted to command her to stop, or at least to see thing my way, the same way that I could in the OR."

"You knew that wouldn't work with her Dr. Renowski!"

"I certainly know that now. But she seems so caring, so focused on me. I like that. She doesn't place the focus on herself at all, she keeps it squarely on me."

"She's certainly empathic."

"Really, she's lost her legs, but we never talk about that, we only talk about me."

"I think that's her humility."

"There's no ego in her, either she doesn't have one, or she learned somehow to put it in its place; she's certainly not ego driven like I am."

"What makes her like that, I wonder?" asked Jan in her most facilitative voice.

"She made me realize that my life was always all about me ... and it was. Everything was for me; I somehow bullied the people around me to be submissive. I emotionally pushed everyone into admiring me, at least to my face; God only knows what they said behind my back."

"But Dr. Renowski you were, I mean are, a world renowned surgeon; doesn't a slightly elevated ego come with that territory?"

"Perhaps a little, but I made it my life. I wasn't Stanley, Jan; I was *the* Dr. Stanley Renowski. I could never take my profession out of my identity equation. Not only was I a surgeon, I had to be the very best surgeon."

"Well some surgeon has to be the best one, why not you?"

"Because my motivation wasn't pure, it wasn't real. I wanted to be the best for all the wrong reasons. I had to be best for me, not to help mankind, not even to further science; it was always about me, Jan ... always!"

"But you did help people, you did further science. Aren't we better off because of you?"

"In some small ways perhaps, but *I* wasn't better because of me, I was worse, and becoming more so all the time. I was obsessed, addicted to my own ambition drug; I was addicted to the image of Dr. Stanley Renowski. Like all drugs, the deeper you descend into them the more confusing your life becomes, until it spirals out of control. That's what happened to me Jan, I was out of control; I think I have been for years."

"But you achieved so much."

"That may be, I achieved a lot but I lost me; I lost the real me. Do you know, I can remember many nights leaving the hospital and practically running to my car, passing the housekeeping people, you know the people who clean everything. I'd actually have the thought rocket through my mind as I passed them that they may not have a prestigious job like I did but I'd bet they were in charge of their own life. Wasn't that crazy? I saw their peace ... something I didn't have at all. When I think back on that now I get the smallest glimpse of just how out of control I was. I had no self-agency, I wasn't in charge of my life – my ambition addiction had control of me. My ego had constructed this imaginary image and instructed me, really insisted, that I serve this image that had no reality. I was totally controlled. This image was the force that controlled me; the real me was pushed further and further away to a point where I lost contact with him entirely. I rejected my own real self – I abandoned him."

"He's still around," said Jan.

"No, I could have never retrieved my real self by myself; you forget, I was out of control. No, it was only when Sister showed up in my life, she's the one who found my real self and now I'm trying to get him back so I can find out who I really am."

"Well, good for you, you've done it then."

"No, I need Sister. Without her I'll remain lost. I'm powerless, I need a guide, and I need her right by my side at all times. I need her in my life. I can't live without her!"

"Wow, Dr. Renowski, I had no idea."

"Jan, you can help me. You know Sister and she respects you. Talk to her Jan, tell her how much I need her, tell her I can't live without her ... she has to marry me."

"Dr. Renowski, even if I could agree to what you ask, I'm professionally barred from doing anything like that; it's totally against our professional ethics."

"Screw the professional ethics! If we abided by all the ethics nothing would ever get done. Jan, don't let ethics stop you from helping where help is really needed."

"Dr. Renowski, I could never tell Sister that she had to marry you, just because you need her. There's so much more to the marriage bond than one person's need. Marriage is a blessed union that's designed to bring both partners closer to themselves and closer to God."

"She would be closer to God. God is a benevolent God, he already knows that by helping me, by being with me, married to me, that she'll get closer to him – it's simple."

"But Dr. Renowski, she's a nun, she can't marry anyone."

"Well, she can leave the monastery, can't she? Doesn't she have a free will; can't she make her own decisions? I don't see why she can't."

"Dr. Renowski, from what I've seen of Sister, she is a devout, reverent, and totally committed religious woman, my guess is that she could never loose those bonds."

"Jan, you have to help me; there's no other way, she has to come home with me."

"Dr. Renowski you can't command someone to marry you, it's not right. You're just very on edge now because you know that your time here at St. John's is getting short; anyone would be scared, I've seen it over and over. You'll be OK, we'll work with the social workers in discharge when the time comes; they can arrange almost anything."

"No, no, it must be Sister, it has to be Sister."

"OK, I'll bring this up when I next see Sister, but Dr. Renowski, I can't cross any professional boundaries, I can't be a match maker."

Jan walked back to the nurse's station in semi shock. She was deep in thought: What was this about? What should she do?

Chapter Eighty-Four

I've learned to meditate well. I begin with formal prayer, sometimes a rosary. I then deepen to centering prayer using a word or phrase to help me move to my spiritual core. I use deepening images of walking down a long spiral staircase around and around until I enter a vestibule off of which is a beautiful chapel through two large oak doors. I proceed to the altar and there, at my spiritual center, I sit with Jesus. We talk together. Today I have many questions.

How can I deal with Stanley, Lord?

I listen.

I don't want to hurt him Lord, but he must come to realize my position ... I'm married to you.

I listen.

Help me find you, dear Lord, in Stanley and help him find you in himself.

I listen.

Help him see a vision of his future that rest on his shoulders, that's directed by him, and not dependent upon me.

I listen.

Help me stir him up, Lord, as you have all along, so your Spirit can find a foothold in his confused mind.

I listen.

Help me find new eyes for him he needs to see more clearly.

I listen.

Help me clarify his thinking, soothe his feelings, motivate new decisions, and activate healthy action in him.

I listen.

Help me to help him get a grip on his heart and soul like never before.

In the silence of my inner sanctuary the only answer I get is the realization that I am powerless over Stanley. I'm stunned that I have done all I can do for now and that it's Stanley who needs to change.

Chapter Eighty-Five

"Sister, Sister, I'm sorry to disturb you but I must talk with you. Are you awake Sister?" Jan asks.

I rouse myself back to consciousness.

"Oh, oh ... yes ... Jan. What's going on – what's wrong?"

"Sister, I've just caught my breathe after a conversation with Dr. Renowski. I can't believe what he's saying; Sister he wants to marry you."

"I know, Jan, I know."

"You know ... how?"

"He told me last night."

"Well, what do you think?" asked Jan.

"I think Dr. Renowski is scared."

"Scared of what?"

"He's scared of starting his life anew without taking his old self along. He knows he has to leave it here at St. John's, but he can't yet see how he can live without it."

"But what will he do? I've never seen Dr. Renowski like this; he frantic, he can't stop talking about you, about how much he needs you ... can't get along without you. Sister, Dr. Renowski is lost."

"No, Jan, he's not lost, actually he's taking the first steps toward finding himself."

"I can't see that at all."

"Jan, until yesterday Dr. Renowski was in utter despair – that's when he was lost. Today he thinks he's found a plan, a way out of his despair. His plan includes me; he thinks he'll be OK, he thinks he'll stay out of despair if he has me with him on his journey. He's scared that if I won't follow him that he'll slip back into the horrible emotional abyss he's been in since he came here to St. John's."

"Well, Sister, there may be some truth to that, don't you think?"

"What I think is that Dr. Renowski needs to take the next step. I only hope and pray that he can."

"And what's the next step, Sister?"

"He's always suffered a deep tension within himself, a terrible uncertainty about who he was – what his real identity might be. Because he didn't know who he was, he invested all his energies into medicine, and he took his identity from that."

"Doesn't everyone do that, Sister? I see myself as a nurse, I've been a nurse for a long time, it's sort of become a part of me."

"Of course, a part of you, but not all of you. The question is, are you first a nurse and then a person, or the other way around? Before yesterday, Dr. Renowski saw himself as a surgeon and that's all – the person part was seldom, if ever, nourished, consequently the person of Dr. Renowski became very anemic."

"Sister, how did you figure all this out?"

"Jan, I'm sorry, I shouldn't be saying all this. God has given me the gift of empathy and this allows me an insight into people, at some level anyway. I can't seem to help it, I quite naturally look to the deeper levels of a person; God has given me a spiritual intuition that always seeks truth – the most noble parts of a person, and Dr. Renowski has mountains of truth in him. He really wants to help, but when a person has forfeited himself to forces outside then he loses control of what's inside."

"Sister, you have so much wisdom; where does it all come from?"

"Certainly not from me, Jan, certainly not from me."

Chapter Eighty-Six

I wanted to continue my personal retreat, a retreat toward God and away from Stanley. After lunch I took a nap, said my rosary and my afternoon Liturgy of the Hours, and meditated. I simply wanted to be close to God.

"Sister, are you feeling any better?" asked Jan as she rounded the corner from the hall into my room.

"I'm just trying to be at peace now Jan. I'm listening to God as best I can."

"May I give you an update on Dr. Renowski?"

"I guess, but I really need to detach Jan."

"Well, he was restless when the aide brought and served him lunch after his morning exercises. The therapist said he couldn't concentrate on his therapy; his mind seemed consumed by thoughts of you and how he could woo you to him."

"You know Jan, I don't think he sees what he's doing as wooing at all, he is simply followed his fear. His only thought is that I'm his ticket out of fear. Without me, he thinks of himself as lost."

"Sister, it strikes me that this is Renowski's way, he identifies a target that he thinks will satisfy him, ease his pain ... an appendage that can somehow complete him."

"I know Jan, his first target was medical school, then surgery residency, then research, his reputation, trophies, then Anne, house, cars, status ... more ... more ...more."

"Now you're his target Sister. As he has done before, Dr. Renowski will invest the full measure of his energies into persuading you that you simply must be his bride."

"I know Jan, I know."

Late that afternoon, Sandy, the aide who was helping Dr. Renowski with his evening meal, was unsuccessful in her attempts to make small talk with him between his bites until she asked, "So, Dr. Renowski have you made any plans for when you get home, you know, when you're finished with your rehab here at St. John's?"

Renowski lifted his eyes squarely at Sandy and gave her a look that unnerved her.

"Sister and I are getting married; we're both going to start new lives together," he said matter of factly.

"Oh, that's wonderful," said Sandy. "When's the big day?"

"What big day?"

"You know, Dr. Renowski, the wedding day."

"No, no, we haven't set a date. It won't be a big wedding, something simple, just close friends."

"You know, we had a wedding right here at St. John's one time."

"Really, when was that?"

"About seven years ago I think. I wasn't here long at all. Two patients who met here married in the chapel. It was real touching ... most of the staff and patients at the time filled the chapel to over flowing."

"Is that right, Sandy? I wonder if we could have another wedding here, wouldn't that be nice."

"Oh yes, Dr. Renowski what a thrill – you and Sister. But wait, how can she marry anyone? She's a nun!"

"Oh, we haven't worked out all the details, but we will. I'm sure that Sister would like knowing about a wedding right here. I wonder if you could tell her?"

"Oh sure, I'd love to tell her, right after we're finished here."

Sandy went directly across the hall to Sister's room and announced with enthusiasm, "Well Sister, I understand that congratulations are in order."

"Why Sandy, congratulations for what?"

"You can't hide it very well Sister. I was just with Dr. Renowski and he told me."

"Told you what?" I asked sharply.

"That the two of you are getting married – how wonderful!"

"He told you what? Sandy, Dr. Renowski and I are definitely not getting married," I said with a stare.

"What? But he said ..."

"No Sandy, no marriage. I'm a consecrated nun, I can't marry anyone," I protested.

"But Sister, he seemed so sure – so definite."

"Sandy, I'll have to talk with Dr. Renowski, he can't be saying things like that, and he just feels scared that his time here at St. John's is getting short."

Chapter Eighty-Seven

"Stanley we have to talk," I said as I wheeled into his room.

"Sister, hello, I was hoping you'd come over."

"Stanley you can't be telling people that we're getting married. We aren't getting married; I've already told you that Stanley."

"Sister, Sister, don't get upset. I want to tell you what I heard from Sandy. She said there was a wedding right here at St. John's. Two patients who met here got married in the chapel. Most of the patients and staff were there; it was beautiful. Can you imagine Sister, we can be married right here ... right here in the chapel."

"Stanley, how many times have you been in the chapel here?"

"Well none, but how could I -- like this?" he said looking down at his immobile limbs.

"Any day you could have asked to go to the chapel. The fact is that you didn't want to ... you didn't see the need. The chapel is only important to you now because it meets your needs, or should I say, it meets your wants."

"Sister, I thought it was the perfect solution to our problem."

"And what problem is that, Stanley?"

"You wouldn't have to return to the monastery. I'm sure it would be hard for you to face all your Sisters there. If we got married here you wouldn't have to face them, you wouldn't have to go back at all."

"Stanley, if I were to get married, the first place I'd go would be back to the monastery to explain the full measure and depth of my reasoning in heart and mind. I'd very much want my Sisters to know; I would seek their advice and counsel ... their spiritual direction."

"Well good, I didn't realize that. We can go back together as soon as we're married."

"Stanley, you're not listening, you don't want to hear what I'm saying. We went through this yesterday and I'm not going to insult your intelligence by going over it again."

"It's OK Sister, it's OK. I do get the picture; you don't want to get married right away. This must have been a shock to you when I popped the question yesterday. You need more time, anyone would, and I've been obtuse with you. Take your time Sister, I want you totally comfortable when we get married ... absolutely at peace."

"Stanley, you don't get it do you? Stanley, read my lips; I'm not getting married, to you or anyone else. That's really all I have to say. I'd thank you not to bring up the subject again."

Stanley was saying something as I rolled out of his room, but I neither heard it nor reacted to it.

Chapter Eighty-Eight

Once again I was alone with God.

Lord give Stanley deeper insight into himself, into his real need. He's alighted on me as his savior, yet he has no savior but you. Stanley only seems to understand control, he identifies what he wants and then seeks to control it. He doesn't want to love me, he only seeks to possess me, to have me serve as a prop on the stage of his life; he's lost all his other props and now he wants me to be at his service. Oh Lord, I don't want to impute malevolence into Stanley's intentions, he's not a bad man; he's simply a lost man. Of course he was lost before his accident, even when he had his former props in place, but now he's more desperate still, trying to use the same tactics that worked before. Lord, illuminate his mind and heart and soul; enlighten his perspective so he can come to see his own distorted motivations more clearly. Help him get a grasp on himself so he can capture his true self and in so doing gain you as well. Let Stanley take himself back from what he has given himself over to, back from the world and over to you. Amen.

I drifted off to sleep and dreamed my now familiar dream about the big dog charging at me along the park sidewalk. The aide awakened me with my evening meal.

"Hi Sister, I'll just drop this off on your rolling table, is that OK?" said Helena, another aide on the floor.

"Oh sure, Helena, that will be fine."

"Well, I heard the good news, it's all over the floor. How wonderful that we're having a wedding right here at St. John's."

"Oh no," I cried. "Who told you that?" I snapped.

"Well, like I say, it's all over the floor. But I heard it directly from Dr. Renowski just minutes ago when I checked on him."

"Helena, it's not true, we are not getting married. I've already told him over and again that we are not getting married."

"Oh Sister, but he really wants to marry you ... he needs you!"

"Helena, he thinks he needs me, what he needs is to own himself, not own me. I don't know what I can do to make him understand."

My words hit me, 'make him understand.' I can *never* make him understand. I have to remember that I'm powerless over Stanley. I need to detach, for his sake and my own I do need to detach from Stanley ... let go ... completely let go. When I do fully let go I'll release myself and release Stanley as well. Right now, we're still attached to one another at some level. When even the most remote possibility exists that we may get together Stanley will not relent. I didn't want to have to do this but now I have no choice. I must talk with Jan.

Chapter Eighty-Nine

"Jan, I need to leave St. John's immediately, I cannot tarry, I must leave."

"Whoa, Sister, whoa. I can't arrange for that so quickly. I need to present your progress at morning report and retrieve all your numbers and opinions from all the therapists who've worked with you. We can't just snap our fingers and fly the coop. We also have the matter of your UTI."

"Jan, my fever is gone. I'm fine now and I must leave. I cannot stay any longer."

"Sister, what's the hurry? What difference will a few more days make?"

"Jan, it's the only way. Dr. Renowski can't hear what I'm saying to him about marrying me, and as long as I'm here, his entire focus will remain on me. The only way he will survive, let alone thrive, is to look more deeply into himself, he can't continue to rely on others, it has to be himself. For his good I must leave now."

"OK, OK Sister, I'll call Dr. Pollack right now and see what he says."

"Jan, please don't try to stall me, please convey the seriousness of the situation. This is not a request, Jan. For the good of Dr. Renowski's life both here and in eternity I must leave; it's very, very important."

Jan Left and I filled the time with prayer. She returned ten minutes later.

"Sister, Dr. Pollack says we can start making arrangements for your discharge right away. But he made it clear that the earliest we can get everything together for discharge is probably the day after tomorrow."

"Jan, that won't do, I need to leave tomorrow morning at the latest. I simply must leave."

"Sister, I'm afraid that's the best we can do."

"Jan, I'll leave against medical advice if I have to."

"Sister, how can you do that?"

"Jan you forget I'm Mother Superior, I can call the monastery right now and I can assure you that my nuns will be here in the morning to get me."

"Sister, please don't do that, let me call Dr. Pollack again."

Ten minutes later Jan returned with the news that I would be discharged by noon tomorrow if I could have transportation ready. I immediately called the monastery and gave special dispensation for two of my sisters to take the monastery sedan and drive the five hours to be here at St. John's by noon the next day. It was arranged.

I slept a disjointed sleep and awakened to the pelting rain on my window. It wouldn't be a great day for travel. Jan reported that all was ready for my noon discharge.

"Aren't you going to say goodbye to Dr. Renowski," asked Jan.

"I'm afraid not Jan, it's better if we don't see each other; I know what he'll say. I can't bear his level of need right now."

"He'll be very angry I'm sure, Sister, when he finds out you're gone."

"I'm sure he will, but I can't control his emotions. I'll leave him a note but my sense is that he'll descend into depression again. I can only hope however that the true Stanley Renowski will stop his freefall into complete despair, that's my prayer."

I prepared a note for Stanley.

Chapter Ninety

Dear Stanley,

I've been discharged and I'm gone. I've asked Nurse Jan to give you this note. I know this is a blow to you, I know you wanted our relationship to continue ... but it can't, not for my sake nor for yours. I'm leaving so abruptly Stanley because I love you. Not the romantic kind of love that perhaps you hoped for, but a love resting in Jesus, a love that can take the pain of not seeing you again, because it's a love that is not of this world.

As I've related to you before, you have grown dramatically since our arrival here at St. John's. The Holy Spirit has continually softened your heart day by day. Right now your heart is able to see a future for you, but your mind can only grasp that future if I'm in the picture – but that cannot be. I am already married to Jesus and I must remain so ... it is my destiny; I know that.

My prayer for you right now is that you will allow the work of the Holy Spirit to proceed in you. There is much work still to be done. In time Stanley, it's my prayer that you will realize that you can rely only on the true you inside, the holy self that is God's presence within you. You have made a lifelong career of finding things outside yourself to define who you are. You have been so successful at this task that you have lost your true self in the process. We've discussed this before, but you weren't ready to take it in. Stanley, you need to come to peace about this, you need to realize who you are. I know I must sound like a broken record to you, but what I'm saying here is true.

I pray that you pray. I pray that you can develop a relationship with God. Seek the help of a spiritual director, which will help immensely. Stanley, get back to your source.

In loving, fond, and warm regards,

Sister Theresa

Chapter Ninety-One *Back Home*

Two of my sisters arrived at noon the next day. I departed St. John's with quick stealth, no good-byes to anyone, except Nurse Jan. I made no farewell rounds through the gym; I gave no thank you to all the therapists, aides, doctors, or ancillaries. I simply rolled past the chapel and the bookstore, and departed through the front entrance as though I'd be back that afternoon.

My sisters were giddy with joy to see me again and eager to de-brief every facet of my stay at St. John's. I simply said that I was tired and hoped they would understand if I just closed my eyes for a time. The Holy Spirit gave me sleep almost the entire journey home to the monastery.

As we pulled through the front gates of the monastery, I gasped at its reality. I was home again where I longed and needed to be. "*Thank you Lord.*" After a small meal attended by all the nuns, where their questions were voluminous and my responses sparse and diverting, I made my way to the chapel. I peered through the brass bars separating our chapel from the public chapel and spied the overhead fan from which I launched this chapter of my life. Somehow I knew it wasn't over yet.

Dear Lord, you know I can't yet make sense of my behavior over the last three months. I trust you will give me insight when I'm ready. Right now, dear Lord, I ask for peace. I need a retreat from the tumult of these past few months. I need to regain my spiritual balance and find myself in your arms once again. Lord, I also need your guidance. What do I tell my sisters about Dr. Renowski? Is it fair to them to give details; is it fair not to? Help me, Lord, align my heart with your will so I can do what's right and good for all of us. Lastly Lord, be with Stanley; give him your gift of hope to fight back the terrible depression that I know has gripped him. Lift him from himself and help him find your Self inside him. Lord, he must find his true self. Amen.

Chapter Ninety-Two

I plunged into the cloistered life again, quite against the advice of my Sisters who thought it better to rest a few days. I needed to be a part of the monastery again and the only way I could do that was to start. They were all so patient waiting to hear of my adventure beyond the confines of the monastery walls, but I simply didn't have the energy, or perhaps I didn't have sufficient internal direction to give words to my thoughts. Yet after several days I gained strength, and succumbed to their anticipation. I began telling them the story ... *sans* Stanley.

I described the hospital and the rehab gym; I told them of the competent and compassionate professionals at St. John's. I gave them verbal snapshots of my room, my floor, the chapel, and the pool, even the bookstore. I extended all this out and filled our community recreation time for three days. Still I left Stanley out of every detail; the person who I realized played the central role in my healing was not part of my story to my sisters. I felt awkwardly guilty about this omission.

One week into my newly regained life, Sr. Dorothy, who was on phone duty that afternoon, announced that I had a call from a Nurse Jan.

"Who?" I inquired. Certainly I recognized her name, but I was too shocked to react more accurately.

"All she says is to tell Sister that it's Nurse Jan,' said Sr. Dorothy.

My heart pounded in anxious anticipation.

"Jan, is that you?" I asked.

"Yes Sister, it's me, Jan. How are you, Sister?"

"I'm fine, I'm acclimating myself back into the monastery."

"We're all worried about you Sister, everyone keeps asking me about you ... every day. 'Have you heard from Sister? How is Sister? Why did she leave so abruptly? Is anything wrong with her?' They ask me over and over."

"Jan, I'm so sorry. I never meant to put you in such a difficult position."

"Sister it's OK; I just don't know what to tell them. But Sister, that's not why I called."

"No, well what is it Jan?" I asked, halfway knowing what was coming next. My heart rate quickened as my fear level rose.

"Sister, it's Dr. Renowski. I'm afraid he's in rather a bad way."

"What's wrong?" I said innocently, but fully aware that I left Jan in a mess with Stanley.

"Well, just like you predicted he withdrew into a deep depression. He refused to eat anything for three days. We were ready to start IV fluids when he suddenly and completely flipped from despair to anger; the most intense, demanding anger I've ever seen."

"What's he angry at?"

"Everything ... the food ... the care ... the place ... his therapy, but most of all he is angry at us for letting you get away, as he puts it."

"Jan, that's horrible ... but I can't say I'm surprised."

"He still wants you Sister, you are all he talks about. In between his angry outbursts, which are tirades, he speaks of nothing else but you. 'If Sister were here I'd be fine. If Sister were here you wouldn't be so blunt and uncaring.' Over and over, we all hear the same thing every day."

"How is he progressing with his therapy?" I asked.

"All the therapists say that they've brought him as far as he can go given his negative attitude. He's actually ready for discharge anytime. Some of us think his discharge can't be soon enough. Sister, he's just a bear to deal with."

"Is there anything I can do?" I asked, hoping that she would say 'no', but certain that she had a plan that involved me.

"Well, that's why I'm calling. Dr. Renowski wants to talk with you; he says that you're the only person who can understand him. The social workers are trying to find accommodations for him in Detroit, perhaps an apartment with a live-in aide, or at least someone who could come several times a day to check on him, provide meals, and perform his elimination program."

"That's exactly what he needs Jan," I responded. I tried to divert any personal responsibility, even though I knew that I had culpable responsibility for Stanley's emotional state.

"But Sister, that's just it, the social workers can't get things arranged for another month ... they need time. In the meantime we're all afraid that Dr. Renowski will simply explode. Not only that, he says that he's not going anywhere without you."

"Jan, that's impossible. I can't be involved with him anymore ... I simply can't help."

"Sister, we were wondering if you could just talk with him, just on the phone, it might calm him some. We don't know what else to do."

"I don't know Jan, he might calm down but he also might go the other way, become even more insistent that he must have me with him."

"We know Sister, but like I said, we just don't know what else to do. Something has to give or else Dr. Renowski will self-destruct."

"Give me a day to think about this, Jan, it's risky for all of us."

"I know Sister, I know, but we're stumped. I'll call tomorrow around the same time; is that OK?"

"OK Jan, I'll talk with you then ... take care."

"You too, Sister ... goodbye."

Chapter Ninety-Three

My hand shook as I placed the phone back in its cradle. I was angry, I was sad ... I was confused. What could I possibly say to Stanley that would make any difference in his life right now? He'll only demand more of me, demand all of me. He was unreasonable, and in his current state, he seemed irrational; he wasn't in touch with reality. I understood where he was emotionally, I understood what he wanted. He was desperate, and he was emotionally flailing about. But, what could I do? *Dear Lord, give me your guidance.*

If I did talk to him maybe he could come to some understanding, however blunted, that I was here to stay, that marriage was out of the question, and that he needed to get on with his life. Perhaps just a short phone call; I guessed I owed it to Jan after all she had done. Even if the call accomplished little or nothing, I could at least say that I tried, and Jan would have a better idea of what her next steps could be. All right, I reasoned with myself, I'll call Jan right now to set it up, the sooner the better.

Jan worked fast. Within a half-hour Sr. Dorothy announced that I had a call from a Dr. Stanley Renowski. This was it; I needed to be strong.

"Hello ... Stanley," I said.

"Sister, thank you for talking with me, since you left I've been through hell in here. Sister, they don't understand what I need, they don't understand my predicament."

"And what is that predicament Stanley?"

"Sister, you know how I feel about you. You made me a new man, you showed me how to feel, how to get out of myself, how to be real. I know how I must have scared you with all my talk of marriage. I was totally out-of-line, and I'm sorry. Sister, I apologize from the bottom of my heart; I never wanted to scare or hurt you at all-- never!"

"Is that why you wanted to talk with me Stanley, to apologize?"

"Well, yes, that and another thing, too."

"What's that Stanley?"

"They want to discharge me but they're having a tough time making the necessary arrangements. I have no family, no one, and finding the right place and the right people takes time."

"Yes, so what does all this have to do with me?"

"I was thinking; I remembered you saying that you had guest quarters at your monastery and that they were separate from where the nuns lived."

"Stanley, I can see where you're going, and the answer has to be *no*. The guest quarters are for temporary visitors that have deep relationships with the nuns, usually family, or a priest here to give us a retreat. There are no permanent residents ... there is absolutely no possibility of that!"

"No, no Sister, I'm not talking permanently; just until the social workers here can get arrangements made for me in Detroit."

"And how long will that be Stanley?"

"About two weeks they tell me."

"Why can't you simply stay there at St. John's?"

"For two reasons; the first is that they tell me my therapy is essentially complete. The second is that I'm afraid that I'll lose my mind if I have to stay here any longer."

"Stanley, you're not serious."

"Yes Sister, I'm quite serious. You know how to take care of me, and you mentioned yourself that two of your nuns are former RNs."

"Yes that's true, but their vocation now is prayer, not medical care."

"This wouldn't be real medical care, just assistance with some things that they could handle easily."

"Stanley, you're asking too much."

"Sister, I'm not asking ... I'm begging you. I'm right on the edge, I'm circling the drain, I need a retreat. Sister, I'm scared! I need to continue my spiritual journey. If I could have two weeks there with your help and spiritual direction then I think I can slowly begin a new life; if not, I'm afraid what might happen.

The silence between us spoke loudly. Finally I said, "Stanley, I need to think about this, I need to pray about this. I'll call you tomorrow with the decision."

"Sister, you won't regret this. I'm a lost lamb."

"Stanley, don't think that this is a done deal. I have a lot of thinking to do and my Sisters need to be apprised too."

"OK, OK Sister, I understand, and I know you do too."

"I'll call you tomorrow, Stanley."

"Thank you, Sister."

"Goodbye, Stanley."

"Goodbye, Sister."

Chapter Ninety-Four

Stanley was scared, and now I was scared! I wasn't simply frightened; I was shaken to my core. What could I do? Where could I start? I couldn't hide this from my Sisters; if I brought this up for discussion, I'd have to tell them everything ... could I do that? Was I ready? Was this fair?

I made my way back to the chapel for prayer.

Dear Lord, are you in this, or is this simply a human problem? The way Stanley said, 'I'm a lost lamb,' touched me, it seemed real, and he seemed so genuine. Maybe he's more advanced on his spiritual path than I thought. Perhaps two weeks here will enable him to gather himself up so he can start a new life. But, he's also a manipulator ... a controller. Is he simply setting me up? Once he's here it might be next to impossible to wrench him out. It's a risk Lord, a dilemma; I need your help. What's my next move? I'm afraid for me also. There is something in me that is clearly attracted to Stanley. What is this part of me? What need in me is aroused by this man? Perhaps it's only the residual of that childhood fantasy of a happy marriage; perhaps it has to do with bringing profound closure to the adultery of my youth, perhaps it's just the co-dependent caregiver gene making itself known -- I want to care for the lost soul, I want to fix him. And certainly Lord, I am not the innocent victim in all of this. I have no doubt that my actions spoke to Stanley, the woman in me spoke to him in ways I never intended, but nonetheless in ways that gave him occasion to wonder about my intentions at the very least. What part, dear Lord did I play in suggesting to Stanley that I might consider leaving my life here at the monastery for him? And one final thing, dear Lord, what is my responsibility to Stanley regardless of his intentions and/or my own fears? Lord, illuminate my mind and heart; I am your child in need.

I felt compelled to stay in the presence of God, yet I knew it was past time for the evening meal. I rolled myself to the refectory. I was in great distress. All my Sisters were at table and each turned her face toward me as my wheelchair caught the doorframe with a thud. I gave a look of frustration that sent their faces back to their food. Haltingly I rolled through the serving line and took my place at the head of the table. Only occasionally did I spot an eye edge-up as if to check on me; it quickly returned to the business of eating once I caught its gaze. Each Sister took her turn in this visual dance.

I was bursting inside; I was so full of doubt and indecision. I felt they were waiting for a spectacle ... and I didn't disappoint them. All restraint both internal and external was breeched; the sacred mealtime silence was broken as I simultaneously erupted into tears and words ... "My Sisters ... I need your help!"

Now all eyes were fixed on me, they knew as they had anticipated, I was sure, that my story about St. John's was incomplete. Now was the time of truth.

"My Sisters ... I'm very troubled. Let us finish our meal and make haste to the recreation room. I'm suspending solemn silence this evening, we have a very important decision that cannot wait."

We gathered quickly. I began with an overview of the situation.

"Sisters my time at St. John's was more eventful than I have so far reported to you. The reason I needed to leave so abruptly was because of a man. His name is Stanley Renowski. The same auto accident that left him paralyzed from his neck down also took his wife's life. He has no family whatsoever. He is a world-renowned surgeon who has won many awards. We happened to be placed across the hall from each other at St. John's."

With this statement their eyes noticeably widened and I thought I heard a muffled gasp.

"When I found him he was a man in despair; all he wanted was his life to be over. If he could, he would have taken his life. Naturally, I felt it my spiritual duty to form a relationship with him in the hopes of helping this man, with God's grace, find Jesus. He was more than difficult, compounded by his narcissistic and quite demanding personality. I'm afraid that my efforts to assist him toward God challenged me beyond my limits, for on two occasions at least I found myself kissing his tears away."

This time the gasps were not muffled.

"I never did become what could be called romantically involved with him, but I know that his deep level of need enticed me to spend too much time with him, all under the unconscious guise of helping him. I know now that his need was but a cover I used, albeit without conscious awareness or intent, to keep returning to him over and over. Many times I had to force thoughts of him out of my mind; I had to exercise intense self-discipline. For the most part I was successful."

"I left St. John's so quickly because I was running away from his very public proposal of marriage ... he actually thought that I could marry him. I suppose I also thought that my leaving would take away his desires."

"I've received word from a nurse at St. John's, a nurse who is very well acquainted with this entire situation, that upon my departure Dr. Renowski at first lunged into a morbid depression for three days, so deep that he refused all food. This was followed by intense and ubiquitous anger. I spoke with Dr. Renowski just this afternoon at the nurse's advice in an attempt to calm him. What I found was a contrite man who asked if he could stay here in our guest quarters until the social workers at St. John's can arrange for his needs in this home city of Detroit. I seek your advice and counsel on this matter."

My Sisters erupted into excited questions, never before had they heard of, nor even imagined such a request coming from any of them, especially me as mother superior.

"How confined is he? What level of care will he require?"

"Is this even permissible under our rules?"

"When might he arrive?"

"What kind of a person is he? Tell us about him."

"Mother, do you want him here?"

Most of the questions dealt with Stanley and his needs. I answered each as factually as I could. Then came the question that gave me more than pause.

"Mother, what impact will having Dr. Renowski here have upon you?"

This of course was the question that was at the core of my confusion. Even though I appeared confidant and assured, I knew this was little more than a veneer -- underneath was turmoil. How indeed would I react to Stanley under the roof of the monastery?

In the end, the Sisters embraced the idea of temporarily assisting Stanley. Although there were dissenters who rested on community legalism; they were swayed, no doubt, by their innate compassion for a person in need, as well as by the novelty of having such a prominent person at the monastery. But most of all, I was sure; they perceived that I both wanted and somehow needed Stanley to come so that I could reconcile myself with him and more importantly -- with God.

Chapter Ninety-Five

I was still so confused about my own motivation. Were my actions guided by the noblest parts of me, or by my own ego needs? I rolled into my office where I placed a call to Stanley. After being connected to the nurse's station, when I told an elated Nurse Jan of our decision, I got Stanley on the line.

"Stanley?" I asked.

"Yes, Sister. Is that you?"

"Yes, Stanley, it's me."

"I'm so glad to hear your voice."

Was he? Or was he merely ingratiating himself?

"Stanley, the Sisters have met and discussed the possibility of your staying here at the monastery only until arrangements can be made for you in Detroit."

"Yes, Sister, yes. What did they decide?"

"They've agreed to a temporary stay here, only a short maximum two week stay; Stanley ... no longer than two weeks."

"Sister, that's wonderful. Sister, I want you to know that I prayed for this continuously since we talked yesterday."

"Prayer works Stanley."

"Yes it does."

"Stanley, one thing ... no talk about marriage."

"Of course not, Sister."

I heard the words, but there was something hollow in them.

Chapter Ninety-Six *Review*

Late the very next day an ambulance deposited Stanley on our doorstep. The transfer process was laborious. The physical transfer itself was more than smooth; it was Stanley's attitude that was laborious. The old Stanley, or maybe the real Stanley, roared out of him. He barked at the two attendants in the same manner that I remembered from the early days at St. John's. Perhaps his transformation was only for me. Maybe he hadn't really 'changed his strips.' Maybe he was simply suffering from road fatigue due to the long drive from St. John's.

"Be careful bringing me in here. Don't bang the doorframe. Watch out for the statue. Be careful of this highly polished floor. Keep your voices down, don't you know this is a holy place?"

Commands paraded from him with the regularity of marching soldiers. The two sisters who accompanied me glanced at each other in horrified disbelief. I'm sure they were already wondering what the monastery was in for.

In the midst of all this, Stanley broke from his orders and planted his eyes squarely onto mine. His gaze denuded me. I thought I saw his eyes begin to melt as he said, "Sister, you look wonderful, so natural here in your own environment. I can't thank you and your Sisters enough for having me here. You can't know what this means to me."

I could do nothing but nod at him; I had no words to respond. What was real about Stanley? Was the real Stanley the bully, or was the real Stanley the man whose words and demeanor could warm my heart. Perhaps he was some strange combination of the two, possessing some schizophrenic ability to convert from one to the other. On the other hand, maybe I was so disconnected from the secular culture that I was appalled by rudeness that may have been common in Stanley's former world.

The aides finally got Stanley settled in our guest quarters and retreated to their ambulance as quickly as they could, trying, I'm sure to escape more of Stanley's barrage. The sisters, who by virtue of their RNs were assigned to Stanley's care, had prepared the room, given our less than state-of-the-art resources, with thoughtful acumen. All in all he appeared quite comfortable and professed likewise.

Chapter Ninety-Seven

As the Sister/nurses completed their work, and after giving Stanley a light meal, he turned to me and asked, "Sister, do you think you could stay just a while?"

Again his tone of voice and demeanor were so empathic that I felt coerced to accept his request.

"All right Stanley, I can stay just a bit, we do have night prayers soon and I can't be late."

"Oh, thank you," he said.

As the two sister/nurses left the room Stanley signaled me to come closer.

"Sister, when I realized you were gone I didn't know what to do, I felt cast away, spun off, and abandoned. The person in whom I had placed all my trust had left me alone. I felt like a motherless child. I became completely despondent, abjectly confused, and without cause. I felt that whatever small steps toward personal integration I had made were now obliterated; I was lost."

I don't think that Stanley meant it but his words came across as self-serving; the unspoken message is that I was acting selfishly when I departed St. John's. The entire focus of his statement was on him, from his perspective, his wants, and his world. There was no hint in his statement that he considered my volition, my needs and desires at all. His only implication was that I abandoned him.

"Stanley, I can't discuss any of this tonight. You must be tired from your long trip, and right now I need to go to night prayer. Let's call it a night, all right?"

"Certainly Sister, you're right ... as usual."

"OK then, the sisters will be in every two hours to check on you tonight. Sleep well."

"Thanks for everything Sister; you know how much I believe in you."

"Good night, Stanley."

"Good night ... you're wonderful."

Oh, he'd gotten sappy ... what next? It felt so surreal that Stanley was here; he seemed so different, and yet so much the same. My mind wandered thoughtlessly during night prayers; I couldn't concentrate. Stanley's presence here, right here in the monastery, simply overpowered all my focus on prayer.

My sleep was fitful and punctuated by dream fragments all with a threatening theme. I awakened with tension in my heart, uncertain of the reason why all this was happening. I wanted to believe that the providential hand of God was guiding our progression toward wholeness, but my faith was tainted by fear, a fear that shook me deeply.

The next morning I visited Stanley while he was having his breakfast, facilitated by one of our sister/nurses. He asked me a question that I hadn't anticipated.

"Sister do you think I could participate in the prayer life here in the monastery?"

Wow, where was he coming from? Was this a genuine attempt to find himself, or just a manipulation designed to gain my respect and favor?

"Why do you want to do that?" I asked curtly.

"I've always been interested in prayer and I know that the highest forms of prayer are practiced right here. Maybe I could finally learn to pray like I should. Don't you think I'll need that competency with the road ahead of me?"

This man was full of surprises. He had never talked about prayer before, but, I couldn't argue with him, certainly prayer would serve him well in the coming years. What could I say but ... "Certainly Stanley, we could teach you the basic order of prayer that we follow here in the monastery; it's called the Liturgy of the Hours. Actually, we're in constant prayer, but we go to the chapel for formal prayer seven times a day."

"Could I accompany you?"

"Well no, our private chapel is reserved for consecrated nuns only. I guess however you could go to the public chapel where you could hear us and follow along silently on your own."

"That would be great, Sister, thank you."

That afternoon I gave Stanley a crash course on the Liturgy of the Hours. He was a quick student; he immediately saw the sequence and progression of our prayer life. I realized however that Stanley couldn't be alone in the public chapel; for one thing he couldn't turn the pages in our prayer book to follow along. Stanley needed a prayer helper. I called one of our lay associates who quickly created a schedule of people to be with Stanley during prayer times. I guess there was no way I could keep Stanley's presence at the monastery even partially guarded; now all of our world would know.

Chapter Ninety-Eight

For the next few days Stanley settled into our routine. The two sister/nurses reveled in their new duties, and the rest of the sisters exuded an almost palpable upswing in their general energy level and mood. All seemed well. God's hand was bringing harmony; perhaps my fears were unfounded.

The next day, one of the Sister/nurses handed me a note from Stanley saying that he would very much like to talk with me as soon as my schedule permitted it. Apparently Stanley had enticed his sister/nurse to write the note for him. Several hours later, after mid-day prayer, I appeared at Stanley's door.

"Sister, great to see you. Thank you for coming."

"You're welcome Stanley."

"I was wondering if you had heard anything from St. John's about any arrangements for me in Detroit?"

"No, Stanley, nothing yet, but I'm sure they'll be calling soon."

"I was just curious that's all. I'm not in any hurry to leave this little piece of heaven; I think I could stay here with you forever ... it would be so nice."

"You know that's impossible Stanley."

"Oh yes, I certainly know I can't stay here with you, but I still pray that you might reconsider and come live with me; I think we'd have a full life together."

"I thought we agreed that we wouldn't talk about that."

"I know, Sister, I was just testing the waters you might say."

"The waters are dangerous for anything like that Stanley."

"OK, I promise, but I still want to make the best of our time together."

"It's my hope that your time here is productive and helps you get a firmer grip on your life. It wasn't too long ago when you wouldn't give much for your life at all."

"That's changed, Sister, thanks to you. I'll always be in your debt; there's no way I could repay you for that."

He seemed so sincere ... maybe he was for real.

"That's generous of you to say, Stanley, but you know it wasn't me. God provides the power behind all good things."

"What about the bad things?" he retorted.

"Bad things just happen. God has created this world to give us the opportunity to show us love; if bad things didn't happen how could we learn God's love?"

"That sounds a little paradoxical to me, Sister."

"It sounds like a paradox because it is. A paradox always points up a truth. The truth is that love is the primary power in the universe."

"It's still hard for me to see why we have to experience bad things just so we can show love. Can't we just show love without the bad things?"

"That sounds like it would work, but without bad things there would be no motivation to show good. Strange as it sounds we need the bad things so we can show our goodness, which is actually God's goodness."

"It still sounds like a hell of a way to run a railroad."

"What?"

"It's just a figure of speech Sister, meaning it doesn't make sense, there must be a better way."

"If we were given charge of organizing the world I'm sure we would do it differently than God has put it together, but that doesn't mean it would be better. You've noticed I'm sure that we humans don't naturally do a good job making things work for goodness, at least not for long."

"Yeah, we do manage to screw things up pretty well."

"Stanley, I've got to ask you; have you made any decisions yet about your future?"

"Decisions ... I don't know. I don't have a plan if that's what you mean. My original plan included you, but that seems to need modification."

"I don't mean you need a full-blown life plan, but what about your next steps?"

"I'm simply glad that I'm out of the hospital and here with you. I know I need to get closer to God, and I guess I'm hoping I can take a step closer while I'm here. I never imagined that I'd live in a monastery."

"How is your prayer life progressing Stanley?"

"Very well, I think. I like the regularity of the Liturgy of the Hours. There's a rhythm to it that seeps into your soul ... it's soothing ... it gives me solace; something I haven't experienced for a long, long time – if ever."

"I'm very pleased to hear that. The volunteers that help you, your prayer partners I guess you could call them, have mentioned to me how much they enjoy being with you in the public chapel. I think your example is helping them find more depth in their own prayer life as well."

"Who would have thought that I, Dr. Stanley Renowski, would ever, or could ever, be an example in prayer for anyone!"

"God's grace is always at work."

"I hope so, because I'm gonna need it."

Chapter Ninety-Nine

"Stanley, with all that you've learned about yourself and about life in the past four months, you should be able to open yourself up wider and wider to let God's grace and power inside you."

"Really, Sister, what have I learned? I do feel differently than I did, for sure, but I don't think I would be able to itemize exactly what I've learned."

"Most of our learning tasks are life bridges we don't even know we've crossed, even when we have; we just awaken one day and know that we're different than we were, and we live in a different world. That's the way it is with God's grace too, if we're aware of it at all it's generally after it has done its work; we sense, or feel its effects but we very rarely see the thunderbolt strike."

"Is that what grace is ... a thunderbolt?"

"Actually I see grace more like a spring rain on parched earth. The rain falls on all of us but some of us are standing face uplifted and arms outstretched to receive the rain as fully as possible, while others of us are holding umbrellas so we don't get wet."

"I like that Sister, remind me to go outside the next time it rains. Seriously though, what would you say that I've learned so far?"

"Stanley, you've been on the fastest spiritual growth track I've ever witnessed."

"Tell me about it."

"Well, the first big barrier I saw you burst through was that you're no longer looking behind you, to your profession, your role, to define who you are today. This was a huge hurdle for you. You had invested so much in your profession, and had succeeded so well, that you couldn't imagine a life without your past, without being a heart surgeon."

"Sometimes I still feel that way but I try to push it aside, I try to replace the thought with something else. At first I replaced it with you; now I don't have a clear picture of a replacement, all I know is I can't go back to what was, I just don't know what to move forward to."

"None of us knows what's ahead, we simply have to live today as fully as possible."

"I know, Sister, but that's not easy. Even when I was an active surgeon, once I was finished with a case ... it was over, all I could do was look to the next, and the next, and the next case. My life was simply a parade of heart surgeries."

"The second thing that I noticed was that not only were you stuck in your professional identity, but you were also caught in your youth. Even though you're physically in your mid 50s, you were psychologically still the age you were when your first put on the mantle of surgeon, you hadn't progressed. You were still thinking with the same attitudes and perception as that young man you were long ago."

"But that's what I tried to do. I tried to remain fresh and youthful. Isn't that what we're supposed to do?"

"Certainly we want to remain current, you needed to keep up with the latest advances in medicine, for example, but remaining youthful is quite different. You can remain current and still mature psychologically and spiritually. Maturation takes a certain detachment from what you do so that you can see more clearly who you are, and how to develop that who into its fullest sense. When you accomplish this you become the most authentic Stanley possible."

"How do you know all this, Sister; I wasn't aware of any of it."

"That's it Stanley, like I say, our most vital growth happens when we're not even looking. For most people it happens as they grow older and confront some of the losses that punctuate life. In your case, you were so successful in insulating yourself from these losses that you inhibited your psychological and spiritual forward progression. It wasn't until your accident when you encountered big losses, that you were brought up short, so to speak."

"Do we have to lose?"

"Yes, Stanley, we covered all this months ago at St. John's. I think this brings us to the third dimension of your growth."

"What's that, Sister?"

"Contradictions."

"What do you mean?"

"Stanley, the third thing that I noticed about you, and that I think you've grown beyond somewhat, was that you found it most difficult, if not impossible, to let life's contradictions into your little life sphere. You wanted everything to be perfect, right, and correct, always according to your beliefs. Of course that meant everything had to be your own way, anything that wasn't your way was a contradiction for you and couldn't be allowed. You demanded that everyone and everything conform to you. This adolescent attitude prevented you from addressing even the possibility that you, like the rest of us, might somehow be broken. You refused to let the inconsistencies and the paradoxes that are implicit in the world break into your conscious mind. You kept all of this out by selective vision and selective listening."

"What's that mean?"

"It means you saw and heard only what you wanted to see and hear ... you lived in your own world. The upshot of all this selection was that you became more and more unhappy. Again, your accident broke through the mental dikes you had constructed and gave you a new perspective on life."

"Sister, you just can't stop telling me how lucky I was to be injured. I wish I could appreciate it like you do."

"You have no other choice, you must see it as an opportunity. What's your option?"

"Well, like most folks I could see it as the tragedy it was."

"Stanley, of course your accident was a tragedy, just like my accident was a tragedy, but I think you've learned that you can redefine the tragedy by how you see and think about it."

"Is that so? Help me out here Sister."

"If you persist in seeing it only on your own personal level, you're sure to continue feeling cheated and punished."

"I certainly felt that and lots more."

"Stanley, this brings me to something else I've noticed about you. What number is this now? I think it's the fourth dimension of your spiritual growth. This one still requires a lot more work on your part. If you can get outside of yourself and view your injury as a ticket to a new world, a world where you can help others in new ways, then you'll grow in emotional and spiritual stature like never before."

"Go on, I guess I need to hear this even though it's tough. I thought I was helping others – look at all those surgeries that I performed!"

"I know. We've been over this before. Were you performing surgery for the people you operated on, or were you primarily performing surgery for your own self? If you really develop a focus of helping others rather than simply serving yourself, your whole personality transforms into something wonderful because the full measure of what God has implanted in you can pour forth. This is still a big challenge for you.

"Sister you say those words so easily, they sound beautiful and enticing, yet who can really live up to them?"

"You can Stanley, but you'll need lots of faith, and that takes prayer, spiritual reading, the sacraments, and discipline. You have it all Stanley, you just need to put it into practice."

"Sister, I think you have too much faith -- too much faith in me."

"No, Stanley, I see the strength in you. I see the stamina in you."

Just then it happened again. I felt a surge of emotion ripple through me. The wave left me weak and vulnerable. It pushed me toward Stanley and compelled me to touch him. I found myself stroking his arm and touching his cheek. He had to know that something had taken me. As he looked into my eyes with both question and anticipation, I responded by looking away.

"Sister, you're so real, you're so present to me. I just know we'd be so right and so happy together."

"No, Stanley, no; we can't be together, no matter my feelings at this present moment."

I gathered my emotions and composed myself.

"Stanley, I must say goodnight."

"OK, Sister, I understand ... certainly I understand."

But how could he understand? I didn't understand myself. What caused this temporary lapse? What did it mean?

I thought I had eclipsed feelings like this, and yet the impulses to be near him, to touch him, and even wanting to kiss him were so real.

I rolled directly to the chapel where I outstretched my arms, uplifted my hands, and hung my head. *Dear Lord, I need your help to get a grip on myself. I need your vision to give me insight into my behavior. Help me be empathic toward Stanley but still remain detached emotionally. I can't let myself be pulled into the dark hole of his neediness. Perhaps it's only his neediness that exerts that pull upon me. I do see his spiritual potential, and I want so very much, I'm sure, dear Lord; I want too much to see Stanley rise to the full measure of spiritual power that you have invested in him. Help me be but a link in the chain that eventually leads him to you.*

The nuns were arriving for Vespers; I couldn't stay, I needed to be alone.

Chapter One Hundred

The next two days I busied myself in anything. I knew this was simple avoidance but I needed the respite from Stanley. Then a note from Stanley invaded my hideaway.

> *Sister,*
> *I've thought a lot about what you said, and I know that you're right. Can we continue our conversation about what you see that I've learned? I need to hear it all, I need to know the truth of God's action within me.*
> *Stanley*

Through the grate I spied Stanley in the public chapel during mid-morning prayer. He looked devout and at peace; I, on the other hand was not. I knew I needed to talk with him again; I couldn't let his cry for help, if that's what it was, go unanswered. I resolved that I must talk to him today. After our midday meal I wheeled over to the guest quarters.

"Hello Stanley. How was your lunch?"

"Sister, great to see you; it was just fine thanks. Everything here is just fine. I'm really getting into prayer, it's a whole new world."

"I'm glad, Stanley; I'm really very pleased. You can thank God for that."

"How are you doing Sister? You look a bit somber."

"I am a bit today, but I'll be fine ... I'm sure."

"Anything I can help you with?"

"Thank you, Stanley, but no. I came by in response to your note, so we can review what I think you've learned."

"You're very sweet to come. I'm vitally interested in your observations ... thank you."

"Stanley, I want you to know that I've given this considerable thought. The process was actually quite enlightening for me too. I've identified six more items that I think are huge spiritual developmental steps that you've started, but you're still in mid-stream, so to speak. These are in addition to the four other ones we talked about the other day."

"Sister, you're so thorough: I love it!"

I didn't respond directly to this, it seemed ingratiating. I simply plunged into a brief description of the six additional spiritual/psychological growth dimensions that I witnessed he had at least started since his accident.

"The fifth lesson I think you're beginning to learn is growing into a more emotionally integrated personality. When you arrived at St. John's you were in pieces ... emotionally fragmented. On a spiritual level I guess we could say that your harmony and wholeness had seriously eroded. Your life was out of balance, you were horribly over committed to your career, but the other arenas of your life: family, relationships, self-awareness, leisure, and especially your spiritual life were dismally anemic. This imbalance made you particularly vulnerable to the depression that gripped you after your accident. The accident unraveled you. The fabric of your personality was so unevenly woven that it couldn't hold up under the pressure. Your accident broke you, it broke you emotionally, psychologically, and it crushed your undernourished spirituality."

"Sister, you express this with such drama."

"It is dramatic Stanley, it's high drama. Actually, this brings us to the sixth dimension of your spiritual growth. Part of the drama was the despondency you experienced; you were emotionally desolate. The profession that gave you everything including your sense of self was gone; you felt abandoned ... naked. Only slowly did this personal desolation begin to thaw a bit, allowing in a ray of hope, a hint of consoling light that just might illuminate a way for you to find new life beyond your accident. Your challenge now is to take the next step and allow the ultimate consolation that only God can give, pour over you like a healing oil. How's that for drama Stanley?"

"Pretty good Sister, in fact very good ... I like it. That's exactly what I'm trying to do here, open myself to God and let whatever can happen, happen. Believe me Sister, I am trying to look inside for that peace and consolation you talk about."

It's incredible to me that Stanley can say things like this and authentically mean them. He is trying so hard to open himself to God; he seems more directed, more centered, and more balanced right now than I am. I'm the one who now feels confused, as though I'm somehow out-of-place even here in the monastery, my home for all these years. I need to center myself. Having Stanley here unnerves me; the other sisters like the novelty but I only feel unsettled.

"Sister, are you all right? You seem like you're miles away."

"Oh yes, I was just thinking."

"About what?"

"Oh, just the next item on my list of what you've learned."

"Yes, please go on; I'm riveted, no one has ever done this. Is this what analysis is like?"

"I've no idea Stanley, these are simply my gleanings over the months. I've got four more on my list."

"Please proceed."

"This next one, the seventh one, builds on the two previous ones; it has to do with finding new purpose. You haven't actually completed this one, perhaps you haven't even addressed it yet, but it's crucial that you do. You must find new purpose for your life. We all need to follow what God has etched on our heart. Make no mistake-- once you lost your former life purpose of surgery, God gave you a new one; you just need to discover it. Your new purpose may be a higher calling beyond the physical plane."

"What do you mean, beyond the physical plane."

"The spiritual plane; God has a purpose for you on the spiritual plane. This requires that you gain new perspective on yourself and on the world in general. Your goal is to be holy and sanctified. You needn't do anything special except be your authentic self; you can live a meaningful life seeing your life situation from a higher vantage point."

"I'm trying, Sister, believe me I'm trying."

"This brings me to the next point on my list; the eighth dimension of your spiritual development. You've only just begun to work on this, you have a long way to go, but it's encouraging to me that you've 'gotten off the dime' as they say."

"Really, and what's that?"

"Change!"

"Change?"

"Yes Stanley ... change. You've been stuck, locked in place, fixated in a mindset that has become a mental antique for you, not to mention a spiritual hindrance."

"A mental antique ... I like that, Sister, even though I don't quite know what you mean."

"A mental antique is an attitude and a corresponding view of life that once were very functional for your life, but now, because circumstances have changed, it no longer gives you life ... it's become a drag on your life."

"You mean like a horse and wagon."

"Well, sort of. A mental antique is a mindset that guided your life very well for a long time, but now it's simply quaint, a curio piece, just a reminder of a by-gone era. Beliefs and attitudes can become antiques, quaint and cute, but utterly non-functional."

"Can you give me an example?"

"OK, let's see. Well, you formerly thought that in order to be a good surgeon you needed to have a commanding personality, to the point of being arrogant. This was an unspoken and even unconscious belief you harbored that rested on several values. You've now gone beyond this perspective ... you've changed. No longer do you need to overwhelm and overpower other people. A self-serving attitude like that simply doesn't work for you anymore, you can't be captain of your own ship anymore, you're beginning to turn that position over to God."

"Whew, Sister, you're like a psycho-spiritual machine gun, you just keep firing and firing. I love it, but I'm also mentally wincing at the accuracy of your fire."

"I can stop anytime, Stanley, the last thing I want to do is hurt you."

"No, no, no, please proceed."

"OK, the next one, the ninth one on my list, I entitled 'life enrichment'. I've already touched on aspects of this one but it has its own distinctiveness. I've noticed that you're just beginning to discover the unique beauty that's inside you. I like to call this interior beauty your gifts because they're the power, the spiritual energy, or the grace that God has planted in you so you can grow and become all that God intends for you. Believe it or not, I think your lead gift is humility."

"Humility, I think you miscalculated that one, Sister! I don't see anything submissive or passive about me."

"Humility doesn't mean either submissiveness or passivity; no, it means being honest and accurate."

"Is that what you think I am, honest and accurate?"

"Well, you do like to be accurate, and I think you're honest in the sense of being fair. This is certainly true with regard to your patients over the years. But that's not why I think that humility is your lead gift."

"Well, why then?"

"It's because you've been so self-centered ... so vain."

"What? What does being vain have to do with humility?"

"They're opposites; vanity is the opposite of humility. Stanley you've been stuck in the opposite of humility for a long time."

"So, if I've been the opposite, how can I have humility?"

"You couldn't be self-centered if you didn't have the gift of humility; one is the opposite of the other, like two side of a coin, they exist together. You've just given more energy, lots more energy, to the self-centered side of the coin, now you're learning to turn the coin over. Believe me, it's a beautiful thing to watch. I've seen it start to grow and I've rejoiced at its development."

"Sister, you are too much. You're incredible, your perspective is so different, you see things that no one else could possibly see. I am simply amazed."

"I think I told you before, one of my gifts is spiritual empathy ... I can discern what God has given to others. It's a beautiful gift but it can be frustrating at times when you can see the truth and goodness, the power and the potential that God has bestowed upon a person and that person is blind to it all. That's the way I felt about you when I first met you. I could sense the spiritual energy in you but you had completely overlooked it, you were limping along. Oh Stanley, sorry for that reference, it just slipped out."

"Don't give it a thought Sister."

"Thank you. But can you see that you were only using a fraction of the spiritual energy God gave you, and even misdirecting that? I was sad for you."

"Sister, I can't believe you. I had no idea. When I first met you I thought you were misguided and naïve at best. Now I can see that from the beginning I was on a completely different plane than you. You were working so hard and I was just stuck. Wow, what a dummy I've been."

"You know you're not a dummy, you were just on a different wave length, as they say. You weren't tuned in to God."

"Sister, that is a fact!"

"This brings me to the tenth, and last, point on my list Stanley – taking back your life."

"I haven't lost it Sister."

"Yes Stanley, you have lost it; you're now in the process of taking it back. More accurately, you're in the process of requesting it back from God."

"You'll have to unpack that one for me Sister."

"I'll try Stanley. I've seen you begin, just begin, to progress toward taking a fuller ownership of your own life. Surgery formerly dictated the direction of all your energies. When you did this, you remained distracted from the core of you. You busied yourself with mountains of tasks; volumes of details, and piles of issues, all of which were outside of you; in the process of all this busyness, you lost sight of you. Consequently, you forfeited ownership of yourself to these mountains, volumes, and piles, all of which assaulted you relentlessly. Now you're taking your real self back, retrieving your true self from the limbo where you left it. You're coming to new life, Stanley, new possibilities; it's a joy to watch it all unfold."

"Sister, I feel like you've just performed psycho-spiritual surgery on me. Now we can hope that the surgery is successful, and more than that ...we hope the patient lives."

"I think that's quite probable from what I see. I also see that it's time for me to retire. See you tomorrow."

"That will be great, Sister. I'll look forward to it. I've got a lot to digest."

Chapter One Hundred-One *Emancipation*

I didn't see Stanley the following day, nor did I choose to see him the next, nor the one after that. He sent word several times that he would like me to visit, but I felt that I had already said what I needed to say to him. I realized that I was afraid my feelings would overpower my personality again and lead me in directions I didn't want to go. This I certainly wanted to avoid. My feelings were always strong ... and not very smart. I needed to take note of them for sure, but I learned a long time ago that I simply couldn't trust my unexamined feelings to be my primary guide. I kept telling myself that I was not rude to Stanley by not seeing him; I was simply taking care of myself.

On the fourth day after my conversation with Stanley, I got a phone call.

"Hello Sister, this is Jan at St. John's."

"Jan, how wonderful to hear from you. How are you?"

"Sister I'm just fine. Once Dr. Renowski left we all felt relieved. How are you doing with him down there?"

"I guess I could say something nondescript like, 'it's been interesting', but the truth of it is that it's been a challenge for me. I think it's a healthy challenge however and with God's help it's been growthful and spiritually productive challenge."

"Sister, you always did have a way with words. Look, I have news. The social workers have made the necessary arrangements for Dr. Renowski in Detroit. They've put it all together; it was a real chore for them but they've got an apartment for him in an assisted living complex. They've also got private nursing, and a live-in homemaker who's had training in care of spinal cord injured patients. They're delighted with the package they've managed to piece together."

"Jan this is music to my ears; I'm so relieved. Stanley's stay here has been most generative for him. He seems at peace; he's very vibrant, but he continues to stir me up inside. Frankly, for both our sakes, Stanley needs to go, and needs to go soon. I think he's ready to go, even if he doesn't realize it. I know that I'm ready for him to go.

"Well, we can start the ball rolling. The social workers are investigating airline transportation for him; when they can finalize that, then we'll be ready to roll."

"Great, do you think I should tell him Jan?"

"Oh, by all means, he needs to begin his psychological preparation for the move."

"OK, I'll tell him today. Have you any idea when this might transpire?"

"I would think in a couple of days."

"Wow, it doesn't seem possible."

"It's been a long haul hasn't it?"

"Yes it has, Jan ... yes it has."

Chapter One Hundred-Two

I all but stumbled over myself as I rushed to Stanley to tell him the good news. I wasn't at all sure however, that he would agree with my assessment.

"Stanley ... good news. I just got off the phone with Nurse Jan. She tells me that your arrangements in Detroit are pretty much put together. She says you'll probably be able to leave in two days or so. Isn't that great?"

Stanley looked out the window. He was silent ... and he was somber. Finally he said, "I'm not sure what kind of news it is."

"Stanley this is your big transition; this is what we've been preparing for all this time. This is the big bridge ... you can cross it ... you're ready."

"Your confidence in me exceeds my own, Sister."

"You're not alone, God is with you. Maybe this is a good time for us to say a rosary together. You know the rosary don't you Stanley?"

"Sister I haven't said a rosary since I was in high school."

"Well it's time you did. You can follow along with me."

I started, and Stanley followed my lead very slowly at first, but by the time we got to the second decade he had found his way and remained with me through to the end. I looked up at him after the final 'Amen' and witnessed tears streaming down his cheeks. I couldn't stop myself; I rolled over to him and wiped several tears away. He smiled faintly but tenderly. I felt tears swelling in my eyes as well, and soon our tears mingled as our cheeks touched sweetly. So much was communicated in our touch, so much healing shot through us both; for as we parted our cheeks and caught each other's eyes, it seemed apparent that we were not alone – the Holy Spirit was there. The Holy Spirit was working spiritual magic. I knew that a miracle was erupting between us. We witnessed it in awe even though no visible signs were discernable; miracles always happened on the transcendent plane. Our eyes fixed on each other's in a visual laser embrace that spoke silently of love, and gratitude, and mercy, and hope, and peace, and grace. This was our last communication at the monastery.

Two days later an ambulance appeared in the front circle. From my office window I witnessed Stanley's transition over the front threshold, beyond our protective care, and out into his new life ... whatever it would be. As the ambulance glided out our drive I did two things: I thanked God, and I began a long sobbing cry.

Chapter One Hundred-Three

It had been nine months since Stanley left the protective care of the monastery. With God's care and grace I had plunged into the Liturgy of the Hours with renewed enthusiasm. I recited prayers that I had recited many times before, but now they seemed new, fresh, delightful, and full of personal meaning. I noticed that colors seemed more colorful, the grain in our wood floors was richer and deeper, the chalice sparkled anew, the statues were more real, and our many pictures echoed a brilliance that first inspired them. The whole world was more real, or perhaps I was simply more awake to what had been there all along. I felt a new potency course its way through me. I felt stronger than ever before, the barriers had fallen, a new light and new life was streaming into me. I was made brand new! I rejoiced, and rejoiced, and rejoiced; I knew this was God's work.

Each day I wondered about Stanley, a part of me wanted to know that he was settled and that his spiritual growth was progressing well. Yet, there was a stronger part of me that resisted the temptation to take any action to find him. At some point I noticed that this stronger part of me propelled me away from Stanley and toward a fuller embrace of the beauty of the cloistered life of prayer God's grace had given to me.

Each time I entered the chapel I felt an excitement, a graced anticipation of a new spiritual intimacy I was experiencing with Jesus. I often remembered the spiritual dryness that I felt before my accident, and actually found myself thanking God for giving me the accident. This seemed so strange to be thanking God for what I formerly thought of as a tragedy, yet it was gratitude I was experiencing; I guess not for the paralysis itself, but for the journey that the accident brought me.

I realized that, like Stanley, I too had grown spiritually. I enumerated what I believed I'd learned from this chapter in my life, and was surprised to discover the parallels between my growth and Stanley's. While the content of the growth was different, the themes were remarkably similar. I looked at the list of spiritual growth items that I had made for Stanley and I could easily find myself there too.

This self-analysis paid dividends in abundance, mostly in a new closeness I felt with God that seemed at times to be nothing short of profound. It was as though God was re-igniting the flame of my vocation that now burned hotter and brighter than ever before. This improvement was not minimal; my relationship with God now was far beyond what it had been before my accident.

A shift of mammoth proportion had taken place in me, as if two tectonic earth plates had collided and caused a gigantic up-thrust of land producing high, high mountain tops; promontory points from where I could survey an entirely new personal landscape and discover in the terrain a new beauty I hadn't seen before. The terrain was abundant with hills and valleys too green to describe, verdant fields, meadows of flowers, and inviting streams.

Everything seemed to have taken on a new luster, a distinctive patina that seemed luminous and oh so beautiful. Most of all my view of my sisters was transformed. I remembered how burdened I felt by them before my accident;

how obtuse I was to their uniqueness that I saw only as troublesome and certainly unnecessary flaws of personality. I failed to see their luminosity and their inner beauty. Now I had found a new respect that honored their individual idiosyncrasies as behavioral badges of their diversity, given as gifts by God. They were truly my teachers, showing me how to love better. I looked at them file in the chapel for Vespers and I marveled at their virtue. They were all very human, but they were at the same time paragons of humility and patience, of kindness and mercy, and of perseverance and charity. They were beacons of God's love, reflections of his grace, and vanguards of hope for the world. I was blessed. I always thought that I was blessed but now I *knew* that I was with a new and profound surety.

I pondered ... what ancient yet fresh forgiveness had purged me of whatever psychological and spiritual encumbrances had impeded the free flow of God's streams of love through me? What dams had I erected that had created stagnant pools within me that were now being flushed and freshened so they sparkled clear and productive? I knew what caused them; the answer was evident.

These dams rose in me as a response to my selfish rejection of the new human life that was conceived and had grown within me so long ago. This was a distinct, and oh so innocent human life that was created by my adulterous relationship with Jay. I had flushed that life from me. At the time I regarded this new life as only a reminder of my sin, a sin I wanted to run away from then. My action blighted my potential for deep joy from that fateful moment till now.

How many times had I confessed this sin ... this hurt? How many prayers had I offered in atonement for my unthinkable and selfish act? Yet, not until now, not until I was the instrument God used to bring new life to Stanley, was I fully released from its curse. In some mysterious way my accident, and what ensued from it, sparked internal explosions that eventually burst the thick, high dams and emancipated my soul, allowing my confined guilt, that long festering emotional effluent, to gush out from its internal cesspool.

I now understood the miracle of conversion in ways I never did before. I'd been taken up by the rivers of grace flowing freely now through me, and I'd been transported into a new garden, an Eden, where I now basked in the fullness of God's sunshine. This must be what the great mystics, St. John of the Cross, and St. Theresa of Avila spoke of in their writings – a new ecstasy penetrated my consciousness making me so vibrantly aware of God's presence everywhere. I felt so free!

I found a new grandeur all around me – and in me. The world had taken on new meaning, generated, I think, from an intensification of my original purpose, a purpose that I had no doubt, God had invited me to pursue – a lifelong pursuit of him. How strange that my road to this new state of awareness led me through Stanley. In our coming together we both were able to off load unnecessary baggage that we had carried for so long.

Each day I prayed for Stanley; I probably would for the rest of my life. Each day I also wondered how he was doing. Yet, I couldn't ... or wouldn't try to find him. I was afraid of what I might encounter within myself if I tried; still ... I wondered.

Chapter One Hundred- Four

My wondering was fruitful ... the very next day I received a letter. I didn't know whose handwriting graced it but it was Stanley's name on the return address. My heart jumped with excitement along with a strong mixture of fear that now overtook me. I don't know how long I stared at the envelope before my curiosity overtook my trepidation ... I opened it.

Dear Sister,

I've written this letter in my head and heart so many times before I committed it to this page. I'm astonished (and probably so are you) to report that I'm fine. What's so surprising is that I could never say this before my accident because I never did feel fine. I was so cramped inside my armor I had no room to feel anything. How can you be fine when you're so squeezed? It took my accident and especially you to free me from my self-imposed confinement.

I learned the meaning of paradox from you and now I find I'm living paradox – I found my freedom in my paralysis. I continue to find new fields of freedom. Every day I think of you and every day I pray for you ... and your spirit. I know you're not God but I also know that God is in you and works through you and that's more than enough for me to carry on.

Life is hard; I struggle each day. My struggle with my unresponsive body is not half as tough as my struggle with my formerly paralyzed mind that still wants to command and control. I work each day to gently move away from its tyranny. I read all the time; actually I listen to audiotapes of books. I've discovered the new world of the Christian Press; they publish libraries of audiotapes that offer so much clarity and inspiration.

My nurse/companion is writing, I'm just dictating. Her name is Margie; she's just what I need. I'm her biggest admirer. I live in a small, ground floor condo that has no steps at all. I can roll right to my van parked just outside my door. Margie drives me anywhere and everywhere.

I got an invitation from my medical school to give the commencement address – I'm actually thinking of accepting. If I do, I'll send you a tape of it ... if you want. I'd love to hear from you, that is if you're allowed to write. I just needed to thank you in my own way – you saved my life – you saved me!
Love, Stanley

I sat back in my wheelchair and wept, clutching the letter as though it were a message from heaven. I immediately wrote him a return letter.

Dear Stanley,

I'm so happy to know that you're feeling well, and I'm thrilled beyond what words can express to learn that your spiritual nature has emerged from the deep freeze of your previous years. How can I thank God for your letter and an answer to my prayers that I've prayed continuously since the day you left the monastery? Your short note is so rich – I find new solace and new hope in it.

It's wonderful that you've been asked to give your medical school commencement address. This is an honor, and beyond that, it's an opportunity to help shape the minds and hearts of the next generation of physicians. You have so much you can tell them; the story of your journey can undoubtedly inspire them as they step out into their new profession. I do hope you will accept.

I want to let you know that I've also been fine. It's true that each day is a challenge, as you said, but I find that each day is also a treasure so much richer than I experienced before my accident. Some days, Stanley, I'm actually moved to tears by a new profundity I'm finding by living simply in "the now" of life. I'm so much less concerned with what was and what will be – far beyond these I look only for the presence of God in all things, all persons, and in all circumstances. It's amazing how refreshing and rejuvenating this new awareness of the holy present is for me.

I do often think about how you're doing. I pray each day that you find God's grace within you, the power that gives you direction and purpose, peace and strength, and wisdom and steadfastness. I shall pray a prayer of thanksgiving this very night for your continued healing and happiness.

In Christ's love, Sister Theresa

PS: I'll look forward to receiving the tape recording of your commencement address.

When I sent off the letter I immediately felt a new wholeness grow within me. Stanley was OK! This simple thought rolled over and over in my mind and with each revolution generated new peace and a quiet affirmation that what I did with Stanley was good, wholesome, and Godly. The fact that he was healing of mind and spirit justified the extreme behavior that overtook me at times while at St. John's. Stanley was OK! The very silent mouthing of these words caused a celebration within my heart. Stanley was OK! Stanley was OK! Stanley was OK! I threw my fists into the air in jubilation. Stanley was OK! Yes!

Chapter One Hundred-Five

Two months later I received a small package; it was from Stanley. Inside, I found a cassette tape and a note.

Dear Sister,

I hope you enjoy this tape recording of my commencement address as much as I enjoyed giving it. All is well!

Love, Stanley

I retrieved the monastery's tape player and popped in the tape. There were three separate introductions; the final voice was identified as Dr. Howard Shepherd, president of the university.

Dr. Stanley Renowski is a giant among all the physicians who have graduated from this medical school. His now famous accomplishment in the specialty of cardiac surgery, known as the Renowski technique has been adopted by the length and breadth of the profession. Dr. Renowski has twice received the National Cardiac Honors Award; in addition he has brought distinction upon himself and upon this institution by receiving the International Cardiac Surgery Honors Award for his pioneering work in surgical technique, which now bears his name. Dr. Renowski's work is found in every new surgery textbook. Dr. Renowski is a very special and unique individual, a man who you will see has triumphed in spirit over what medicine has yet to conquer. The commencement address today is Dr. Renowski's first public appearance since his very unfortunate accident. Let's hope that it will not be his last; the medical profession still needs his mind and his heart even though it is deprived of his hands.

After lengthy applause, Stanley's voice broke onto the tape.

Thank you Dr. Shepherd for your kind words, but I must correct one misperception I think you may have inadvertently given. While I was awarded the International Cardiac Surgery Honors Award, I never physically received it – my own arrogance robbed me of that pleasure. That arrogance, my friends and graduates, is the theme of my remarks to you today.

Stanley proceeded, with the zeal of a missionary, to describe in detail all the emotional and psychological barriers he had erected over the years, barriers that had separated him from the people he had vowed to serve on the day of his graduation from medical school. His talk was a confession of his transgressions. He accused himself of a litany of faults: haughty and presumptuous, blunt to the point of being brutish, caustically perfectionistic, self-centered and obtuse to the real needs of others, and an addicted fault-seeker who indulged himself in contention with all who dared approach him as an equal. In short, Stanley confessed that he violated every tenet of the Hippocratic oath. He continued ...

My fellow physicians, I relate my personal shadows and compulsions to you today not to unburden myself at your expense, but rather to caution you against taking yourself too seriously. Someone once said that angels can fly because they take themselves lightly. I wish this for you, that you learn to fly in your chosen specialty that you soar to new heights heretofore unknown. This possibility is yours, but it is only achievable if you learn to shed the terrible weight of your own ego. Learn to let go of any need for self-adulation – learn to fly. This is my first wisdom light, if you please. The second is this – find yourself a spiritual mentor. Find yourself a person who can call out the spirit in you. Learn to trust this person, learn to heed the questions this person poses. Their questions may be provocative indeed, yet these are the questions that matter, if you are to find that authenticity inside you that a power greater than us has placed uniquely in you. Here is the real you. Try, try, try, and try again and again to meld the professional in you with the real in you. Bring these two together into a unified whole. This task is of course a lifelong, ongoing process. We may never achieve it perfectly, but it's in your attempts that will emerge a new peace, a new vitality, and a new light that radiates wellness onto all whom you touch.

Lastly, don't ever, ever forget that while doctors treat, it's only God that heals – I am living testimony to this great truth.

I heard the applause immediately erupt from the audience. I imagined them rising to their feet in admiration for a man who spoke so plainly and with such authority and power.

In my mind's eye I saw Stanley in his wheelchair alone on a vast stage, flanked by flowers and palms, tears on his cheeks and a look on his face that straddled gratitude and transcendence, all with more than a trace of humility. Here was the new Stanley.

And also in my mind's eye, there was the new Sister Theresa, also in her wheelchair – who felt exactly the same.

THE END

Study Guide and Supplementary Materials

I hope you have enjoyed reading this novel. In addition to being a "good read', this book can be used as the centerpiece of group and individual study. The underlying "curriculum" of this story is the ten spiritual developmental tasks of the middle years.

Our psychological and spiritual growth is ongoing. Each stage and each phase of life offers specific opportunities for growth. Each of us grows in our own unique way within the framework of the specific "work" of that life stage. Spiritual growth is to some degree intertwined with all other human growth, emotional, psychological, and physical. We are holistic beings, one level of growth cannot dramatically outpace the others; we are body, mind, and spirit.

It is usually in our early 40s when our midlife story begins, for it is generally at this time when the first pangs of what will become a full-blown transition first become evident. Eventually these growth pangs will surface and resurface until they confront us in ways that we cannot escape; we are forced to address them. This book and the supplementary materials that support it form an intriguing curriculum that leads us through the sometimes bumpy terrain of our 40s, 50s, and 60s and brings us to a clearer understanding of our emerging authentic spiritual self.

If you'd like to learn more about how to use this novel in group study, log onto www.LifelongAdultMinisty.org/thenunandthedoctor where you will find study guides, assessments, and a home-study or in-person course that offers a certification to those who wish to bring the message of this story beyond these pages.

Blessings to you always,

R. P. Johnson